Praise for *Under the Rainbow*

We hope you enjoy this book. Please return or renew it by the due date.

You can renew it at www.norfolk.gov.uk/libraries or by using our free library app.

Otherwise you can phone 0344 800 8020 - please have your library card and PIN ready.

You can sign up for email reminders too.

'*Under the Rainbow* is essential reading – both heartbreaking and hopeful. A novel that will stay with you.' Laura Kay, author of *The Split*

'*Under the Rainbow* marks the arrival of a wildly talented, observant, political, feminist writer to the literary ranks. Celia Laskey is a true original, and she's here to stay.' Emily Rapp Black, author of the *New York Times* bestseller *The Still Point of the Turning World*

'I absolutely love this book. With wit and empathy, Celia Laskey has written a kaleidoscopic portrait of queer, rural life at a crossroads… The result is a novel that made my heart feel full.' Joseph Cassara, author of *The House of Impossible Beauties*

'The best sort of novel, one that leaves you sad it's over but already looking forward to the author's next.' Lori Ostlund, author of *After the Parade*

'Laskey inhabits each of these characters with skill and grace in a tour de force of first-person narration… Energetic and compelling, a promising first book from a writer to watch.' *Kirkus Reviews*

UNDER THE RAINBOW

CELIA LASKEY

ONE PLACE. MANY STORIES

HQ
An imprint of HarperCollins*Publishers* Ltd
1 London Bridge Street
London SE1 9GF

www.harpercollins.co.uk

HarperCollins*Publishers*
1st Floor, Watermarque Building, Ringsend Road
Dublin 4, Ireland

This edition 2021

1
First published in the United States in 2020 by
Riverhead Books, an imprint of Penguin Random House

First published in Great Britain by
HQ, an imprint of HarperCollins*Publishers* Ltd 2021

Copyright © Celia Laskey 2020

Celia Laskey asserts the moral right to be
identified as the author of this work.
A catalogue record for this book is
available from the British Library.

ISBN: 9780008481025

For my queers

Under the Rainbow

Year One

•••

Avery

I'm sitting in second-period biology, where I should be diagramming a chain of DNA but instead I'm diagramming something way more fascinating: the back of Jake Strommer's neck. The spot where his light brown hair meets his suntanned skin looks like a bird in flight, with two arches connecting in a V in the center. I imagine what it would be like to reach out and touch it, trailing my fingertips down to where his skin gradually pales at the rim of his gray, frayed T-shirt. I'd pull the shirt off with my teeth—I'd rip it right in half—then I'd kiss my way down his spine, stopping at each bony knob. When I get to the two dimples at the base of his back, my hetero shame hits.

Hetero shame: *noun* \he-tə-rō\ \shām\
: fear of coming out as heterosexual to your lesbian mom who you know wishes you were a lesbian, too

That's right—I'm a straight fifteen-year-old girl with moms who basically raised me like a dog-show poodle to be the most perfect lesbian ever, with just the right amount of feminist theory and fall flannels and whale watching. Not that there's any whale watching here, and not that my moms are even together anymore.

A few weeks ago I moved from Los Angeles with my mom Karen and my brother Cory to Big Burr, Kansas, a charming little hamlet of ten thousand people that has definitively been labeled the Most Homophobic Town in the U.S. Try not to be too jealous. The "most homophobic" thing is for real—this huge LGBTQ nonprofit called Acceptance Across America had a whole process for how they narrowed it down.

They started by looking at which states had the most hate crimes and conversion therapy and all that fun stuff, then they combed through people's social media and saw who was dumb enough to publicly say things like "I hate faggots" or "Choke on a dick, you dyke," then once they had a few front-runners they visited the towns, incognito, to see what was up. Big Burr was the clear winner.

Finally, in an exciting experiment to see if bigots can be transformed into reasonable people, Acceptance Across America sent a task force to actually live in Big Burr. A task force that my mom promptly volunteered to be the head of, which brings me to how I found myself in this classroom. I'm pretty sure they're hoping the task force will work like that old MTV show *The Real World: This is the true story of fifteen queers and lefties, picked to live in the most homophobic town in America, to work with its residents and find out what happens when people stop being polite and start getting real.*

4

We're supposed to stay in Big Burr for two fucking years. My other mom, Steph, was not down for the ride. She's the head of programming at Netflix and wasn't about to move to what she calls "the grundle of the United States." My moms fought nonstop for the six months before we left about whose work was more Important with a capital *I* and whether my brother Cory and I would stay or go. Since Steph travels all the time for work, they decided we had to go with Karen. I threw a shit fit, which obviously didn't change the outcome, but Cory said he *didn't mind* going. He said he thought it was "important to his development" to "experience how queer people are treated in other parts of the country."

Did I mention Cory is essentially a seventeen-year-old Dan Savage? At our high school in L.A. he had a column called "The Fag Rag" and he starred in the theater group's renditions of *The Birdcage* and *A Chorus Line*. He and Karen are two peas. All of this is why I'm a little hesitant to be like, "Hey, Karen, while I totally realize all the ways the patriarchy has held us down and while I completely appreciate the female form on an objective level, when I fantasize in class it's about guys, specifically Jake Strommer, and how I'd like to lick his body up and down."

Mrs. Stark tells us to pair up with someone and compare our DNA diagrams. Jake turns around and smiles at me, the little gap between his front teeth making my stomach dip. "Let me see your genes, girl," he says in a deep, jokey voice.

I stand up and do Vanna White hands around my Levi's. Jake laughs, and I want to yell at no one, "SEE HOW WE GET EACH OTHER?!?!"

"Now let me see your other genes." He flips a page of his notebook to his diagram.

I sit down and look at my blank page. "I didn't do it," I whisper.

"*Tsk tsk*, Avery." He puts his notebook on my desk. "We can look at mine." His drawing looks like two magnified strands of hair with twisted ladder rungs between them. The perspective and the shading make me think he draws outside of class.

"This is really good. But you missed a thymine." I point to the spot on his drawing where it should be.

Jake scoffs good-naturedly. "You didn't even do it, and you're correcting mine?" He draws in the thymine and asks, still looking down at his paper, "So are you going to Billy's party tonight?"

"I don't know," I say, trying to make it seem like I'm debating between Billy's party and other plans, even though I haven't heard of any party and I don't know who Billy is.

"I haven't seen you at any of the parties since school started. What are you always doing?"

I lean in and lower my voice. "You can't tell anyone, but I'm actually in the CIA. I'm undercover as a high school student for a top-secret case."

"So what happens when you fall for the smooth sophomore?" He pulls his front teeth across his bottom lip and looks right at me.

My cheeks heat up like the coils of an electric stove and I look away, scanning the class. "Oh, you mean Franklin?" I say, tipping my head toward the other side of the room. Franklin sits at his desk, a spit-filled pen cap dripping from the side of his mouth, his pleated khakis bunching around his midsection.

"Dang, it's like that, huh?" Jake laughs and shakes his head. "Well, I heard Franklin is coming to Billy's tonight, so . . ."

"So I'm there."

AT HOME, I drop my backpack next to the couch with a thud. Karen and Cory stand at the kitchen counter chopping vegetables.

"If there's a *hunting* club, then I don't see why there can't be a GSA," says Cory, perfectly symmetrical slices of red pepper falling off his knife in rapid succession.

"I'll come talk to Chuck next week," says Karen. Chuck being our principal. "He'll listen to me."

"Seriously, Karen?" I say, stealing a slice of red pepper from Cory's cutting board.

"What?" She places the flat side of her knife over a bulb of garlic and whacks it with the heel of her hand, then winces and rubs her arthritic knuckles. Her hair, cut in a classic mom pixie, is just starting to gray at the temples, and the other night when I walked by the bathroom I noticed her patting baby oil under her eyes.

"Can't you leave some things alone?" I say. The school year just started a few weeks ago, which means no one knows who my mother is yet, and I'd like to keep it that way for as long as possible. Thankfully I have Steph's last name, and I told anyone who asked that we moved here to take care of my ill grandmother, who lives one town over in Dry Creek. "You do know no one's going to join a GSA, right?" I say to Cory.

He narrows his eyes at me. "You would, wouldn't you?"

"Well, yeah," I lie. "But you and me would be the only members." I grab a handful of pepper slices and chew them with my mouth open.

"Did you have a bad day at school, Avery?" asks Karen, reaching over to pet my hair.

"I had a fine day." I duck away from her hand. "I'm going to a party tonight."

Karen and Cory make eye contact. "Billy Cunningham's?" Cory says.

"How do *you* know about it?"

"Because Billy told me during history class that if I go, I'll be . . . How did he put it? Beat till I'm a dead horse." He laughs exaggeratedly. "Such a nice guy, that Billy. He's gone out of his way to introduce me to Kansas customs like drawing dicks on my locker and reminding everyone my name is Faggot."

Karen puts down her knife. "Honey, are you serious?"

Cory shrugs.

"Now I'm *definitely* coming to talk to Chuck," says Karen. "And I don't want you going to a party at some homophobe's house," she says to me.

"Fine, I won't go," I say, and quickly change the subject. "Are we having stir-fry *again*?"

"There's nowhere decent in this town to get Chinese," says Karen, removing a paper-towel-wrapped block of tofu from underneath a dictionary. "So yes, we're having stir-fry again. Did you

8

know I had to order fish sauce online? None of the grocery stores in a sixty-mile radius had it."

Cory winces. "I'm so desperate I would even eat P. F. Chang's. Compared to Pu Pu Hot Pot it's, like, gourmet."

"You guys are the ones who wanted to come here," I remind them.

Karen looks at me from the corner of her eye while she slices the tofu block in half horizontally, then cuts vertical strips from the top. "So who were you planning to see at that party tonight?"

"Jana," I say, who is my one friend so far in Big Burr, "and some other people from school." I shrug. "No one in particular."

"No one in particular, huh?" Karen makes a self-satisfied face like when she solves the Sunday crossword. "Does Avery *like* someone?" she asks Cory in a teasing, singsongy voice.

What is it with mothers? Sometimes they don't know anything, and other times they know the one thing you wish they didn't. She's always so careful to use the right words: *someone, anyone, she* or *he* or *they*. But her bias shows anyway, like a bra strap underneath a spaghetti-strap tank top. I can see it in how she holds her face when she asks questions like these, expression deliberately neutral. I can hear it in her tone, overly disinterested and nonchalant. Most of all, I can feel it in the pressure underneath her words, her hope for an answer that will mean I'm just like her.

It's not like she's ever outright said, "I wish you were gay." But on any given day Karen's sound bites would include the word "hetero" said like a slur, "Divorce your husband!" (yelled at the TV during

House Hunters; said under her breath to women at Target), and, "Every day something makes me sad for straight women." The take-away being: heterosexuality is inferior, and all straight people must be miserable idiots.

AFTER DINNER, KAREN and Cory nestle on the couch and cue up *Queer as Folk*, which they must be re-watching for at least the tenth time. I hover near the window, waiting for Jana to pick me up. I told Karen we were going to a movie even though we have no plans of abandoning the party. When I see Jana's white Toyota Corolla with the dented door pull into the driveway, I sprint outside before Karen has a chance to invite her in.

As soon as I open the car door, I'm smacked in the face by the sickly sweet smell of Jana's vanilla-scented perfume, magnified by the Yankee Candle vanilla air freshener hanging from her rearview mirror. "Jesus, Jana, it smells like you fucked the Cookie Monster in here," I say, rolling down the passenger-side window.

Jana pauses to roll her eyes, then continues applying mascara using the tiny mirror on the back of the sun visor. She's wearing her standard black V-neck and black jeans, her long black hair parted down the center. She's not a goth or anything; she says she just likes her clothes to match her soul. I don't think my floral-print sweat-shirt matches my soul, but I have no idea what would. Probably that gross purply brown color you get when you mix all the colors in the paint palette together.

"Hey, can I put some on?" I ask, gesturing to the mascara. I rarely wear makeup but we *are* going to a party. Maybe it will entice Jake to make a move.

Jana hands me the mascara and the second I bring the wand near my lashes, I poke myself in the eyeball.

"Oh my god, have you never done this before?" Jana licks her thumb and wipes the mascara from my eyelid, then takes the wand back. "Blink," she directs me as she makes small upward strokes. My lashes catch in the brush, sticking together and getting heavy.

When she's finished, I flip down my sun visor and behold myself. "Wow. I never knew my eyelashes were so long." I wonder how I would look with a full face of makeup: my acne foundationed into oblivion, my barely visible cheekbones contoured into sharp lines, my normal-sized lips plumped to Angelina Jolie proportions.

Jana laughs at me batting my eyelashes at myself, then backs the car out of the driveway. "So where are we going?"

"I thought you knew where Billy lives."

"Nope," she says. "Why don't you just text Jake and ask him for the address?"

"And reveal what a loser I am? No thank you."

Jana presses her lips together, thinking. "It's cool. We can just wait at 7-Eleven until someone from school shows up to buy Slurpees. Then we follow them." The rumor is that to be allowed into one of Billy's parties, you have to be holding a Slurpee, like some kind of offering. He dumps all the Slurpees into a huge bucket and then adds a few handles of vodka. The resulting slop is called pussy punch, supposedly because it gets girls so wasted that they'll have sex with anyone. Sometimes I can understand why my mom hopes I'm a lesbian.

After we've waited twenty long minutes in the 7-Eleven parking lot, a black hatchback pulls in and two people from school get out: Zach Roland and his best friend Ramona. Jana tells me they're kind of loners, not really friends with anyone except each other, and she wouldn't expect them to be invited to a party of Billy's, but when we follow them into the store they buy two Slurpees, so we do the same. Armed with a Mountain Dew Kickstart and a Fanta kiwi-strawberry, we follow them back out to the edge of town, past the gravel pit where yards become car graveyards and it's harder to tell which houses are lived in or abandoned. Finally we turn into a long, potholed, tree-lined driveway, thick branches scraping against the side of the car as we creep toward the house.

Jana parks in a dirt lot next to about fifteen trucks, her head-lights illuminating a barn and some kind of animal hanging upside down from a post. When we get out of the car, I can tell it's a deer by the antlers that graze the ground. It's been slit from ass to chest, the empty red body cavity gaping, white fur flapping from the sides. A group of boys I vaguely recognize as juniors stand wide-legged around the deer, drinking beer and gesturing to various parts of its body.

Jana and I try to pass by quickly, but one of the boys holds out his arm to stop us.

"It's a beaut, huh, ladies?" The bill of his Jayhawks hat sits low over his eyes, and he flicks it up to get a better look at us.

"Sure," I say, swallowing a mouthful of sour spit. "A real beaut."

12

Tiny strings of white tendon hang from the ribs of the deer like remnants of a spiderweb. Between two ribs, there's a jagged V-shaped hole. The boy sticks his finger through it, and I jump.

"Killed the old-fashioned way, with a bow and arrow," he says proudly.

"Did *you* kill it?"

"Billy's dad got this one," he says. "But I'll get mine when firearm season starts."

"Why's it hanging upside down?" I ask, immediately kicking myself for a question that might mark me as an outsider.

"The tenderization process," he says, slapping its haunches.

"You've got to wait for the rigor mortis to pass," says another boy, his words slow and sticky from drinking. He tips his head back to finish the last of his Colt 45 and tosses the bottle in the bushes. "About five days will get you some nice, delicate meat." He smiles at my mortified expression. "Not from here, are you?"

"I'm new," I say, hoping he won't ask for more details.

He looks me up and down, his body lilting back and forth like he's standing in a rowboat. When he sways toward me, he holds his face close to mine. His breath smells like rotting leaves after it rains. "No one here is new. Why would you come to Big Burr?"

I switch my Slurpee to my other hand, wiping the cold condensation on my jeans.

"She's on a top-secret mission," Jake says from behind me. I breathe out, not realizing I had been holding in air, and step closer to him.

"What kind of mission?"

Jake rolls his eyes. "It wouldn't be top secret if I told you, would it?"

The boy regards Jake, then me. His pale blue irises bob near his eyelids. Then he stumbles back against the wall of the barn and falls sideways into the brambly weeds. His friends laugh, help him up, and pass him another Colt 45.

Jake puts his hand on the small of my back, my skin lighting up under his touch, and guides me past the deer. "Let's go inside."

As we walk into the living room, I can't help but stare at the animal heads mounted above a gaudy rose-patterned couch. I recognize deer and moose, but can't figure out exactly what the other ones are. Below each head hangs a picture of a handsome bearded man, who I assume is Billy's father, holding up the head when it was still attached to its limp body in the wild. Two large windows flank the couch, framed by yellow tulip-printed curtains. I've never seen such a straight-looking room: something for the husband, something for the wife. It's a very democratic, if not visually cohesive, form of decorating. I can practically hear Karen yelling at Billy's mom, "Divorce your husband!"

A girl who's just funneled a beer climbs onto the couch and holds her red Solo cup up to the moose's stiff mouth. Just as she begins to tilt the cup, Billy comes tearing across the room, grabs her arm, and pulls her to the front door, tossing her out. "What is Billy's one rule?" he asks the room.

"Hands off the taxidermy!" everyone yells back.

Jana and Jake and I wander into the kitchen to see what there is to drink. The infamous bucket of pussy punch sits on the kitchen table, which is covered with a vinyl daisy-printed tablecloth. We dump our obligatory Slurpees in, then stir the sludgy dark purple liquid with a plastic ladle.

Jana dips a Solo cup into the bucket. "When in Rome." She takes a sip, then shakes her head back and forth and smacks her mouth like a cat after you force a pill down its throat. "It's good," she croaks. "Tastes just like a Slurpee." I reach for her cup.

"Don't drink that," Jake says to me. "You, either," he says to Jana. He hands us each a can of Bud Light and we head back into the living room.

The TV is tuned to the local news, which I'm assuming is just the default channel, because no one is paying attention. The anchor, who looks like she can barely hold her eyes open with all the eye shadow weighing down her lids, is talking about how a man with a shotgun held up a combination KFC/Taco Bell. When it turned out there was only forty-four dollars in the till, he demanded one of each menu item from both restaurants and was arrested halfway through eating a Beefy Fritos Burrito.

"He should have been arrested just for eating a Beefy Fritos Burrito," jokes the woman's co-anchor, a man wearing a striped tie almost as wide as his face.

The female anchor gives a small, forced chuckle and then moves on to the next story. "Today, task force members from the gay rights organization Acceptance Across America met with the mayor and council members of Big Burr." My stomach jumps. I pray no one notices, but the name "Acceptance Across America" triggers some kind of Pavlovian response and everyone in the room snaps their heads around to look at the TV.

"The head of the task force, Karen Roxford, spoke to us today about Acceptance Across America's main objectives, and the strategies that businesses and residents can use to make their communities more LBGT-friendly," the anchor goes on, botching the order of the initials, but it doesn't seem like anyone noticed. I fight the urge to bolt out of the room or huddle into a ball on the floor as the camera cuts to my mother, wearing a white blazer with a large AAA pin fastened to the lapel. As shouts of "Dyke" and "Go back where you came from" echo across the room, I make eye contact with Zach, the guy we followed from the 7-Eleven, who seems to be the only other person not yelling some kind of epithet. He pulls his mouth into a grimacey smile and starts walking toward me. Oh, Jesus. Has he somehow realized that Karen is my mom? Is he going to out me right now, in front of everyone? He has a gentle, dopey face, the kind of guy who looks like he wouldn't be able to grow a full beard no matter how hard he tried, but appearances can be deceiving.

He leans against the wall next to me and widens his eyes at everything going on around us. "You're new here, right?" He shakes his head. "That's a stupid question. I know you're new. I would ask how you're liking Big Burr so far, but I don't think this party is doing us any favors."

I cross my arms. "I'm having a fine time."

He laughs. "A *fine* time. What everyone wants to have at a party!"

I laugh, too, but keep watching the TV out of the corner of my eye, waiting for Karen's face to disappear.

Zach leans in close to me and lowers his voice. "I'm having a terrible time, to be honest. I'm only here because my best friend Ramona has a crush on Seth Braun." He shoves a fist into his mouth. "Oh, shit. Don't tell anyone I said that, will you?"

I roll my eyes. "I don't really have anyone to tell."

"Oh, right. I heard you're from L.A.?"

I nod.

He smiles a big, goofy smile. "I've always wanted to go there. Have you ever met a celebrity?"

I shrug. "Sure. Not, like, been introduced to them, but I see them around all the time. One time Kristen Stewart tried to pet my friend's dog, then the dog growled at her."

"That's crazy." He shakes his head in disbelief. "What was it like at your old high school?"

My *old* high school—the word sends a jolt through my gut. "It was like a different country," I say. "A way more developed one." Karen is still on the goddamn TV, talking about how businesses can put rainbow flags in their windows to signal acceptance. When I look back at Zach's face, I see that it's fallen. "Sorry, that's so rude. I only said it because you don't really seem like everyone else."

He gives me a sheepish look. "Is it that obvious?"

We both laugh, then stop when we see Billy sauntering up to the TV with a mischievous look on his face. He unzips his fly and pantomimes taking his dick out. He cups the air in front of his pants and guides his imagined member into my mother's mouth.

Someone hoots. A few people laugh. Encouraged, he humps the screen, starting out slowly, then quickening to a frenzied pace. His pants sink lower as he thrusts, and the top of his boxers becomes visible, little red hearts on white fabric. I wonder why someone like him would wear boxers like that. Maybe they were a gift from his mom. Maybe it's laundry day. Or maybe he's actually a very sensitive person.

"You like that, huh?" he says, looking into my mother's eyes with an amount of hatred I've never felt for anything. He jerks his crotch forward and groans enthusiastically, pretending to come on her face, as the room cheers. My heart beats in my ears, and I realize Zach has disappeared from my side. I look for Jake and Jana and they're not cheering, but they're definitely laughing—either because they actually think it's funny or because they feel like they have to, and I don't really want to know which it is.

THE NEXT MORNING, I wake up to "Let's Have a Kiki" by the Scissor Sisters blasting from the other side of the house. I shove in earplugs but can still hear the bass vibrating through the floor. I throw off my covers and stomp into the living room, where Karen and Cory are having a dance party. "A kiki is a party for calming all your nerves," Ana Matronic sings. Karen is doing her mashed-potato mom dance, while Cory does his inexpert version of voguing, which involves a lot of wrist-flapping and falling backward onto the carpet with one knee bent behind him. Karen mashed-potatoes over to me and grabs my hands, moving them from side to side. I stand completely still, obstinate. She places one hand on my hip and points the finger of my other hand, pulling it up to point at the ceiling and then down to point at the floor à la John Travolta. I smile a little bit against my will, and Cory runs up behind me, placing his hands on my hips and rotating them in wide circles.

"I'm not a puppet," I yell over the music.

"Then dance on your own," yells Karen, letting go of my arms. Cory releases my waist and shimmies in front of me, holding his arms out to his sides and shaking his chest. I laugh and shake mine back.

"More!" he shouts. "Work those B cups!"

I shake more earnestly, my braless breasts swinging from side to side in my oxford pajama shirt. I lean my head back and close my eyes, spinning in a circle, my hands above my head, spreading my fingers as wide as they can go. My breath glides in and out of my body. I imagine tiny silvery beads of bad energy forcing their way out from under my skin, floating into the air and popping in a Technicolor burst of gas like a miniature supernova. Who cares if everyone at school thinks I'm a weirdo? Who cares if they find out Karen is my mom? Who cares if Karen finds out I like boys?

The song ends and I open my eyes, the last wisps of Technicolor vanishing. We all flop down onto the couch.

"That's what we need," says Karen. "A kiki."

"A good ole Kansas kiki," Cory says sarcastically, giggling.

"I'm serious," says Karen. "Let's have a party tonight. A fancy one with classic cocktails and canapés. I'll invite everyone from the

19

task force, and you kids can invite whoever you want from school." She looks at me and winks as she says the last part.

"I think Billy Cunningham would love to attend our kiki," Cory says. "Just the other day, he was asking me for canapé recipes."

"Venison sausage and spray cheese on a saltine would be to his taste, I think," I say.

"I don't know about that, but we'll need something to eat," says Karen, standing up and clapping her hands. "Let's go to the grocery store."

"I have to write a paper about World War II," says Cory, face-diving into the throw pillows.

Karen looks at me. "Shall we?"

"So HOW ARE things going at school?" Karen asks as we drive to the store in what's probably the only Prius in all of Big Burr. I stare out the window as we pass by a field clustered with silver grain silos, all huddled together like they're cold. A metal structure with long poles connects the silos at the top, and from far away it looks like a daddy longlegs.

"I don't fit in very well," I say.

Karen shrugs and puffs her cheeks, blowing out a long breath of air. "That's high school for you."

"I fit in fine in L.A." It physically hurts to think about what I'd be doing on a Saturday back home—getting the best breakfast burrito ever at the bakery in Los Feliz and people-watching in Silver

Lake, then seeing an indie film at the ArcLight on Hollywood, where my friends and I once saw Chris Pine buy a ticket to his own movie. We'd have Sugarfish for dinner, which puts all other sushi to shame, and we'd end the night at my friend Scout's house, whose mom is internet-famous and would let us take over her Instagram account whenever we wanted.

When I first left L.A., my friends and I texted all day every day, but as the weeks have gone on, everything is suddenly a long story they'll tell me later, though later never comes. It's even been hard to keep in touch with Steph—half the time I don't know what state or country she's in, and when she tries to FaceTime me her screen always freezes. She keeps telling me to "hang in there," which makes me think of this poster I had when I was little, of a kitten dangling off the end of a tree branch, over big blocky text that says OH, SHIT.

"Transitions are hard," Karen says. "Growing up as an army brat, I had to move every two years. It was tough to maintain relationships." She honks at the car in front of us as it slows to a crawl and turns without using its blinker.

"Were you out in high school?"

"I came out to just my best friend during my senior year, while I was living in Virginia," she said. "That was 1988. Needless to say, it didn't go very well." I know it didn't go very well with Karen's parents, either, who never came around to her being gay, and thus whom I've never met. It's why Karen dedicated her life to fighting homophobes—when I think about that, I feel pretty guilty about how much shit I've been giving her for being here.

"If you were a teenager living here, would you come out to anyone?" I ask.

"Definitely not." She pulls into the strip mall and parks in front of Dillons, then shuts off the engine but stays in her seat, buckled. "Is anyone giving you a hard time?"

I replay the look of hate in Billy's eyes as he thrust into Karen's mouth on TV. What would they have done if they discovered I was her daughter? What would Jake have done? I picture myself hanging upside down from the beam in front of Billy's barn, a long slit from my crotch down to my neck, my internal organs fed to the dogs, the white bones of my ribs scraped clean from the surrounding red flesh. "No," I say.

"Good." She puts her hand on the door handle but doesn't open it. "Your friend Jana sounds nice." She looks out the window as she says it, playing aloof, but her voice has that saccharine, suggestive quality.

I nod, trying to forget Jana's laughing face from the night before.

"I'm glad there's someone here you've connected with," Karen says. "You should invite her to the party tonight."

THE DOORBELL STARTS to ring around eight o'clock, and I'm introduced to a stream of Karen's coworkers: a woman named Tegan who kind of looks like Carey Mulligan and who's wearing a jean jacket that says VULVA on the back; a striking androgynous person named Harley; a tall man in a bowler hat named Jamal, who is also the only Black person I've seen so far in Big Burr; a handsome pair of middle-aged men named David and Miguel; and a bunch of other people I can't remember. They all give me a kiss on each cheek or a heartfelt hug. The house smells like warm cheese and caramelized onions, and a mix that Cory's made rotates through LCD Soundsystem, Robyn, and Calvin Harris. Karen even lets me have a glass of champagne. It feels so much like we're back in L.A. that I expect to look out the window and see palm trees. I go into the kitchen for a goat-cheese-and-fig crostini, where Jamal is in the middle of telling a story to a rapt audience.

"The pastor says, Raise your hand if you're alive, so obviously, we all raise our hands. Then he says, You know who you have to thank for being alive? Your mother and your father. That's right, not your mother and your mother or your father and your father. For all of us to be here, you need a man and a woman, the way God in his ultimate wisdom intended."

Everyone groans. "Ignoring the fact that straight couples are the ones who keep having queer babies," says David.

"Let's not talk about all that tonight," says Karen, waving her hand in the air as if to dispel a swarm of gnats. "We're here to have a good time."

"You know what?" says Tegan. "I know we're supposed to be better than them, to keep our poise while they fling around their First Amendment rights, but I just have to say this." She slams her highball glass down on the counter and teeters a little bit, making me wonder if she's already drunk. "When this is all over, when we're in charge and doughy half-wits like that pastor are stuck

23

doing line work in our glitter and dildo factories, we're not going to forget the bad old days. We'll mumble slurs when we pass them on the street, we'll pick a disease and say it's just for them, we'll stand by doing nothing as they get beat up and raped and murdered all because of who they fuck."

Everyone blinks, stopping mid-chew or mid-sip.

"Whoa," says Harley. "That's intense, Tegan."

"Well, I say Amen to that!" says David. He raises his glass, and a few other people raise theirs. "Amen!" they yell.

I hold my glass in front of my chest, wondering if I should raise it, too. Then my phone buzzes in my pocket: a text from Jake.

U wanna hang tonight? I stare at the gray speech bubble, then switch my phone to silent, putting it back in my pocket. I eat another crostini, and David pours me another glass of champagne after checking to make sure Karen isn't looking.

"When in Rome." He grins at me deviously, topping off his own glass. "So how are you surviving here? Teenage girls in small towns are even cattier than gay men."

"Treading water, I guess."

He licks champagne from his mustache. "I'd like to think I'm doing the butterfly. Which reminds me, I need some Mariah Carey." He pats my arm and floats away to the stereo in the living room.

I swallow another gulp of champagne and take my phone out of my pocket. Underneath Jake's initial text, there's the ellipsis that means he's typing. I hold my phone in my hand for what must be a full minute, watching the dots, until his next text finally appears. *It'd be really cool to see u.*

The champagne has pulled at my principles, loosening them like a sloppily tied knot. Images flash by: his warm mouth on mine, his hands raking my hair and then sliding down my neck, my chest, landing on my breasts, a thumb snaking into the cup of my bra, rubbing back and forth slowly across my nipple. *Pick me up on the corner of Walnut and Pine*, I text back. I chug the rest of my champagne, then grab an unopened bottle before sneaking out the back door.

I'm outside before I realize I forgot to grab a jacket. I button up my thin cardigan and cut through the neighbor's backyard, the silver springs of a trampoline gleaming in the moonlight. The black spindly tips of pine trees reach into the sky like the claws of a Maurice Sendak monster. I shiver and pick up my pace, sprinting through the next few yards until I reach the corner.

Jake pulls up in his old Honda Accord. I get in and pull the bottle of champagne out from under my cardigan.

"First you tell me to pick you up on the corner, then you have champagne?" he says. "I think you really are in the CIA." He takes the bottle and puts it in the back seat, unbuckling his seat belt and leaning his body into mine to reach. "I think I'll have to check you for a wire," he says, his face so close I can smell the Big Red gum he's chewing.

I let out a nervous laugh and pull away, pressing my back against the door. I have nothing witty to say in return. My stomach gurgles and I hope he doesn't hear it. I've imagined kissing him so many times, I never thought about how nervous I'd be if it ever actually happened.

Jake hesitates. I force myself to make eye contact, giving him a look that says yes. He places a hand on my thigh, leans in, and kisses me once, softly. He pulls away and smiles. "You've already had some champagne."

I nod and grab the back of his neck, pulling him in. This time he kisses me more forcefully, his tongue eddying against mine in a telepathic rhythm.

He stops again. "You're not drunk, are you?"

I shake my head. My insides feel warm and viscous, like melted candle wax.

"Good," he says. "I wouldn't want that to be the reason this is happening." As he leans back in, his phone vibrates. "Oh, shit, I think we're late."

"For what?" I ask, surprised and disappointed that there are plans involving other people.

He grins. "You know that lesbian who was on the news the other night? Billy followed her home from work the other day. We've got about twenty cartons of eggs with her name on 'em."

And just as suddenly, the candle wax inside me stiffens, forming a hard shell around my lungs and my heart. When Jake leans in again to kiss me as he starts the car, his mouth feels like nothing.

We meet a group of about twenty people in the high school parking lot, mostly clustered on the hoods of cars, smoking cigarettes and sipping from bottles of Mad Dog. The girls wear the boys' Carhartt jackets, the zippers low enough to show the dark valley of their cleavage, and the boys stick their T-shirted chests out, pretending not to be cold. Hip-hop blasts from Billy's truck, and there's an air of excitement, like before a football game.

Jake puts his arm around me, and I really do feel like a double agent. Billy walks around passing out Styrofoam cartons of Sunny Farms eggs. He hands me one and I accept it, the fat cartoon sun on the package smiling at me menacingly.

"Okay, people," Billy says, and kills what's left of a bottle of Mad Dog. "Let's do this." He lobs the bottle over everyone's heads and a few seconds later it shatters on the pavement. They all whoop and get in their cars, revving their motors. Competing bass lines bump against each other as radios turn on. I slide into the passenger seat of Jake's Honda, the carton of eggs on my lap. He drums the steering wheel as we follow the line of vehicles out the long school driveway, everyone unrolling their windows to flip off the 15 MPH speed limit sign as we race by.

"You're quiet. Is everything okay?" Jake asks, reaching over to put a hand on my thigh.

"Yeah, everything's fine," I say, then remember Zach's joke from Billy's party about having a fine time. Based on the vibe I got from Zach, it figures he's not participating in the egging. I wouldn't have thought Jake would be down, either, but here we are. As much as I want to leave, it feels like some kind of outside force is keeping me pinned to the passenger seat.

As Jake drives, he spreads his fingers across the width of my thigh, drags them back in, then spreads them again, like he's picking something up and dropping it over and over. My chest tightens as we drive past the Acceptance Across America billboard that just went up on top of Barb's Boutique, a store that unabashedly has a sign in the window that says WE SERVE ADAM & EVE, NOT ADAM & STEVE.

27

Karen told me she overheard some women in the Pancake House talking about how the boutique hadn't been doing well, so Barb sold the ad space to a media company who, unbeknownst to her, promptly rented it to AAA. And now there's nothing Barb can do about it. Karma, man. The kicker? The billboard features two femme, fashionable women holding hands underneath cursive type that reads *Equality has a bright future in Big Burr, Kansas.*

Jake laughs, then pulls his hand across his mouth in an attempt to smother it.

"What's funny?"

"You know Keith? He took a picture of those lesbians and jerks off to it."

"Typical," I mutter under my breath.

"What do you mean, typical?"

I sigh and look out the window so I won't have to look at Jake. "Men thinking lesbians exist for them."

"Huh." He shakes his head good-naturedly. "You're a funny one, Miss Los Angeles."

I cross my arms. "It wasn't meant to be funny."

He presses his lips together and widens his eyes. "Are you sure you're okay?"

Before I can decide how to reply, we turn onto Pine Street and he says, "Hey, this is near where I picked you up. You live around here?"

"I was at a friend's," I say. As we get closer to my house, my throat spasms with the urge to vomit. Part of me wants to blame Karen for my current predicament—who did she expect me to hang out with, bringing me to this town? Or was I supposed to be a social pariah, just like she was? But another, larger part of me knows I'm only blaming her because I don't want to blame myself. In L.A. I would never be stuck in a situation like this—at least half my friends there are queer, and if anything I was always slightly *less* cool because I'm straight and cis. My life there seems unthinkable now, like some alternate universe. I know I should just make some excuse to Jake about why I can't go with them. But I stay silent, thinking about Newton's law of inertia as we speed down the street: an object at rest stays at rest and an object in motion stays in motion unless acted upon by an external force. In science class, our teacher showed us a video of a car crash to illustrate the point. I find myself hoping for one right now—that someone will accelerate through a red light or merge blindly into our lane, sending us careening in the opposite direction.

Billy pulls over a few houses before mine, the others following suit. Everyone slams their car doors and runs down the sidewalk. The guys whoop and punch each other in the arm, the girls following behind them, smiling uneasily. I pray they'll get the number wrong and end up egging one of our neighbors. But then Billy stops in front of my house and nods. The party still appears to be going strong: the high soprano of Kylie Minogue and the screech of laughter make their way through the closed windows.

"Perfect, a homo party," says Billy. He opens his carton of eggs and balances one in his palm. Then he flicks his wrist and whips the egg at the beige siding of my house. It hits with a hollow, sloshy crack. Another one hits, then another. Jake hands me an egg, then joins the firing squad. Arms move in steady circles as eggs fly through the air and explode against the house. The glossy whites drip and shine in the streetlights, the shells collecting on top of the yew bushes. Karen and the others must not be able to hear the noise over the music inside. Then an egg whaps into one of the living room windows. The music turns off and the front door opens, Cory's face appearing behind the glass of the storm door.

"Come on out, faggot!" Billy yells to Cory, who pushes the storm door open and walks slowly down the sidewalk, his mouth set in a hard line. I know I should duck behind a car before he sees me, but my feet stick to the ground.

Karen rushes into the doorway. "Cory! Get back inside right now." Cory ignores her and keeps walking, his eyes fixed on Billy. "I've called the cops," Karen yells.

Billy scoffs.

Cory walks right up to Billy and, without hesitating, reels his arm back and punches Billy square in the face. Billy blinks, his eyes wide and disoriented. He looks like someone who's just woken up in a hotel room in a strange city and has no idea where he is. A bright red spot of blood appears below his left nostril, tracing a thick line to his mouth. He touches the spot and holds his hand in front of his face. Then his rage kicks in and he snarls, lunging at Cory. They both fall to the ground.

Karen runs out from the house, but not in time to stop Billy from returning a punch that lands directly on Cory's right eye. Cory yowls and writhes. "Please," Karen says, trying to pull them apart. She looks at the group of teenagers standing on the sidewalk.

"Won't someone help me?" Her eyes scan the group until they come to rest on me, standing at the edge of the lawn, an egg in my hand. "Avery?" She blinks and pulls back her face like someone's thrown sand in it.

Billy turns to look at me, everyone else's eyes following. "You know her?"

Karen waits for me to answer, her lips pressed together. I look down at the grass.

Billy's eyes dart from Karen to me to Cory, then back to me. "They're your family, aren't they?" He shakes his head, his eyebrows pulling together. "That's fucked up. Why would you egg your own house?" He releases Cory from his grasp and Cory stumbles to stand up, touching a finger to his eye and grimacing. I look at Cory and expect him to be seething, but he makes a face like *he* feels bad for *me*, like I'm the one who's hurt.

"Good question," says Karen, crossing her arms and staring at me.

Everyone waits for an answer. I look up to the sky, hoping a simple explanation will appear there. Sometimes it's hard to remember that the moon is an actual astronomical object, with rocks and craters and sweeping lunar plains formed by ancient volcanic eruptions. From the ground it just looks like a translucent projection, which would be a good description for how I feel most of the time—letting people see what they want to see on my blank surface. My eyes drift down and land on Jake, who won't look at me. Karen follows my glance, and her eyes widen in understanding.

Just then a cop pulls up to the curb and gets out of his car unhurriedly. He has a face like a toddler's, with ample cheeks, a short, upturned nose, and a grin as if he's just covered a wall in Sharpie. He strolls up to a guy I recognize from Billy's party and claps him on the shoulder, saying, "Nice touchdown last week. Think you can do it again this Friday?" Then he turns to a girl from my science class and says, "Tell your mom thanks for that apple cake. It put my wife's to shame, but let's keep that between us, huh?"

"Excuse me," Karen says to the cop, her voice raised. "These kids just egged my house."

"Yup, that's what you said when you called."

"Well, what are you going to do about it?"

The cop gives her a look like she's about to step over an imaginary line. "Seems like a harmless prank to me."

"Really?" says Karen. "Because it seems like a hate crime to me."

He smirks and puts a hand on his hip, right above his gun in its holster. "I'm sure these kids didn't know whose house they were egging," he says, his eyes on Karen. "Right, kids?"

They all nod eagerly.

"And I'm sure they won't do it again, right, kids?"

Their heads keep bobbing.

"Problem solved," he says. "You all can go home now." Everyone races to their cars like they're being timed, Jake included. I hope he'll turn back and look at me, but he doesn't. The cop saunters to his own car.

Karen follows him. "Your department will be hearing from me."

"I'm sure they will," he says, before closing his door.

The cars roar to life one after the other, like thunder rolling

32

across the air. They all leave the same way, disappearing in an orderly line around the bend, the hum of their engines fading. The neighborhood feels eerily quiet: the calm after the storm. I look down at the egg still cradled in my palm.

"You might as well throw it," Karen says.

"I don't want to," I say.

"Throw it."

I rock the egg back and forth in my hand. It feels light as a feather, heavy as a rock.

"Throw it!" she shouts.

I gasp, startled by her anger, and wind my arm back. The smooth shell glides past my fingers, the white orb arcing through the dark air. When the egg cracks against the house, something in my chest cracks, too, like a wishbone snapping apart at the forked bone.

Christine

It's appalling," says my best friend Pammy at our kids' weekly playdate. We're sitting in her living room on chairs we've pulled up right in front of the AC window unit. It huffs like it's running up a hill, struggling to cut through the ninety-eight-degree humidity of an October heat wave. Pammy's talking about that new billboard, the one you can't miss on the roof of Barb's Boutique.

"It's more than appalling, it's horrifying," I say. If I stand on a chair and look out the top left corner of my bedroom window, I can see the back of it, casting a long, dark shadow down the street. And it's impossible to avoid—I have to drive by it every single time I leave the house. The photo on the billboard shows two women holding hands, standing in front of the old wooden gazebo in the park on Walnut Avenue. The women are looking at each other and smiling, like they're just so content with their life choices. Like God and everyone around them approves.

"I bet they're not even real lesbians," I say. The one on the left is tall and thin, with long, dark brown wavy hair, defined cheekbones, and an extended, upturned nose. There's a sharp severity to her face, like she might be from Russia or one of those Eastern European countries. She's wearing a flowy black blouse over jeans so snug her thighs don't even touch. The other one is a few inches shorter and curvier. She has a platinum-blond pixie cut with side-swept bangs that fall over wide blue eyes. Her full lips jut out from her profiled face even as she smiles. She's wearing a gray T-shirt dress with a black belt cinching the waist. On the bottom of the photo, in folksy cursive, it says *Equality has a bright future in Big Burr, Kansas*. In a much smaller font below that, it says *Brought to you by Acceptance Across America*.

From what I've gathered, Acceptance Across America is a gay nonprofit all about shaming the rest of us, like we're somehow to blame for being straight. They decided that out of the tens of thousands of towns in the United States, Big Burr was the "most homophobic" of them all. And how did they make that decision? By nitpicking our laws, hacking our social media to look for "hate speech," and barraging our homes with phone calls asking inappropriate questions, all of which I later realized was a precursor to them sending people here to investigate us in person, like the gay Gestapo. The way the media outside of Big Burr reported the investigation's findings twisted everything around. They said a teacher at the high school was fired for being gay, but I heard he resigned completely of his own accord. They said a lesbian-owned bed-and-breakfast was purposefully burned down, but the fire department said it was actually due to faulty wiring. And the one that really takes the cake: they said members of my church almost strangled a young boy to death in an attempt to "banish his homosexual demons," but the boy refused to press charges, which seems awfully convenient. Now a task force is here on all these false premises, invading our workplaces with "inclusivity trainings," ruining our social events, and erecting gay billboards.

Pammy shakes her head. "Katie kept asking me, 'Mommy, why are those two ladies holding hands?' So I told her, Those ladies are best friends. Do you know what she does now? She makes all her dolls hold hands and says, 'Look, Mommy, they're best friends!'"

"Claire and Carson haven't asked me about it, thank God," I say, lifting my hair up and leaning closer to the AC, trying to feel the barely cool breeze on my damp neck. "I got some of those mesh window shades for the back seats of the minivan, and I always make sure to have a movie playing when we drive by, so I don't think they've noticed it yet."

Katie screams out. Over in the play area, she points at Claire and says, "She took my frying pan!"

Claire stands at a Fisher-Price kitchen play set, placing perfectly round fried eggs and wavy pink-and-white strips of bacon in a pan.

"Claire, give Katie back her frying pan," I say.

Claire tightens her grip around the pan's handle, her tiny arms shaking with stubborn resistance. "I have to cook my husband his breakfast."

"Why don't you bake some muffins?" Pammy says to Katie.

Katie eyes the frying pan sulkily, then picks up a bowl and pretends to add various ingredients from the cupboard.

"POed in the kitchen," Pammy says. "The apples don't fall far from the tree, do they?" She laughs, then pulls her mouth into a scowl. "Do you ever cook vegetarian meals?"

"Not really, why?"

"A girl at work gave me a recipe for vegetable lasagna, so I made it the other night. We all sit down and Doug takes a bite and makes this face. Then he starts taking apart the lasagna with his fork, layer by layer, asking where the meat is. When I tell him there is none, he looks at me like I might as well have put arsenic in the food."

"Men and their meat." I shake my head.

"So you know what I did?" Pammy smiles impishly. "I took a can of beef dog food out of the cupboard, opened it up, and dumped it on his plate."

My hand flies to my open mouth. So much for Ephesians 5:22: "Wives, submit yourselves to your own husbands as you do to the Lord." When I'm mad at Jeff, my rebellions are so invisible I pray God won't see them: I'll overcook his piece of chicken breast, use his loofah to scrub my feet in the shower, or leave his clean laundry in the washing machine overnight before drying it so it smells ever so slightly of mildew. But I would never tell even Pammy about these small acts of resentment—the struggles of a relationship aren't meant to be shared. "What did Doug do?" I ask her.

"Oh, you know," she says, waving her French-manicured nails in the air. "Looked at me like he was gonna throw me across the room, then got in his truck and peeled out of the driveway. When he came back later that night, he made sure to leave two Arby's bags sitting on the kitchen counter."

"Wow," I say. "All because of some vegetables."

Pammy lowers her voice. "I swear, Christine, sometimes—"

I reach over and place my hand on hers, stopping her before she says something too true. "I know," I say. "Sometimes I feel like I'm at the end of my rope, but then I just remind myself that I shouldn't fight to be right. Reconciliation is the true victory." The other day I made a wallpaper quote of that sentiment, over a close-up photo of a man and a woman holding hands, the woman's slender fingers positioned so you can see her engagement ring stacked on top of her diamond wedding band. When I posted it to my *Righteous Wife* Facebook page it got 176 likes, one of my best-performing pieces of content.

Pammy rolls her eyes. "Do you *always* practice what you preach?"

"I try."

She sighs. "Don't you get tired of it?"

AT HOME, I put some chicken in the Crock-Pot and put the kids in front of *The Little Mermaid* with popsicles. Then I sit down at the computer to write my daily blog post for Media WatchMoms. Today's topic is the Viagra commercial that came on last night at seven p.m., while the whole family was watching the Chiefs game. I title it "No Touchdown for Prime-Time Viagra Commercial." I'm not one to toot my own horn, but I'm kind of known for my clever headlines. After I finish, I re-post the article to the Media Watch-Moms Facebook page and instantly get one like and one love. My last piece, about the inappropriate sexual innuendos in a Dove chocolate ad, got almost three hundred likes.

Pammy says I have a way with words, and that if I devoted more time to *Righteous Wife* and found a way to integrate my Media WatchMoms angle, it could become a full-time job. After a while, she said, brands might pay to advertise on my site, and it could lead to things like TV or radio appearances or even a book deal. I mentioned it to Jeff once, the idea of turning my blog into a real business, but he just laughed and asked if I went to school for writing or knew anything at all about running a company. I'm sure he's right—I should get my head out of the clouds, stop daydreaming about something that'll probably never come true. But sometimes when I'm alone in the bathroom, I still like to practice my smile in the mirror for the book jacket photo—just for fun, mind you.

I scroll through my Facebook timeline, liking a photo of my friend Sarah's baby wearing oversized sunglasses, a Pinterest recipe for Oreo pie, and an article titled "Justin Timberlake and Jessica Biel Share Family Values." My old high school friend Gina Townsend has updated her profile picture to a full-body shot of herself in a skimpy, sparkly dress. According to Facebook, she got divorced a few months ago. So much for holy vows.

I click on her profile. There are photos of her on a rooftop drinking a margarita and laughing; her at a museum posing in front of some kind of abstract sculpture; her at a concert making the rock 'n' roll hand symbol, sticking her pointer finger and her pinkie up in the air. It's hard to believe we're the same age—thirty-two is a little old to be running around footloose and fancy-free, isn't it? After a divorce, she should be trying to get right with God, but instead it looks like she's having the time of her life. Doesn't she want kids? I remember how in high school we used to sit up at night planning our future children's names and what color we'd paint their rooms. How lucky I am that everything went just as planned: Claire and Carson, pink begonia and willow springs green.

I search through the pictures on my phone and find one from the previous weekend, when we were all out to lunch at the diner after church. Claire and Carson were eating tomato soup and grilled cheese, their mouths stained goofy red, and Jeff had his arm around me in a loving embrace. My upper arm looks a bit wider than I'd like, but at least I had gotten my hair freshly highlighted the day before, and my makeup looks nice. I post the picture with the caption "Family life. ☺ It doesn't get any better than this!" A few minutes after we took the photo, Claire spilled her bowl of soup and it got all over Carson's comic book and my white dress. I yelled a little bit, like I tend to do when I forget "the anger of man does not produce the righteousness of God," but I was able to get the stain out with some OxiClean, so no harm, no foul.

The clock reads 5:58. I should get the rice pilaf and salad started, but if Jeff's running late, then so will I. I go sit with the kids and watch the movie. It's the part where Triton comes to Ariel's grotto after he finds out she's rescued Eric from drowning, disobeying his rules about mermaid and human contact. Ariel blurts out that she loves Eric, and that's when Triton loses it. His face turns dark under the glow of his magic trident, and he destroys all her human artifacts. Her globe of the world, her candelabra, her stone statue of Eric, all smashed to bits. Afterward, he gives her a guilty, resigned look and squeezes his eyes shut as he turns to leave.

The scene reminds me of my mother. The littlest things could set her off: if I slouched, if there was still a wrinkle in my skirt after I ironed it, if I snuck a bite of mashed potatoes before we said grace. Once, after a particularly nasty blow-up about how I had set the table wrong, I asked her why she even had me, since she seemed to hate me so much. "Children are a gift of the Lord, the fruit of the womb is a reward," she said in a sarcastic singsong voice, before adding darkly, "What they forgot is that fruit rots."

When Jeff's truck pulls into the driveway, I pop up off the couch to put the rice on and chop vegetables for a salad. The kitchen, with its west-facing, sun-filled windows, is like the seventh circle of hell. A rivulet of sweat snakes between my breasts. The front door opens and the kids squeal in excitement, their little feet drumrolling the floor as they run to jump in his arms. It must be nice to be the one who gets the welcome party. They babble to him about our day: I got a booboo, look at my new video game, did you know butterflies have thousands of eyes but they're just clustered together so they look like one eye?

Jeff sets the kids down and walks into the kitchen, unbuttoning his blue dress shirt, which is stained with wide, dark circles around the armpits.

"October fricking seventh," he says, tossing his shirt on a chair, then giving me a quick peck hello.

He smells like beer, and I tell myself not to comment on it; to at least try not to be the stereotypical nagging housewife, but then again, why should I stay quiet about things that bother me just because I don't want to seem annoying? If he doesn't want me to be a nag, he shouldn't give me things to nag about. "You smell like beer," I finally say, wrinkling my nose and turning back to the cutting board, chopping broccoli florets into halves and quarters.

"You know farmers," he says. "They live for a beer at the end of the day, and once you've told them how to save their business, they're grateful." He opens up a bag of grated cheese from the counter and leans his head back, dropping a fingerful into his mouth. "How was your day?"

"I'm thinking about starting a petition against that Acceptance Across America billboard."

Jeff opens up the snack cabinet, diving into a box of Wheat Thins. He takes another fingerful of cheese out of the bag and drops it on a cracker, then sandwiches another cracker on top. Shreds of orange cheese fall to the floor. "What billboard's that?"

"Are you kidding? It's a giant photo of lesbians, and it says equality has a bright future in Big Burr." I hold a glass of ice water to my cheek. "You would've had to drive by it."

He coughs up a piece of cracker. "Lesbians? I thought they were clothing models or something."

"Exactly. They're too pretty to be actual lesbians."

"Well." He opens the refrigerator. "Could be worse. It could be two men."

"How is that any different?"

"It's just . . . more gross."

"So because it's two women, you don't care?"

He sighs. "Babe, I'm exhausted. I'm not gonna get all riled up about something that doesn't affect me." He takes a container of spinach dip out of the fridge and I swat it out of his hand. "Hey! I'm starving. If dinner was ready, I wouldn't have to snack."

IN THE MORNING, the heat still hasn't broken, and the news says it'll be at least three days until it does. After a strawberry-banana smoothie and a cold shower, I type up and print out a petition, making sure to leave plenty of spaces for signatures. Then I strap Claire into her stroller and remind Carson to put on his helmet before passing him his scooter. Having both of them with me will be a pain, but they'll help my cause. Slowly, we make our way down Pine, the sidewalks shimmering in the heat. After just a block, every crevice on my body is slick with perspiration, even the creases of my eyelids.

As I approach Main Street, just the top of the billboard is visible, the roof of the neighboring building cutting off the picture below both women's eyes. They gaze at each other like there's nothing else in the world to see, like they're standing in front of Stonehenge or the *Mona Lisa* but they'd rather just look at each other.

By noontime I have forty-nine signatures and a bladder full of lemonade. Claire is starting to writhe in her stroller, arching her back against the belt across her chest while emanating high-pitched whines, and Carson has resorted to chucking rocks at plants, but I want to get at least fifty signatures before the end of the day. There's one house left to visit in the neighborhood—our across-the-street neighbors, the Ivingstons. I ring their doorbell. No answer. I ring it once more, and just as I'm about to give up, Linda comes to the door wearing a long black T-shirt that goes down to her knees, and moccasin slippers. She's obviously not wearing a bra, her oblong breasts hanging in her shirt like small eggplants.

"Are you here for your casserole dish?" she says. "Let me go get it." As she pads away, I peer past the open door into the living room, where all the shades are pulled down and piles of cards with pictures of flowers and setting suns teeter on the coffee table and overflow onto the floor.

She returns with my dish, a brown, crusty rim around the top. "Thanks, Linda, but that wasn't why I stopped by." I wish I had thought better of coming to her house, but I'm here now, and every signature counts. I force a smile and hand her the clipboard.

She reads the petition and laughs under her breath. "Can't say I've noticed it." She hands the clipboard back to me.

I pull my smile wider. "I know you haven't been out much recently, which is completely understandable. But if you were, you'd definitely see it. It's not the kind of thing we should have to look at every day."

She smiles back and looks me dead in the eyes. "You know what, Christine? I couldn't give a flying fuck about that billboard."

Carson giggles. "She said a no-no word."

Acid churns in my stomach. "I understand you're grieving. But God needs us to protect the children who are still here from this kind of sin."

She laughs and laughs. She puts her hand on the doorframe and leans over, catching her breath. "You know who else doesn't give a flying fuck about that billboard?" she says, her eyes shimmering. "God." Then she slams the door in my stunned face, waking up Claire, who starts screaming.

"Mommy," says Carson, his face bright red and slick with sweat. "Can we go home now?"

SATURDAY NIGHTS ARE date night. There are really only two nice restaurants in town, Giovanni's and Bistro 46, and at both places the food is nothing to write home about, but it gets us out of the house and gives me a night off from cooking. We went to Bistro 46 last week, so this week it's back to Giovanni's. As we walk to our table, we pass two young women sitting across from each other, one with dirty blond hair and a plain face and the other with curly black hair and dark features, clearly not from around here. I don't think anything of them dining together until the one with dark features reaches over to wipe a crumb from the other woman's mouth: a version of the billboard come to life. I can't get a moment's peace. They're engaged in a lively conversation, talking a little too loudly and smacking the tabletop as they laugh. I would bet anything they're from the task force. I ask to be seated near the window, across the room from them.

After Jeff and I order our usual—spaghetti and meatballs for Jeff, salmon and green beans for me—Jeff reaches across the table and holds my hand.

"You look beautiful tonight," he says, like he says every Saturday night.

"And you look very handsome," I say, reminding myself that he *is* handsome and wondering why I no longer think so. I look at him closely, trying to see him the way I did in the beginning, back when we were eighteen. He has kind brown eyes, even if they are a tad too close together, a strong nose, and full, long lips. I watch his lips as they move—he's talking about work again—and I picture the very hungry caterpillar crawling across his face, eating one apple, two pears, three plums, four strawberries . . .

"So I told them, if they switch to an aboveground pivot system instead of the pipes, they'll have way less flooding," Jeff says.

What was it the very hungry caterpillar ate after the strawberries? It wasn't so long ago I read the book to Claire every day. Was it some kind of citrus? Five grapefruits or five oranges? Or was it tangerines?

"And then aliens landed in the field and took us to their home planet," Jeff says.

"What?"

"I might as well be talking gibberish, for as much as you care."

He takes a gulp of wine, lowers his glass, almost setting it on the table, then brings it back to his mouth, taking another gulp.

"I'm sorry. There's just a lot on my mind." On *Righteous Wife*, I recently posted twenty-five conversation starters to spice up date night—questions like "What are three qualities you love about me?" or "What's your favorite activity to do together?" or "If we could go on another honeymoon and money was no object, where would you want to go?" But I don't feel like asking them now. I imagine how Jeff would answer. For the three qualities he loves about me, he'd probably say I'm kind, I'm a good mother, and I'm devoted to my causes. I don't think it's all that true that I'm kind or a good mother—certainly not all the time—but that's what every man says about his wife. And I think it actually annoys him how devoted I am to things like the billboard and Media WatchMoms. After all, *devoted* is just a synonym for *stubborn*, and no one likes a stubborn woman. He would probably say his favorite thing to do with me is to watch TV, even though he's always shushing me as I criticize commercials and ask logistical questions about *CSI*. And he'd probably outright refuse to answer the honeymoon question. "But money *is* an object," he'd say. "What's the point of daydreaming about something unrealistic?" We went to the Florida Keys for our actual honeymoon because Jeff had read in some travel magazine that it looked just like the Caribbean but without all the expense or inconvenience of traveling outside of the U.S. Never mind that I thought it would have been nice to leave the country, since we never had. Still haven't. Italy-themed paintings line the walls of the restaurant: cliffy seaside towns, bright pink flowers spilling over pastel buildings along a cobblestone street. I wonder if it looks like that in person, so charming and picturesque. One of my friends who went to Rome said it was actually quite dirty.

Jeff blows air out of his nose and rolls his eyes. He grabs a roll out of the bread basket and stuffs half of it in his mouth.

My chest tightens. I know I should leave it alone and try my best to act interested in what he says for the rest of the night. "What?" I say instead, crossing my arms. "What do you want to say?"

"Nothing." A wad of half-chewed bread sits in his open mouth. He shakes his head and smiles meanly.

"Say it." Heat crawls up my neck, and I know he must see the red splotches forming there, a dead giveaway that I'm upset.

He swallows the bread in his mouth and washes it down with another glug of wine. "I provide for the family and give you everything you ask for. What could possibly be on your mind all the damn time?"

"I'd like to see you spend one full day with them by yourself," I say. "You'd go crazy."

He laughs. "And what would you do if I stayed home with the kids? How would you provide for an entire household? I don't think a *blog* would cut it."

"I guess we'll never know. Since you shot that idea down pretty quick."

"Were you *serious* about that?"

I shrug. "My posts have been getting more likes and comments.

A lot of women have built careers off of blogs that started with just a few followers. And I did take a creative writing class in college. My professor said I showed promise."

"Please," he says. "We both know why you went to college." He looks down at the small oval of diamond on my ring finger.

Before he can see my face crumple, I stand up and walk to the bathroom, cloistering myself in a stall where I sit folding squares of toilet paper into tiny fans, willing myself not to cry. It's true. I never intended to use my sociology degree. My mother said it was the perfect major, because it made you seem smart but nonthreatening. What would I have majored in if I had actually planned to pursue a career? Back then, it didn't occur to me that I could choose something like writing or business. All I ever wanted was to be a wife and a mother. But do I actually enjoy spending every minute of every day with my kids? Does it float my boat to vacuum the house three times a week, to fold boxer shorts and tiny T-shirts, to scour the internet trying to find a dinner recipe I haven't made before? Do I cherish talking to my husband every night when he gets home? I used to save up little things from my day to tell him—how the smell of a campfire reminded me of childhood vacations to my grandparents' lake house, where we'd roast foil-wrapped potatoes in the fire; or that I read an article about how smelling an orange can reduce your stress by over seventy percent. Lately, though, there hasn't seemed to be any point.

When we get home, we try to make up by making love. As Jeff moves above me, I repeat the verse from Matthew in my head, "Do not withhold forgiveness from your spouse." I imagine pushing my anger out through my pores and shooting it into space. When we each turn off our bedside lamps, the image of the two women from the billboard pops into my head. I wonder if there's such a thing as lesbian housewives. Some lesbians have kids, right? Using a stranger's sperm. How is it even *your* kid at that point, really? I'd be afraid I'd end up with an ax murderer or something. I guess they could adopt, too, but then it's the same problem—you have no idea what you're getting. Regardless, some of them find a way to do it. I wonder how they decide who goes to work and who stays home to raise the kids. Or maybe one of them isn't expected to stay home—maybe they both have jobs. Then how do they decide who cooks dinner? Who fixes the car and kills the spiders in the bathroom? Who has the final say on decisions? It's all so unclear.

AT CHURCH THE NEXT MORNING, we all dab handkerchiefs to our damp faces, sweating through our Sunday best, as Pastor Jim reads from Ephesians 4:26–27: "'In your anger do not sin; do not let the sun go down while you are still angry, and do not give the devil a foothold.'" Sometimes I swear Pastor Jim can see inside my mind, and tailors each sermon to what I most need to hear.

"Within the past week, how many of you have gone to bed angry?" Pastor Jim asks. "Let me see some hands."

We all peer around the room sheepishly, our eyes lingering on banners that say things like OPEN THE EYES OF MY HEART, LORD, or SEE THE NEED, DO THE DEED. Our hands stay clasped in our laps.

"Come on," says Pastor Jim. "We're here to be honest before God." Someone coughs. Then a man near the front lifts his arm. A few other guys follow suit. Then Jeff raises his hand, keeping his eyes forward. Is he thinking about last night? After we had sex, he didn't seem angry anymore. He seemed positively unburdened, snoring away while I lay awake. I want to reach over and yank his arm down. Carson notices that Jeff's hand is raised, so he raises his own hand, grinning like it's a game.

Jeff grins back at him and whispers, "What are you angry about, champ?"

"I don't want to be here," Carson says, full-volume. "I never get to do what I want to do."

"Shhhhh," I hiss at them.

Jeff rolls his eyes at Carson, and Carson giggles.

None of the women in the room have raised their hands. "Ladies," Pastor Jim says. "Do you really expect me to believe none of you were angry this past week? Denying it doesn't do any good."

"Heck, I'm angry right now!" yells a woman in the front row, shooting her hand up and wiggling her fingers like she's trying to catch a prize. The woman next to her raises her hand, then the woman behind her. When almost everyone in the church has their hands in the air, I put mine up, too, holding it at shoulder level.

Pastor Jim chuckles. "Men, remember this the next time your wife says she isn't angry." He pauses to let the room laugh. "Okay, we've established we're all angry. Now, what can we do about it? The first step is to identify what you're really mad about. You know when you stub your toe on the edge of the couch, and you look at the couch like it's to blame? We do that with our emotions, too. We think we're mad about thing A, when we're actually mad about thing B. Right now I want everyone to close their eyes and think about the number one thing in your life making you angry. Go ahead, I'll give you a minute."

I close my eyes. The number one thing? Options rotate through my mind like I've spun *The Price Is Right* wheel: Jeff, the kids, housework, the billboard. The kids, Jeff, the billboard, housework. The billboard, Jeff, the kids, housework. That feels like the right order.

"All right, does everyone have your answer?" Pastor Jim says. "How many of you said you were angry about, say, your bills?"

A few people raise their hands.

"I want you to ask yourself if it's really about the bills. Or could it be fear that you'll never have the financial comfort you dream of? Insecurity about a promotion you didn't get? Anger is usually a secondary emotion that's covering up the primary one, because the primary one is harder to deal with. It's usually fear, or dissatisfaction, or insecurity, or sadness. Think about which emotion could be hiding *behind* the anger."

I don't always agree with Pastor Jim's sermons. This one seems a little off base. Anger, the emotion you're feeling, isn't actually the emotion you're feeling?

"Let's take it back to the scripture," Pastor Jim says. "In verse twenty-six when Paul says, 'In your anger do not sin,' what he really means is, 'Watch out! You better find out what lies behind that anger before it leads you to sin.'"

AT THE TOWN COUNCIL MEETING the next evening, I patiently wait to present my petition. The air-conditioning is, of course, broken, and everyone fidgets in their seats, pulling their shirts forward and fanning their faces with pieces of paper. Some people audibly groan as the audience address section begins. Henry Plummer accuses his neighbor Bruce of moving the property lines between their houses, Martha Wagner is concerned about unfixed and unvaccinated cats in the neighborhood, and Cindi Webber wonders if someone could volunteer to landscape Linda and Richard Ivingston's lawn, since they haven't been up to it themselves. Finally, my turn comes.

I stand behind the podium, unfolding and refolding my print-out of the petition. "My name is Christine Peterson. I'm a resident of 354 Pine Street and a member of Media WatchMoms." The town council members blink at me resignedly. I clear my throat. "For those of you who are unaware, Acceptance Across America has put up a billboard above Barb's Boutique, much to Barb's chagrin." One of the council members covers his mic and hacks into his hand, then takes a long drink out of a red Big Gulp cup. A cell phone in the audience plays the rumba. "It promotes homosexual relationships by showing two lesbians holding hands," I go on. "Myself and a large number of other concerned Big Burr citizens ask that this billboard be removed immediately. It's indecent and inappropriate for a town with family values like ours."

There are a few shouts of "Amen!" and the audience claps loudly, which I'm thankful for. All my neighbors who signed the petition and promised they'd be at the meeting haven't shown up. The next time I see them, they'll say things like "A migraine came on" or "Tim was running late from work and I couldn't get a sitter." They know I'll take care of it while they do whatever they think is more important. The council members look at each other, waiting for someone to speak.

"Terry, do you want to respond?" one of the council members asks the mayor.

Terry wipes his forehead with a blue paisley handkerchief and clears his throat. "Christine, we always appreciate hearing from you, and you make salient points. But in this instance there's nothing we can do."

My neck goes hot. "Why not?"

"Because we already looked into filing a suit and a lawyer said no judge would rule in our favor. It's free speech."

"So you'll let them take over our town because of free speech? Molehills *do* become mountains, you know. What's next? A gay club? A brothel?" A bead of sweat crawls down my stomach, then another follows. "We elected you as mayor because you said you'd protect Big Burr from just this kind of filth."

Terry pulls at his thick gray beard like he's trying to remove it from his face. "Listen, I don't like the damn billboard any more than you do. But legally, we're backed into a corner."

An intense wave of heat rushes from my feet to my head, and the room starts to spin. I close my eyes, and when I open them I'm on the floor, Terry pressing a wet paper towel to my forehead.

WHEN I GET HOME, Jeff is asleep on the couch, the game blaring on TV and a Pizza Hut box on the coffee table. Plates covered in orange-greased napkins and half-chewed crusts are scattered across the kitchen countertop. *God never gives us more than we can bear*, I say to myself while taking deep breaths. Pastor Jim would probably tell me I'm not *really* mad about the dirty kitchen, but that's easy for him to say. I bet his wife picks up the kitchen while he sits in a quiet room writing his sermons.

I stand there for a minute, debating between yelling at Jeff or just picking up the mess myself. A third option presents itself: I pick up a plate and release it from my hands, waiting for the satisfying shatter as it hits the floor. Instead, it bounces against the linoleum and rolls a few inches on its side before hitting the cabinets.

A deep animal sound rises from my throat. I pick up the plate and try again, this time holding it high above my head and slamming it down. It just bounces higher and rolls farther. I vaguely remember the salesperson in Home Depot selling us on the "shatter-resistant" laminate flooring, and curse the fact that we didn't opt for actual tile.

"Honey?" calls Jeff from the living room.

I stand there, wishing I could throw myself on the floor and feel my body break into a million pieces. I try to think of something, anything, that will give me that sense of release. A grating cheer comes from the living room. How many times in my life have I asked Jeff to turn down the TV? My eyes fall on a Giovanni's matchbook on the countertop. I grab the matchbook and my keys off the hook, then storm out the front door, letting it slam behind me.

As I start the car, Jeff appears in the doorway. "Where are you going?" he yells, his voice muted by the rolled-up windows. As I back out of the driveway, he shrugs and closes the door. I blast the AC and turn the radio on. It's story hour on my normal Christian radio station. The last thing I want to hear right now are platitudes about accepting things you can't change and putting your trust in God. I hit the seek button until it lands on a rap station. I turn it up. The rapper sounds extremely angry, growl-yelling about losing his mind and acting a fool. The bass line vibrates through the car, making my thighs tingle. I turn it up even louder, until the speakers reach their limit, the pressure of the music filling up all the space in my brain.

I pull into the parking lot next to Barb's Boutique and sit in the car until the song finishes, then pop the trunk and grab the red plastic can of gas we keep there in case of an emergency. The boutique is dark inside, the metal grates pulled over the front windows. Headlights approach from far off, illuminating the parallel yellow lines of the street. I press myself against the wall of the boutique until the car passes. For once, I'm grateful the town didn't approve my petition to install higher-wattage bulbs in the streetlamps.

I turn on the flashlight of my phone and scan the building, looking for some kind of ladder or fire escape I can climb to reach the billboard. On the back wall, the beam of light illuminates a metal ladder extending up to the roof. A flake of rust falls off when I touch a rung. I press down, testing its stability, and the ladder holds. I place my phone in my mouth, the flashlight facing up, and grab the handle of the gas can with one hand and a rung with the other. Climbing a ladder one-handed is more complicated than it seems. I work in steps: right foot up, left foot up, then balance as I release my hand and reach for the next rung. Gas sloshes in the can as I shakily ascend. Specks of rust stick to my sweaty palms and spit accumulates in my mouth, coating my phone case and dripping onto my chin.

As I reach the roof, a wisp of breeze lifts the hair from the back of my neck. I set down the gas can and take a deep breath. Lights shine in the cornfield past Field Road: combine harvesters working through the night to mow down the corn. From far away, the unloader arms on the harvesters make them look like one-winged airplanes struggling to get off the ground. I wonder if I'll ever take an airplane, where I'd go if I did. I shine my flashlight on the billboard. From close up, the women look like giants, their clasped hands even more sinister. I unscrew the cap from the gas can and hold the nozzle against the bottom corner of the billboard. The material is some kind of water-resistant vinyl, and the gas splashes onto the roof instead of soaking in. Then I notice the wooden support beams leaning from the top to the bottom on the back of the billboard.

I work methodically, soaking each beam in gas. Then I hold a match to the wood. As the flames surge to life, a puff of hot air hits me in the face, pushing me back. The yellow-orange tendrils crawl quickly, making the wood crackle and pop. I scramble down the ladder and run back to my car. I sit there for a minute, wanting to see the first flame eat through the image. A small black splotch appears on the bottom of the billboard, near the women's feet. The picture begins to sag, pulling the women's faces down into jowly frowns. Their eyes melt into their cheeks and their ears drift down the sides of their necks. They look like some kind of abstract monsters. They look incredibly, inexpressably sad.

As the blaze slowly crawls across the bottom of the billboard, the words of Jude 1:7 come to me: "Sodom and Gomorrah and the surrounding towns gave themselves up to sexual immorality and perversion. They serve as an example of those who suffer the punishment of eternal fire."

I wait for the release I was sure I would feel. But anger still floods my muscles like a poison, straining to break through my skin. If this didn't satisfy it, I don't know what will. I watch the billboard for another minute, then turn the key in the ignition and drive home, the flames waving in my rearview mirror.

David

Arturo shuffles up the path to our house, arms trembling as he grips his walker. He's so bent over that his legs and torso make a ninety-degree angle. He places each foot in front of him gingerly, like he's inching through a minefield and each step might be his last. Miguel, Arturo's son and my partner of thirty years, walks beside him, a beige suitcase in one hand, the other hovering above Arturo's back. Durango, Arturo's black Scottish terrier who is almost as old as Arturo, lifts his leg and lets out a trickle of urine onto the frozen grass. Christmas will be here in two weeks, and it still hasn't snowed.

Watching Arturo's approach feels like watching a bullet come at you in excruciating slo-mo. My lungs seize and constrict. A month ago, Arturo had a stroke and lay on his kitchen floor for two whole days before his neighbor, dropping off some lemon bars, discovered him. After that, Miguel was firm: Arturo was coming to live with us. So we converted the office into a bedroom, installed a ramp to the front door, and kissed our freedom goodbye.

As they walk into the house, I contort my mouth into a smile. Arturo's face has changed since the last time I saw him. The bags under his eyes must obstruct his downward vision, his lips have all but disappeared, and the tendons of his neck stand out like metal rods inserted to support his head.

"Hi, Arturo," I say. "How was your trip?"

He looks through me. "Did you see the price of gas at the Shell down the street?" he says to Miguel, or me, or no one. He spits out a laugh. "They might as well put a gun to your head."

"We don't have much choice around here, Dad," says Miguel. "Not much competition."

"I guess no one has much choice around here. You drag me to this shithole town when I was fine back in New Mexico." His brown eyes square on me. "See? David agrees with me. He doesn't want me here, either."

I blink. I have to do better if a half-senile eighty-two-year-old man can tell how badly I want him back in New Mexico.

"I think you're just tired from the long drive," says Miguel, steering Arturo down the hallway. "Let me show you your room."

"You mean my cell?" he says. Durango follows them down the hallway, nails clicking on the hardwood floors.

I go into the kitchen and open a beer. Beyond the window over the sink, the barren limbs of our oak tree look like a bleeding ink splotch on the gray paper of the sky. Across the street, there's a large wheat field that houses two grain silos, a defunct windmill that never spins, and an abandoned farmhouse with a caving-in roof. It could be an idyllic scene, but Arturo is right: Big Burr, Kansas, is a shithole.

Across the flat, sprawling fields, there's a billboard for a jeweler that says SOMETIMES, IT'S OK TO THROW ROCKS AT GIRLS! Another one says EVOLUTION IS A FAIRY TALE FOR GROWN-UPS. Between the billboards are cattle feedlots that reek of manure and burned hair. Before moving here, when I pictured Kansas cows, they were scattered among green, wildflower-dotted fields, the calves at the feet of their mothers, a farmer in blue overalls lovingly slapping their haunches. The reality couldn't have been more different: brown cows, covered in brown mud and their own brown feces, lined up without an inch of space between them at troughs filled with brown feed, the brown mushy ground stretching for miles.

Not so long ago I was in Brooklyn, where I was born and raised and stayed. I was working as a research associate for Acceptance Across America, mostly analyzing and reporting on survey data. I should have been in a much higher position for my age, but I graduated high school in 1982, just when AIDS was starting to rear its head. It was hard to see the point in going to college, let alone pursuing a career, when you might not live to see the fruition of any of it. So I bartended and temped and did all kinds of menial jobs while the men around me disappeared, then in the late eighties I started to get involved with ACT UP. I mostly did policy and medical research that I was utterly unequipped for, but I taught myself a lot and told myself that if I survived, I'd go to college and pursue research as a career. Fast-forward to a few months ago, when I kept asking AAA for a promotion to senior research associate, which meant I'd get to conceptualize, design, and conduct unique research projects. When they told me I finally got the job, there was one large catch—I'd have to move to Big Burr to do the research on the ground.

The charter school where Miguel taught literature had recently closed, and he couldn't find another job. We were barely making ends meet. The lease was up on our apartment in Ditmas Park, and we'd have to move to Coney Island to find the same rent. Two years in Kansas, to catch our breath and improve our finances, didn't sound so bad at the time. But now that we've been here for four and a half months, I know exactly how long a day can feel.

Miguel comes into the kitchen and follows my lead, taking the whiskey out of the cabinet and pouring an inch in a glass. "Don't even say it."

I hold up my hands in surrender. He takes a sip, then leans his body into me, threading his fingers through mine. He looks into my eyes intently. His deep brown irises have lightened and taken on a green hint, something I haven't noticed before. The green creeps in from the edges of his pupils, like algae in a pond.

"I know what you're thinking." He pulls away and tips his head back, drinking half the whiskey in his glass.

I'm thinking that when you're young, it never occurs to you that part of love, part of sharing your life with another person, includes the shitty things. Like compromising on where to live, needing a third person in your bed to be able to fuck each other, or inviting an aging parent into your house. Then suddenly you're fifty-three, and it feels like love is mostly those things. "I'm thinking how, thirty years ago, we would have bet someone a thousand dollars our life wouldn't be this," I say.

"A thousand dollars would have been all our savings back then. Which apartment were we living in?"

"Dean Street, above the barbershop and below the bowling ball family. Where Barclays Center is now."

"That fucking place." He lets out a half laugh. "Remember the night you banged on the ceiling with the broom handle so hard you made a hole? And two dead mice fell out."

I shudder, remembering the mice hitting my neck like furry hacky-sack balls. "I think that was the worst apartment we ever had."

"But we were happy," says Miguel.

We exchange smiles—weak ones, like tea bags that have already been used once and barely color the water.

Miguel opens the fridge. "Dinner?"

"I got an eggplant and some fresh mozzarella yesterday," I say. "Eggplant parm?"

He gives me a little grimace. "Dad says eggplant tastes like a dirty dish sponge. I'll run to the store and get something he likes."

I look down the hallway toward Arturo's room. Even though I've been with Miguel for thirty years, Arturo still doesn't feel like family. When Miguel came out to him, he said, "Well, okay, then. What's for lunch?" After that, they never spoke about it again. The first time I went home with Miguel he introduced me simply as David, and after a few visits I think Arturo understood I would keep coming back. At holidays and reunions, he tolerates me the way you would a persistent bunion on your foot: you'd prefer it wasn't there, but you can live with it. To be fair, I guess I feel the same way toward him. But the thought of having to interact with him on my own makes my lungs clench.

"I can go to the store," I say through a strangled breath.

"You don't know all his little quirks. There's a lot of stuff he doesn't like."

"Great."

Miguel gives me an exhausted look and finishes the whiskey in his glass.

"What am I supposed to do if he needs something?"

He gives me an even more exhausted look. I wonder sometimes why he hasn't left me. Once, years ago, after I berated him for giving ten dollars to a homeless drunk, he told me I had "zero empathy." He took it back later, but I knew he had meant it.

He walks out of the kitchen, his keys jingling. The front door slams, and I'm terrified it might have woken Arturo. I stand absolutely still, holding my breath and listening for a sound from down the hall. It's not that Arturo is so terrible. But it's like having a roommate when you thought you'd never have a roommate again. When you need to shit, someone's in the bathroom. You can't knock on the door and say hurry up, I've gotta go. You just stand in the hallway doing ass-Kegels, cursing humanity. When you want to watch trashy reality TV, guess who's already on the couch drinking your beers, the game only in the first quarter.

A few years ago, Miguel and I decided to stop traveling for Christmas. We decided it would be a day for us, without any airports or useless gifts or pretending to think our relatives' insufferable children were cute. I'm sure our now-normal routine of bingeing western movies and cooking Indian food is a thing of the past, because guess who doesn't like Indian food.

I realize, with a start, that this will be even worse than having a roommate. At least roommates are self-sufficient. Arturo will need care and looking after, like a baby. I never wanted anything remotely close to a baby, not even a cat or a dog or a hamster. I repeat to myself, *There is nothing obstructing your airways, there is nothing obstructing your airways.* In the middle of the kitchen I start doing jumping jacks, my mother's cure for panic attacks.

The first time one happened, I was thirteen, on the way to my first soccer match of the year. I was the goalie. As I pictured a succession of checkered balls flying just past my gloves and hitting the white netting of the goal, I told my mother I couldn't breathe. She pulled the minivan into a Dairy Queen parking lot and told me to do jumping jacks. When I looked at her like she was insane, she started doing them with me. After about twenty seconds, the air flowed freely. My mother smiled, drumming her fake pink nails on her hip, and said, "Told you."

"Miguel!"

I stop my jumping jacks, hoping I've only imagined Arturo calling for Miguel. But then I hear it again, his trembling voice insistent, like he's being held off the edge of a cliff. I sigh and walk down the hallway to his door. Steeling myself, I knock, then push the door open.

"Oh, it's you," Arturo says. He's propped up in bed on one of those backrest pillows with arms, wearing a pair of blue striped pajamas that look brand new, the collar stiff at his neck, the fold lines still crisp. The dog lies next to him under the covers with his head on the pillow. Orange pill bottles make a miniature skyline on the bedside table. A black-and-white photo of Miguel's mom and Arturo standing in front of a vintage Chevy truck leans against the windowsill, in a tacky gold frame. Miguel's mom left when he was three, and he never heard from her again. Arturo never got over it, and it was up to Miguel to take care of his dad after that.

"Miguel went to the store to get something you'll like for dinner," I say.

"Oh." He glances down at the blanket and smooths it. His hands look like they've been vacuum-sealed, the veins and tendons making valleys of his wrinkled skin. "Never mind, then."

"Is there anything I can get you?"

"No," he says, peering at the semi-closed door like I'm lying about Miguel being gone. He clasps his shaking hands in his lap. I picture him lying on his kitchen floor for two whole days, his cheek pressed against spotted pea-green linoleum, watching the sunlight slide across the countertops and fade into darkness, having to piss and shit himself and knowing that either someone would find him lying in a puddle of his own feculence, or he would die that way. I try not to think about who will take care of me when I'm old. I like to imagine myself just falling over one day after a long life of perfect health. I wouldn't have to ask any favors and no one would be inconvenienced. If only we could all be so lucky.

I tell Arturo to let me know if he changes his mind about

needing anything, then I gently shut the door behind me. I grab another beer from the fridge and take it to the couch, where I open up Grindr. I wait for the grid of pictures to load, hoping for someone new while knowing that, in a town with a population of ten thousand, that's about as likely as a flying pig. We haven't found someone in months.

I scroll through a smattering of familiar six-packs, each muscle like a dinner roll you could pick up and wolf down, mirror selfies cut off at the neck, and boxer-brief close-ups. Gay men in small Kansas towns aren't going to risk showing their faces. There are five guys within a few miles—three of them have the thin, lanky bodies of high school students. The rest are at least thirty miles away.

Then I spot the flying pig: a guy I haven't seen before, with a trimmed beard and camo boxers. The top of the photo is cut off just below his nose and the bottom of the photo ends at his groin. Though he's not very muscular, he's also not overweight, and he has nice, full lips. I picture his mouth covering my cock while Miguel sticks a finger up my ass. His profile name is G, and he's tagged his position as "versatile" and his tribe as "discreet." He's only two miles away, which means that he's in Big Burr. I send him a message asking if he wants to meet up tonight, and he says, *Maybe. Check back in a few hours.* When I return to the grid of pictures and try to scroll down, there aren't any more. Fucking Kansas.

Living here has essentially forced Miguel and me into monogamy, which these days just means abstinence. The last time we slept with only each other must have been the eighties, when sex with strangers became a flirtation with death. It wasn't until the mid-nineties, when some of us started feeling like we might actually live to see old age, that Miguel and I started to sleep with other people. We finally felt safe enough to admit we were a little bored. First we had sex separately, never revealing the details to each other but promising to be careful. Soon there was too much we couldn't say. I started getting paranoid that Miguel wasn't just having sex but a full-fledged relationship, and when I finally asked him about it he said he had been thinking the same thing about me. We agreed to never have sex without each other again. Over the years we honed the rules: three-ways only, no friends, no repeats, no overnights, no anal, no one with tribal tattoos, never in our bed, only when we both approved of the guy, and if one of us ever started to feel uncomfortable, we'd talk about it.

Miguel's car pulls into the driveway and I close Grindr. I turn the TV on to a Folgers commercial. A young daughter gives her father a WORLD'S GREATEST DAD mug for Christmas, then the ad flashes forward to the daughter, now older, giving her graying father a WORLD'S GREATEST GRANDPA mug. I cringe.

Miguel walks in with two grocery bags, looking annoyed. "I was going to make posole, but of course they didn't have any hominy. So I got stuff for carne adovada." He unloads groceries in the kitchen, raising his voice over the TV. "Thank god I still have that stash of dried chiles. Remember when you told me not to pack them?" If there was a fire in the house and Miguel could take only two things with him, it would be his dried chiles and his western DVD collection.

I turn up the TV volume even though I'm not listening. Miguel stands in the doorway between the kitchen and the living room, watching me. I know he's waiting for me to be his sous chef, but I'm still annoyed about the eggplant parm we won't be eating anytime soon. I don't feel like New Mexican food. If I'm honest, I barely ever feel like New Mexican food—except for sopapillas, which are really just vehicles for honey. He turns around and goes back into the kitchen, and I think I've won, until he calls out twenty seconds later, "Would you like to help me?"

I push myself off the couch and follow Miguel to the kitchen. He stands over the food processor, dumping in unmeasured amounts of dried coriander, oregano, and rehydrated red chiles. Two onions, a knife, and a cutting board sit on the island waiting for me. "Why do I always have to cut the onions?" I ask, feeling like a petulant teenager.

"Stop being such a cabrón." He pours honey into the food processor, wipes the lip of the jar with his finger, and holds it in front of my face. I remember a night forever ago, when we had only been dating for a few months, when he did the same thing. He had just made me my first sopapillas, and as I licked off the honey, circling my tongue around the tip of his finger, I watched him get hard in his jeans. He coated my lips in honey and kissed it off. He poured honey into his hand, a thick ribbon that coalesced into a sensuous pool, and enveloped my cock with it. He drizzled honey on my ass and lapped it off. Honey ended up in every crevice of our bodies. We had to peel the sheets off our sticky skin, our body hair matted.

I open my mouth and close it around his finger, but it just feels sticky, not sexual. I wonder whether to fake it, act like it's turning me on, but when I look at Miguel, his lips are pressed together and he's looking over my shoulder. When he really likes something, he makes a deep moan that almost sounds like a snore. He goes to the sink and washes his hands, and I go back to chopping the onion.

"What do you think about meeting up with someone tonight?"

He turns around and squints at me. "Seriously?"

"It's the first time in ages I've seen someone new on Grindr." I run my finger along the blade of the knife to release the curved squares of onion clinging there.

"I didn't know you were still looking."

"It's been a really long time. I think we need this."

"It's my father's first night in our house, and all you can think about is finding someone to suck you off?" He takes the pork out of the refrigerator and throws it onto a cutting board, the pink meat slapping against the plastic.

"I just don't know when there'll be another opportunity."

"Then you should go by yourself." He says it with no discernible tone, his back to me. His tricep flexes as he chops the pork into neat cubes.

"But that's against the rules."

He scoffs. "Because the rules have been working so well for us."

I've finished dicing the onions into a sad, jagged snowbank. "You wouldn't be jealous?"

He puts down the knife and sets his palms on the edges of the countertop. His back rises and expands as he takes a deep breath. "You were supposed to say you don't want to go without me."

I throw my hands up. "Then you shouldn't say things you don't mean."

Miguel takes a pan out of the cabinet beneath the counter and places it on the stove. He fills it with a few glugs of oil and turns the burner on. "You should go," he says, his back to me.

"Tonight, or now?"

When he finally turns around, he looks like he's just gotten off a long flight and I'm the last person he wants to see. "Either." He turns back and drops cubes of pork into the hot oil.

If his father wasn't here, we wouldn't be fighting. I turn and walk out of the house. I get in the car and head toward the Cinephile, figuring an insipid blockbuster will be good for shutting off my brain. The sun is setting, wedging directly between the two grain silos in the field across the street. Beams of light shoot across them like spokes of a wheel. At a four-way stop, the car next to me is full of teenagers singing and car-dancing. I want to follow them, unroll my window, and yell, "Do you know what your lives will become?" The houses get closer together and suburbia flashes by: a man in a plaid jacket tosses a garbage bag into a trash can, a woman unloads groceries from the trunk of her silver SUV, kids bundled in down jackets kick a partly deflated soccer ball across their yard.

I turn onto Main Street, passing the remains of our billboard. Someone tried to burn it down a couple months ago, but they only managed to incinerate the bottom of it, up to the women's calves—the top just melted, disfiguring the women's faces as if they had literally walked through fire. I imagine the people of Big Burr forcing the women to walk through flames to prove their love for each other. Their scorched feet and clasped hands make them look like some kind of gay warriors—maybe a more fitting image than the one we used originally. The cops say they can't let us put up a new billboard because the burned one is part of an active investigation, although I have serious doubts about how *active* it really is.

I pull into the parking lot of the Cinephile. Two movies are on the marquee: *Love Is Blind*, a rom-com about a woman who falls in love with a blind man, and *Ramsey & Robot*, a futuristic buddy-cop movie. I buy a ticket for *Love Is Blind* and check my phone to see if Miguel has texted me. He hasn't.

I choose a seat in the back row, one in from the end, and drape my jacket over the seat next to me like I'm waiting for someone. Women wearing those terrible boots that look like slippers and sweaters that look like bathrobes sit in small clusters, each with their own large bucket of popcorn. A teenage guy sits dutifully next to his girlfriend, holding her hand with one hand, scrolling through his phone with the other. A young mother shushes her toddler as he sings some nonsense song, his mouth full of neon candy. From the opposite end of the back row, two women slide in and sit in the middle. One of them opens a bag of gummy bears and places an orange one on the other woman's knee. She walks the candy slowly up the woman's thigh until the other woman swats it off and places the gummy bear in her mouth, looking around guiltily, as if to make sure no one has seen. The women then get into a hushed argument that ends with a furtive yet ardent kiss. As the lights dim for the previews, I take out my phone to text Miguel, *Omg I'm sitting next to covert Big Burr lesbians*, before I remember we're in a fight.

I fall asleep during the movie, and when the lights come on at the end, I jolt awake to a man staring at me, and not kindly. His face is four inches from mine. My heart beats wildly. My sphincter tightens. The man's black pupils move from my face to my Acceptance Across America sweatshirt with the rainbow American flag logo. Fuck. I left in such a rush, I forgot what I was wearing.

The end credits roll as Stevie Wonder's "Signed, Sealed, Delivered I'm Yours" blares. The two women who had been sitting near me have left, and the remaining patrons stream down the two aisles at either end of the room. I want to stand up and follow them out of the theater, but my limbs feel cemented, like one of those terrible dreams where you're trying to run but can't. Warm air from the man's nostrils blows onto my cheek. Dark stubble covers his jaw like splinters half stuck under skin. A drop of ice water trickles from the nape of my neck down my spine. What if this is how I go? Not after a long, healthy life, but in the middle of it, during a quarrel with Miguel, when I'm still a selfish schmuck who can't see anything.

I close my eyes against the reality of the situation. From the darkness, an image of Miguel emerges. He's lying in the grass in Prospect Park, smiling at me lazily—a look of uncomplicated love. It's an image that comes to me, unbidden, in times of great stress or fear. I blink. The man is gone, the theater empty except for a Cinephile employee sweeping stray popcorn into a dustpan.

WHEN I GET HOME, Arturo is sitting on the living room couch. Durango lies beside him, his head on one of the striped throw pillows. Probably drooling all over it. They're watching *The Good, the Bad and the Ugly*, Miguel's favorite. It's the final standoff between the three men in the cemetery. I hang up my coat and peek in the kitchen.

"He went to bed," says Arturo.

I wonder if he knows that we fought. Are fighting. I sit down on the other side of the couch. Clint Eastwood walks to the middle of a stone circle in a cemetery, sets down a square tan rock, and flips his poncho over one shoulder. Miguel calls this "the most diva gesture ever."

My stomach lets out a low whine. "Is there carne adovada left?" I ask.

"Plenty," Arturo says, grasping his walker and pulling himself up off the couch. "I'll fix you a plate."

I protest, but he holds his hand out in front of me, like you do when telling a dog to stay. "My way is the best way," he says.

I don't know whether he's being nice or implying that I'm incapable of warming up food, but I stay put as Arturo shuffles into the kitchen. A burner clicks and then whooshes as it lights. A knife whaps against a cutting board, the sound fast and rhythmic. Arturo seems much more spry than he did this morning, and I wonder if he was just playing the victim. Next to me, Durango twitches in his sleep, his paws clenching and unclenching and his mouth making wet little lapping sounds. I pull the pillow out from under his head, and he jerks upright and blinks at me. When he realizes Arturo isn't on the couch anymore, he stands on the edge and lets out a long, trembling whine. In his old age, he probably can't jump down. I pick him up and place him on the floor, and he goes running into the kitchen. I sniff the pillow his head was on. It smells sweet and metallic, like raw meat that's been left out too long.

Arturo comes back into the room, a plate and two bottles of beer on the tray of his walker. He sets the plate in my lap and a beer on the coffee table in front of me. He keeps the other beer for himself. He's arranged the carne adovada in three corn tortillas, covered in white onions, cilantro, and queso fresco. He watches me as I take a bite. It tastes different than Miguel's—there's a deeper, brighter flavor, but I can't put my finger on what it is.

"Did Miguel do something different?" I ask.

Arturo shakes his head and smiles, a glint in his eye. "I added my secret ingredients."

I take another bite. Maybe I do like carne adovada after all. "Miguel doesn't know what they are?"

"No," he says. "I make him leave the room."

"Will you ever tell him?"

He smiles and holds my stare for five full seconds. "Raisins," he whispers. "And frozen orange juice concentrate."

"Really?" I swallow my bite of carne adovada, searching for the raisins and orange juice on my tongue. "Why are you telling me?"

He shrugs. "Miguel wants us to get along."

After I finish my tacos, I go upstairs. Miguel lies in bed facing the wall, his back rising and falling in sleep or pretend sleep. I sit down and lay my hand on his side, pressing my fingertips into the depressions between his ribs.

"Why do you stay with me?" I ask.

He takes a deep breath. Air fills the space where my fingertips rest, pushing them up. They fall back down as he breathes out. "Good question," he says, his voice quiet and croaky.

I wait for him to give a real answer, but after a long silence, he still hasn't said anything. My heart speeds up, and I pull on his shoulder. "Miguel?"

He turns over and looks at me with vacant eyes. "Was it good?"

"The adovada? Yeah, very tasty."

"Not the adovada," he says. "The *sex*." He snarls the word.

I reach out my hand, but he jerks away. "I went to the movies, Miguel."

He crosses his arms. "What did you see?"

"Some shitty rom-com called *Love Is Blind*. Can you guess the plot?"

I see his wheels turning, wondering if he should believe me. "How does it end?"

"I don't know. It was so boring I fell asleep." I want to tell him about the man, about how sure I was that something terrible would happen, and how Miguel's image came to me and kept me safe, but it was too surreal to describe. "Baby," I say, plaintive. "I know I can be an ass, but I'm not a liar."

He sighs. His crossed arms unfurl. "You do tend to fall asleep at the movies."

I bring his hand to my lips. I kiss his knuckles one by one. He pulls me down next to him. We kiss, and it flashes through my body like lightning. His fingers grasp the hair at the nape of my neck. Our torsos come together, and I feel Miguel's heat through his thin T-shirt. I tug it off.

He leans away. "But my dad is right downstairs," he whispers.

"It's okay." I take a deep breath, and the air flows freely as I pull Miguel to me.

Linda

I'm standing on my porch clutching this package, this ordinary square brown package with one of the corners crushed in and a white label that impossibly reads my son's name, my son who drove his maroon Buick into a tree and died four months and five days ago. I have no idea how or why the package arrived. Could Dylan have bought something before the accident, but it was back-ordered for ages? Could someone who doesn't know what happened have sent him a gift? Could Dylan be alive in some alternate universe, and this is a message for us via Amazon?

Across the street, the Petersons are leaving for their day. Christine pushes Claire in her stroller as Carson karate-chops the snowbanks on either side of their neatly shoveled walkway, while Jeff stares at his phone, rapidly typing with one thumb. In the front yard there's a gigantic snow sculpture of Lady Liberty, a not-so-subtle dig at the task force, I'm sure. They even used green dye on her crown and red and yellow dye on her torch. At night, they shine a spotlight on it and people stop to take pictures. Christine gives Jeff a quick kiss, then uses her thumb to wipe pink lipstick from the side of his mouth. He gets in his beige SUV and she straps the kids into her lime-green Kia Soul, a car to match her personality. As Christine pulls into the road, she sees me on the porch and gives me the usual I'm-sorry-your-kid-died half smile and wave.

A few months ago, I was Christine. I gave Richard kisses before leaving for work, I matched Tupperware tops to bottoms when emptying the dishwasher, and when I found a quarter in the couch cushions, I thought, *Well, isn't that nice?* Now I don't know if that was me or just someone who life hadn't turned on yet.

Richard steps outside and catches me cradling the package. "It's for Dylan."

"What the hell?" He stares at the label for a few seconds, then matter-of-factly takes the box out of my hands and walks around the side of the house. The lid of the trash can thuds closed. He comes back and opens the door of his car.

"I'll see you tonight," he calls out before ducking inside, by which he means he'll tiptoe past my bedroom door, formerly our bedroom door, around eleven p.m. on his way to the guest room, now his bedroom.

When Dylan had been gone a few weeks and I couldn't even bring myself to throw away the rotting Tupperware of lasagna I had made for dinner the night he died, Richard decided it was time to get back to our normal routine. He told me I was wallowing in misery, when really I was just trying to stop thinking of ways to kill myself. I looked up some therapists in Dry Creek, even jotted down a few numbers, but never actually called any. What good was therapy going to do me if it couldn't bring back my son? Instead, I got some sleeping pills. Now my and Richard's routine consists of carefully calibrated avoidance. In the morning we take turns in the kitchen, forcing down bites of dry toast with coffee. He stays at work crunching the numbers at the beef packing plant—at least that's where he says he is—until he thinks I'm asleep. When he gets home late at night, I can hear the guest room door click shut as I lie in bed waiting for my pill to shut off my brain.

It's hard to remember now, but I think we were happy before Dylan died. We'd crack each other up by making fun of commercials, we'd play pranks on Dylan like putting googly eyes on all the food in the fridge, we'd have routine but satisfying sex a few times a month, and most importantly, we hated the same things (rich people, tuna salad, Julia Roberts), which I think is really the key to any successful relationship.

I watch Richard's car disappear down the road, then walk around the side of the house and take the package out of the garbage. It's unfathomable to me that he couldn't have been curious about what it was. Inside the house, I cut the clear tape with a dirty knife from the kitchen sink. A black shoebox with a beige star on top sits inside the larger box. Inside the shoebox is a pair of high-top Converse sneakers covered in a blue graffiti pattern, size eight and a half. *I'll put them in his closet, in case he comes back*, I think. Then I throw the box across the room.

AT WORK, I watch the second hand on my watch sweep around the face. I'm a teller at the Big Burr Credit Union, and I can't think of a worse job to have when the last thing you want is to see every single person from town every single day. What no one understands is how suffocating their sympathy can be. I thought it would taper off after a few months, but people seem to need to prove they haven't forgotten. Sometimes I turn my phone off for a whole day just to get a break from the texts and voice mails. I hide behind the curtains when the doorbell rings, and when I step outside, another foil-wrapped dish is waiting on the steps.

But at work, I can't hide. Every day it's the same: the how-are-you-*doing*s, never just how-are-yous, the hand pats, the did-you-get-my-casseroles, the fear of eye contact, and the-Lord-never-gives-us-more-than-we-can-handles. Even worse are the ones who paste on uncomfortable smiles and talk about the weather, or the Jay-hawks, or celebrity gossip. It's a catch-22—if they say something about Dylan I resent it, and if they don't say something I resent it even more. I've started fantasizing about moving somewhere where no one knows me, where they'll look at me blankly and assume I'm just like everyone else.

Around lunchtime, I get half my fantasy. I call up someone I've never seen before, a Black man in slim jeans, a tailored peacoat, and a button-up shirt printed with small blue flowers. He smiles and asks how I am.

"Oh, I'm fine," I say. "And you?"

He hands me a deposit slip and a check, then threads his fingers together and places them on the countertop. "I'm doing well, thank you for asking, ma'am."

"Ma'am," I say, bringing my hand to my heart. "How polite! Can I see your ID for this?"

He opens up a neon pink nylon wallet and slides a Florida license across the counter.

Jamal Lowe. I match his name to the name on the check. In the license photo, he smiles widely. His street address is listed as somewhere in Miami. "Florida," I say, handing the license back. "Just visiting?"

"I live here now," he says, then shakes his head. "I'm still getting used to saying that."

"Oh, really? What brings you to Big Burr? We don't get many new arrivals."

He picks up the corded pen that's lying off its stand and puts it back in place. It leans and topples over.

"That's broken." I wait for him to answer my question, then curiosity gets the better of me. "So, Kansas?"

"Oh," he says. "Right." He picks up the pen again, then sets it down. "I came here for a job."

"At the beef packing plant?"

He shakes his head and it occurs to me why he must be avoiding the question. "I don't mean to pry," I say. "If you're here with the task force, I'm not one of those people who's upset about it."

"All right," he says, dubious.

I try to recall exactly when the task force arrived. It was so close to when Dylan died I don't think I'd have noticed if the sky turned red, but even still it was impossible to miss. It was on the front page of the *Herald* and on everyone's lips when you'd run into them at the store. People assumed I wasn't outraged because of Dylan. But most residents have lived in Big Burr for generations—the Smiths, who own a big farm on the northern edge of town, claim their family was here when the state of Kansas was founded. They feel inextricably linked to the place, protective of it; convinced that if it changes they'll lose a part of themselves. My family only arrived in Big Burr shortly after I was born, when my father got a job teaching algebra at the high school. He always said people were like equivalent equations: $5 + 3 = 2 + 6$. The total amount is 8, but there are a bunch of ways to arrive at that figure. I don't think many of the kids I grew up with were taught the same thing.

"Dare I ask how it's going?" I say. "With the task force?"

A grimace flashes across Jamal's face, but his features quickly settle back to neutral. He studies me, trying to determine if I'm friend or foe.

"I'm sorry. That's probably a stupid question. I'm sure you're having a terrible go of it."

He looks down at the countertop and clears his throat. "We're having a luau party tomorrow night," he says timidly. "To try to beat the winter blues." He reaches into his bag and pulls out a flyer with a cartoon smiling sun, a pineapple, and a lei. "You should come. Locals haven't really been showing up to our events, but maybe you can be the exception."

AFTER WORK, I cancel plans with my best friend Lorraine for the third time in a row. We were supposed to get our nails done and eat dinner at the diner, but the thought of having to pretend I'm okay for hours on end is too exhausting. Instead, I swing by Applebee's for my nightly curbside pickup. I get one of their new "healthy" items, pepper-crusted sirloin and whole grains, and add on a triple chocolate meltdown cake at the last minute, because what the hell. I eat it off a tray table in the living room while watching Jillian Michaels's *30 Day Shred*. Something about watching people sweat and struggle while Jillian yells at them makes me feel better. Besides, I can't stand to watch anything on TV anymore. Everything is about family and relationships, tidy problems that conveniently get smoothed out in thirty minutes. Even on *Sing Your Heart Out*, where contestants sing a song while doing an obstacle course, everyone has their little sob story that makes me scream at the TV, "Sorry you can't hear out of *one* ear!" or "Sorry you have dust-related *allergies*!"

I fall asleep on the couch and wake up to Richard's keys clattering into the teal fish-shaped dish on the entryway table. I could get up and skitter to my bedroom. The light turns on in the kitchen and the ice machine grumbles as cubes tinkle into a glass. I could turn over, face the back of the couch, and pretend to still be asleep. The refrigerator door opens, making a noise like a Band-Aid being pulled off skin, and the ice cubes crack as liquid pours over them.

The refrigerator door claps shut. Or I could stay right here and see what he says.

Richard jumps when he walks into the living room and sees me. "Oh," he says. "You startled me." His oxford is buttoned down half-way, exposing a threadbare undershirt, and the red plaid tie I got him some long-ago Christmas is tossed over his shoulder. He holds a pint glass full of milk, the light from the TV giving it the barely blue hue of a glacier.

"Heartburn?"

He nods. "These hours are killing me."

I wonder how long we'll keep up this routine, him pretending to work late, like there's some daily accounting emergency, and me pretending I think it's true. He looks at the Applebee's take-out bag, then the TV, Jillian Michaels and her counterparts doing jumping lunges, then at me. His lips part and he looks like he's about to say something, but then he turns it into a yawn, covering his mouth with his hand. "Well, good night," he says, disappearing around the corner.

WHILE DRIVING HOME from work the next day, I notice the flyer from Jamal on the passenger seat and decide to take him up on his offer. It's not like I have anything better to do. And it felt so refreshing, him knowing nothing about me. I pull into the parking lot and count seven cars in a little cluster, none I recognize. As I open the front door, a gust of hot air envelops me—they must have cranked the heat. I take off my jacket and walk through a grid of gray cubicles. An inflatable palm tree is propped in a corner, a pink flamingo pool floatie rests on a chair like it's hard at work, and a yellow crepe-paper sun hangs over the ceiling light. A half-drunk Miller Lite sits on someone's desk, the sweat from the bottle creating a small puddle that creeps toward a cat-face mouse pad. On the computer screen, a PowerPoint slide says, "You cannot identify an LGBTQ person just by looking at them," next to a picture of a middle-aged man in khakis and a checkered button-up shirt.

A teenage boy appears from a hallway and catches me snooping. It takes me a second before I realize it's Zach, one of Dylan's friends from school. My heart speeds up. I wasn't expecting anyone from town to be here. Zach and Dylan were never especially close, but I remember him coming to the house a few times and eating copious amounts of string cheese.

"Mrs. Ivingston?" he says, his face flushing. "What are you doing here?"

"I'm not really sure," I say. "What about you?"

"I'm volunteering for AAA." He crosses his arms and stares at the floor. "It looks really good on college applications, and there weren't any other places in town that needed volunteers."

"That's great, Zach. I'm sure it'll be really good experience."

"Could you do me a favor?" He clears his throat. "Could you, like, not tell anyone that you saw me here? I just don't want anyone to get the wrong idea."

I nod. "Sure, I understand. And if you could do me a favor right back, could you . . ." I run my fingers through my hair, pulling at a small knot until it comes loose. "Could you not mention Dylan to anyone here?"

He gives me the sympathetic smile I was hoping I wouldn't have to see tonight. "Sure, Mrs. Ivingston."

I follow Zach to a large conference room, where a group of about ten people sit around a table, wearing leis and eating snacks. Whitney Houston is playing just a little too softly for a party. Zach sidles up to a girl with long auburn hair and whispers something that makes her burst into laughter.

Jamal gets up and throws a lei around my neck. "Hey, you came! Sorry it's not more lively. We probably shouldn't have had it in our office, but it's the only place we could really turn up the heat. You want some rum punch?" He gestures to a gigantic bowl of bright pink liquid.

"Do you have any beer?"

He hands me a Bud Light and I tip my head back, taking a long swallow. "Wow, tastes like high school."

He laughs as he opens another beer for himself. "I wasn't drinking beer in high school yet. Mostly peach schnapps."

"That's what all the girls drank," I say, my hand flying to my mouth as I realize that might be an insulting thing to say to a gay man.

"Who do you think I was hanging out with?" he says, giving me a wink. Then his face gets serious. "Being here kind of feels like being back in high school."

"In what way?"

90

He shudders a little bit. "All my old insecurities ganging up on me."

"Oh? What kinds of insecurities?"

His eyes move from my khaki pants to my cubic zirconia wedding band to my pale blue eyes. "I don't know if you'd understand."

"I'd like to."

"I'm just a little too *visible* here. The way you looked at me when I walked into the bank yesterday—I could tell it wasn't malicious, but I could also tell you don't see many people like me."

My cheeks go hot. I hadn't realized I'd made a face.

"So I do everything I can not to draw too much attention to myself," he goes on. "Calling employees 'sir' and 'ma'am' and keeping my hands visible so they don't think I'm stealing anything. Or deepening my voice when I talk to strangers, and not saying things straight white people wouldn't understand."

I remember him calling me ma'am at the bank; how his formality seemed strange at the time. "What kinds of things?" I ask, curious about what he thinks I won't understand.

He smiles skeptically. "If I said, 'No tea, no shade,' what would you think that meant?"

"That you were thirsty and hot?"

Jamal bursts out laughing. "Not even close, but a good guess. It basically means 'No offense, but . . . ' Which means you're definitely about to say something offensive."

I laugh, too. "I've never heard that before."

He takes a drink of his beer and looks at me quizzically. "You must be changing the way you're talking to me, too."

"No," I say, thinking he's referring to changing my word choice or speech patterns. But what about my omission of Dylan's death? What category does that fall under?

He tilts his chin downward. "Really? Not even a little bit?"

I nod, my cheeks burning.

"Huh." He shakes his head. "That must be nice." He pauses, then says, "You went to high school around here?" His tone is somewhere between a question and a statement.

I nod. "Right here in Big Burr."

He grimaces, then tries to hide it.

"Did you ever think about leaving?"

"No," I say. "Or not until recently. I met my husband at KU, he got an accounting job at the beef packing plant and kept getting promoted, I got pregnant, my parents were here to help out with the baby, and it just kept going like that. I know it might be hard for you to believe, but for most of my life I've been content here. There are a lot of things I like about Big Burr."

His brow arches. "Like what?"

"Being close to family is important to me, especially for these last few months," I say, before remembering to censor myself. But it's true that I don't know how I would have gotten through Dylan's death without them. After losing my role of mother, I reverted back to daughter, letting my mother stop by every day to cradle me in her arms and scratch her fingernails over my scalp like when I was a little girl. She read to me and cooked me pancakes, the only food I could stomach for weeks. But being treated like a child is only appealing for so long, especially as the weeks stretched on, and finally I had to tell her I needed some space. But I can't say any of this to Jamal, so I speed ahead like my slip never happened. "And most of my friends have known me my whole life. I own my home, and I didn't have to go into debt to do so. I can take walks in the nature preserve without seeing another soul. And the sunsets will blow your mind."

"I'll give you the sunsets," he says, smiling. "What makes you think about leaving now?"

"I don't know. Lots of things. Where did *you* go to high school?"

"A small town outside of Orlando. Kind of like here, actually—real white, real straight. I got to Miami as soon as I could. I don't really know anyone gay who stayed in the town they grew up in. Like, if you want to meet someone, if you want friends who understand you, you get yourself to a city." He takes a drink of his beer and looks at me curiously from over the bottle. "Why did you come today?"

"I thought it would be nice to meet some new people. And because I think equality is really important, obviously," I add on quickly.

He extends his beer bottle and clinks it against mine. "Cheers to that."

I STAY AT THE PARTY until well after the sun goes down, drinking five beers and talking to almost every person there. Eventually the music gets louder and I even dance a tiny bit. I forget about Dylan for whole minutes at a time. But as soon as I walk in the door of my house, the stale air presses in around me and all that weight comes flooding back. As I step out of my shoes and climb the stairs, small grains of dirt stick to the bottom of my bare feet, reminding me that I haven't vacuumed in weeks.

In the bathroom, I listlessly brush my teeth, watching blue foam drip off my chin in the mirror. Then I notice a very faint light coming from under Dylan's door. I squeeze my eyes shut, thinking those beers really must have done a number on me, but when I open my eyes, the light is still there. It seems to be moving across the floor. I spit out my mouthful of toothpaste and wipe my face on the sour-smelling hand towel.

My tongue goes dry and my heart beats in my hands as I walk toward Dylan's door. I am absolutely certain that when I open it, Dylan will be standing there in his patched jeans and maroon hoodie. He'll push his bleached hair out of his eyes and look at me half guilty, half defiant, like when he used to come home after curfew. *Sorry I scared you*, he'll mumble. *But I'm back now.*

I gently push his door open. The beam of light falls first on the Cold War Kids concert poster over his bed, a line-art cityscape with large puffs of pollution pouring out of smokestacks. A small plane is about to fly into one of the billows. Dylan always talked about going to college in New York or Chicago or Los Angeles, and I think about what Jamal said about moving to a city. What was Dylan running from—or toward? Even though I never had a desire to leave Big Burr, I hoped he would, so he could have an interesting, unpredictable life.

I could always feel Dylan's teenage reality crashing against his adult potential. The teenageness of wanting to fit in, of going to a party then speeding across pitch-black back roads, pressing the soft pad of his foot against the gas pedal as he raced to keep up with the car of friends in front of him, until he reached seventy miles per hour per the cop's estimations, but the thing was he hadn't even been drinking, not a trace of alcohol in his blood levels, and I don't know if that makes it better or worse. All that teenage reality smashed up, literally, against his surety that he would escape Kansas and double-major in music composition and computer coding, just in case the whole music thing didn't work out—that's how practical he could be.

I follow the light down to where Richard's face is illuminated by the glow of Dylan's laptop. He's sitting on the floor, his back pressed against the foot of the bed, the computer on his thighs. "What are you doing in here?"

"I thought you were already asleep," he says.

"I was out."

"Out? Where?"

"Do you really care?"

He sighs and turns back to the computer screen. "Did you know Dylan's friends are still writing on his Facebook page?"

"I didn't even know his account still existed."

"Come look."

I lower myself onto the carpet next to him. Seeing Dylan's profile picture is a punch to the gut. It's a photo he took himself, in this room, in half-light, his face blurry and his eyes looking up and to the side.

Richard scrolls past photos that Dylan's friends have posted on his wall. Dylan playing guitar at one of those garage concerts he and his friends used to organize, his eyes squeezed shut, his lips slack. "Remember that night?" his bandmate Steven writes. Dylan and his friend Cady standing in the middle of a cornfield, fog floating up from their feet. Behind the thin layer of fog their hands are clasped together, fingers interlaced. Had they dated? Kissed one night? Been in love, or what they thought was love? "I hope you can see this," she writes. Richard scrolls extra quickly past a photo of Dylan driving his Buick, a hand-me-down from my dad, the wind forcing the waves out of his hair, still the brown he was born with, not yet bleached. He's smiling at whoever took the photo, which means his eyes aren't on the road, which means maybe his accident wasn't a one-night experiment with danger but a routine of reckless driving. In between the photos are poems about God picking flowers, stars in the night sky, and meeting in the light.

"Every time I visit his page, I tell myself I'm finally going to delete it," Richard says, closing the laptop. On the lid, there's a sticker of a zombie Snow White about to take a bite out of the glowing apple logo in the center.

"Why do you need to delete it?"

Richard rubs his finger over the apple. "It lets me pretend he's still here."

It's been months since Richard and I have been so close to each other. I had forgotten the way he smells, like plain bar soap and thyme. I think about reaching out and touching him, but I can't imagine how that would feel, or what would happen next. He's already standing up.

"Richard," I say.

He looks at me tiredly.

"Sleep well."

MY BEST FRIEND Lorraine comes into the bank the next afternoon. She stands beside the red velour stanchion and lets people go ahead of her until I'm free.

"Hi, honey!" She fiddles with a barrette in her permed hair. "Have you gotten any of my messages?"

"I'm sorry," I say. "So many people have been calling."

Lorraine reaches across the desk and squeezes my hand. Her acrylics press into my palm. "We all just want you to know we're here, you know?"

"I know."

"Me and the girls are going to see *My Third Cousin's Wedding* tomorrow night. It's supposed to be funny."

"All rom-coms are *supposed* to be funny. Whether they actually are is another story."

Her bottom lip wavers. "You'd tell me if you weren't okay, right?"

Of course I'm not okay, Lorraine, I want to say. My son is dead, and

I'm supposed to feel bad that I don't want to see anyone? Every time I see her she wants to rehash it. How I'm feeling. If I'm eating enough. If I'm sleeping. If I force her to talk about her own life, she'll catch herself halfway through mentioning some problem at work and put a hand to her mouth. "Look at me complaining, after all you've been through. Everything's just fine with me."

"I'm okay, Lorraine," I say. "Maybe I'll call you tomorrow."

I DON'T CALL Lorraine the next day or the day after that. Instead, I text Jamal. He gave me his number at the luau—the first new number I've put in my phone in years.

Do you need any volunteers at AAA? I'd love to help out, I type.

Sure! he writes back. *Are you free today after work? We'll be stuffing envelopes and could definitely use an extra hand.*

When I walk into the Acceptance Across America office, I find Jamal and a few other task force members in the middle of a heated debate.

"I bet it was Barb, that asshole," says Tegan, who always calls unlikable women "assholes" and unlikable men "bitches," as I learned at the luau the other night. "She'd do anything to get the billboard off the top of her store."

"What about that teenager from our anti-bullying presentation at the high school?" says Harley. "He just stood at the back, dead-eyed, mime-shooting all of us."

"What happened?" I ask.

"You know our half-burned billboard on Main Street?" says Jamal. "Someone spray-painted DEATH PENALTY FOR DYKES across it."

My mouth falls open. "That's terrible. I haven't seen it. Do the police have any suspects?"

Everyone laughs or rolls their eyes.

"I'm sure they're working *very* hard to crack the case," says Karen, the director. "Just like they worked so hard to figure out who tried to burn it down." She presses her pointer and middle finger into her right temple and closes her eyes. "Let's get back to it."

Jamal hands me a stack of forms and envelopes, a sponge, and a dish of water. "We're sending out feedback forms," he says. "We've been mailing them out because so far no one has come to our in-person focus groups. I'm just hoping we get back, like, two of them that don't say 'FUCK YOU FAGS' in all caps."

I glance at the form. The first question reads, *Have you had an interaction with an Acceptance Across America member? If so, how would you rate that interaction?* A question farther down asks, *Has your opinion about the LGBTQ community changed since the arrival of Acceptance Across America? If so, has your opinion become more positive or more negative?*

"Well, if you send me one, I'll give you a positive review."

"What would you say?" Jamal asks.

"I'd say . . ." I try to think of a way to sum it up. "You all make me feel very accepted."

"Awww." He brings a hand to his heart, half making fun of my saccharine comment. "Acceptance Across America, at your service."

BEFORE I EVEN realize it, I'm spending all my time with Jamal and the Acceptance Across America group. Sometimes volunteering, other times just hanging out. Fancy cocktail parties, board game nights, and long weekend afternoons of binge-watching *RuPaul's Drag Race* fill what used to be empty hours. One day, Richard passes me in the hallway and says I look different. *Different how?* I ask. *Kind of like you did before*, he says. So many of the task force members have had terrible things happen to them: Harley was homeless in their early twenties because no one would hire someone whose gender they couldn't figure out. David lost most of his closest friends and countless acquaintances to AIDS. One of Tegan's friends, a Black transgender woman, was shot to death two years ago and the police never even bothered to find a suspect. Jamal said he tried to commit suicide when he was a teenager. Sometimes I wonder if the reason I feel so at home among them is because of our shared grief—even though I still haven't told them about Dylan.

One afternoon I take a walk in the nature preserve and I'm finally able to see the silvery green of new leaves without feeling like they're mocking me. I force myself to do an entire Jillian Michaels workout instead of just watching it. I smile at Christine Peterson unloading her groceries without wanting to punch her in the face. Lorraine leaves messages on the answering machine inviting me to her candle parties or to lunch, but I never get around to calling her back. Richard leaves me notes on our "Yogatta do this" stationery covered in cats in yoga poses. *The plumber called. Dishwasher is clean. Leftover meatloaf in the fridge.*

On a warm spring Saturday, I meet Jamal at the south end of Main Street. He's holding two coffees and two tote bags full of rainbow stickers that read "This business serves everyone."

"Do you ever get tired of looking at rainbows?"

He laughs. "Whenever I see a rainbow, I know it's a good thing, so no. Some kid from Kansas came up with it, actually. He sewed the very first flag."

"That's kind of ironic."

"Someeeeeewheeeeere over the raaaaaainbow," he sings in a Judy Garland falsetto. "That movie is gay as all get-out."

"What do you mean, gay?"

"Friend of Dorothy?" he says in a tone like it should be obvious.

I look at him blankly.

"Think about it. The black-and-white reality of small-town, un-accepting Kansas. Then, somewhere over the rainbow, is the colorful, welcoming metropolis of Oz."

"So Big Burr is somewhere *under* the rainbow."

Jamal laughs. "Come through, Linda! That's a good way to put it." He finally talks to me like a close friend, though I'm still learning the definitions of words and phrases I thought I knew: *come through* means you just said or did something impressive; *sickening* means amazing; *reading* means you're wittily insulting someone.

He hands me a tote bag full of stickers. "So, you can say as much or as little as you want when we go into these places. Just your presence will help."

"What?" The coffee I was in the middle of swallowing goes down the wrong tube. "We have to go in and talk to people?" I croak.

He tilts his head. "What did you think we were doing?"

"I thought maybe we'd just leave the stickers in the door, like solicitors do."

"I'm sure they wish we would," he says.

The first establishment we hit is Barb's Boutique—Barb, who complained about how warm it was at Dylan's funeral reception while wrapping brownies in napkins and putting them in her purse. As we walk in, Jamal's eyes move from a handbag with a bejeweled cross on it to a busty mannequin wearing a T-shirt that says FOOT-BALL: WHAT BOYS DO DURING CHEER SEASON. He squeezes his arms around his body like he's afraid the items in the store will reach out and grab him.

Barb looks up from behind the register as the door dings shut behind us. She zeroes in on Jamal, her eyes narrowing. He smiles at her and interlaces his fingers, holding them in front of his abdomen. I move closer to him.

"Oh, my gosh, Linda?" Barb sits with a red marker poised above a piece of poster board, halfway through coloring in the letter L in SALE. "It's so good to see you out and about! How are you *dooooing*?"

I can feel Jamal looking at me, wondering why this woman is talking to me like I'm an invalid. "I'm fine, Barb. How are you?"

"Can't complain, but I will anyway," which is what she says every time I see her. "The store isn't doing so hot, which is why I'm having a big sale," she says, gesturing to her homemade sign. "If things don't pick up soon, I might have to close up shop. I blame that gosh-darn billboard. It was enough of an eyesore before it was burned, and now it's even worse."

"You know what might help with sales?" Jamal takes a sticker out of his bag and sets it on the counter.

"Let me guess," she says, placing her pointer finger on the sticker and sliding it back across the counter. "You're with that task force."

"The latest study put gay buying power at just under four trillion dollars," says Jamal. "I'm guessing you don't want to end up like all the other boarded-up shops on the street?"

She huffs. "If I put that sticker up, I'd definitely be boarded up. I'd lose all my other business."

"I'd still shop here," I chime in.

Barb looks from Jamal to me with a new kind of recognition. "I know you've been going through a hard time, Linda, but this?"

"I think Acceptance Across America is doing important work."

"You never seemed like much of a *gay crusader*." She rolls her eyes as she says the last two words.

"Well, maybe I am now."

She crosses her arms and looks at Jamal. "Do you believe that?"

"We're happy to have her, whatever her reasons."

"Did you know her son died?" Barb says, looking at me. "A car accident. He was only sixteen. Such a tragedy." She brings her hand to her heart. "So you can understand why we're all so concerned about her."

A whirlpool of rage and sadness dizzies me, bejeweled handbags and shiny graphic T-shirts making my vision starry. Before I can pass out or vomit I bolt outside, knocking over a miniskirted mannequin in my haste, and crouch on the sidewalk, my arms wrapped around my legs and my face buried in my lap, rocking back and forth.

Jamal appears next to me and squeezes my shoulder. "I'm so sorry."

"I should be the one apologizing." I hand him the bag full of rainbow stickers.

He pushes the bag back toward me. "Linda, do you really think we didn't know about your son? It's a small town. You seemed like you needed to not talk about it, so we didn't. But it doesn't change anything."

I shake my head. "It changes everything," I say softly.

When I walk in the house, Richard is sitting at the kitchen table, Dylan's Converse sneakers in front of him. I drop into the chair next to him.

"You know what my first thought was?" Richard says. "I thought Dylan found the shoes and brought them back inside."

"I do the same thing. That night you were in Dylan's room on his laptop, I was so sure it was him."

Richard picks up a shoe and starts lacing it. I take the other shoe and follow suit, crisscrossing the white laces over the tongue. This is the first time I've noticed the black-and-purple cityscape pattern running along the sides. A silhouette peeks out from a skyscraper's window. "They're pretty fierce," I say.

Richard looks at me, confused. "Fierce?" He pushes the plastic-wrapped ends of laces through silver-lined holes. I always thread the lace through the bottom of the hole, whereas he alternates between crossing over and under. I try to remember which one of us taught Dylan how to tie his shoes, but I can't.

"It's like another word for awesome," I say.

Richard looks at me like we've just met. He finishes lacing his shoe and ties a bow at the top. I finish mine, and we set the two shoes next to each other, facing away from us, like we're waiting for them to start walking.

Zach

The phrase *run away* has always felt like such a cop-out to me, like instead of dealing with an issue you're taking the easy way out. People are constantly saying things like, *He's just running away from his problems.* It sounds so passive, so resigned and negative. But what if running away was actually the opposite of all those things? An active choice made in defiance, not running away but running *toward*. That's how I'm choosing to think about it, at least—like I'm fucking sprinting toward happiness and acceptance, which I know I'll never find here in Big Burr, no matter what the task force says. And Avery is coming with.

After everyone at school found out that not only is Karen Avery's mom but that Avery *lied* about it, suddenly I wasn't the only one getting tormented on the regular. At least once a week Avery's locker would get egged, or someone would come up behind her in the hall and crack an egg over her head. But the physical bullying was just the tip of the iceberg—psychological warfare is teen girls' specialty. The cheerleaders who would never have given Jana the time of day before the egging suddenly wanted to be her best friend, not because they had any real interest in her, of course, but because it meant luring her away from Avery. One of the cheerleaders even started dating Jake, constantly texting Avery pictures of them making out. So when I brought up leaving to Avery, she was game.

Since neither of us have a car and hitchhiking is for dead people, our plan is to walk the sixty-five miles to Dry Creek, the closest town with a Greyhound station. Once we make it to Dry Creek, we'll take a bus to Los Angeles, where Avery grew up and where I've been dreaming of living for years. Currently we're just three miles into our trek, trudging through the flat, boring fields that border Route 83. We're walking far from the road, with just the moon to illuminate our path, since flashlights would make us too visible. We left right after dark and told our parents we were spending the night at a friend's house, a classic lie that's been true enough times that they didn't think it was shady. They won't get home from work tomorrow until about six p.m., which gives us a solid twenty-two-hour head start—exactly the amount of time it'll take to walk to Dry Creek and be on the bus before they even notice we're gone.

I can't believe we have sixty-two more miles, or twenty-one more hours, to go. My calves are already tightening and my backpack straps are digging into the soft muscles between my shoulders and my neck. I wonder what those muscles are called. Thank God I got a burner phone with internet—Google to the rescue. *Trapezius!* Must be related to *trapeze* and *trapezoid*. I look up their etymology.

Yup, they all share the same Latin root, *trapezium*, which essentially means the shape of a trapezoid.

"Hey, Google addict," Avery says when she sees me on the phone. "You're going to use all the data and then we'll be fucked when we actually need it."

"Okay, okay." I put the phone in my pocket.

"So what do you think everyone will say when school starts and we're not there?" she asks.

"They'll probably say good fucking riddance."

"You don't think anyone will miss us even a little bit?"

"They'd only miss us because they'd have to find other people whose lives they can ruin."

Avery sighs. "Is there anything *you'll* miss about Big Burr?"

"Just the triple-A crew," I say, who have been my education, my family, and—to be dramatic for a second—my reason for living this past year. When they first showed up, I stayed after one of the anti-bullying sessions they ran at our high school and asked if they needed an intern or a volunteer, pretending my interest in them was strictly professional, not personal. Karen gave me a knowing look and invited me out for pizza with the rest of the task force.

Pretty soon I was going to the AAA office every day after school. There, I got an education that felt so much more necessary than my actual high school curriculum: Jamal gave me books by James Baldwin; Karen told me about all the classic film stars who were queer, like Marlon Brando, Katharine Hepburn, and Rock Hudson; Tegan lent me feminist books by Audre Lorde and Gloria

Steinem; Harley let me read their personal essays and even helped me write one of my own; David told me what it was like to live through the AIDS crisis. Even though the task force was technically sent to teach homophobes about acceptance, I felt like some queer God had heard my prayers and sent them just for me. I finally felt like I wanted to live.

A few months later, I was even feeling emboldened enough to come out to my best friend Ramona. Which, as it turned out, was a huge fucking mistake. Because right after I told her, she made this completely consternated face and said, "What do you mean, *bisexual*? Maybe that's true for girls but not for guys." And she immediately told some girls at school that I was gay. Once that got around, school became an endless grab bag of loogies in my lunch, lockers slammed on my hand, and water bottles full of pee thrown at me in the parking lot. I developed a crick in my neck from constantly looking over my shoulder and was always late for class because I had to wait for my tormentors to go in first.

All the old feelings I thought I'd left behind in my pre-AAA world began to creep back in—the hopelessness, the desperation, the nihilism—you know, all your classic clinical-depression-with-suicidal-ideation symptoms. I finished my sophomore year with a 2.2 GPA, down from 3.8 the year before. The guidance counselor called me in to speak with her and asked if something was going on at home, like she never saw me getting pushed around in the hallway right outside her office.

Avery became my only confidant. When I told her I was bisexual, she barely blinked. "Oh, cool, a ton of my friends back home are bi," she said. L.A. sounded like this magical place where no one even had to come out as a certain gender or sexuality—it was probably just assumed you were somewhere on the spectrum.

Things finally came to a head—literally—near the end of the school year, during a game of dodgeball. Tiffany McGackin, the star of the girls' basketball team, threw a ball at Avery's face so hard that it broke her nose, then everyone teased her about getting a "Los Angeles nose job." (Don't ask me how a Los Angeles nose job differs from a regular one.) Avery tried to convince Karen it had been an honest accident, knowing that if she got involved the bullying would only get worse, but Karen saw through her and went straight to the principal. Tiffany got suspended for a week, and that night she messaged Avery on Facebook: *Hope u enjoy ur summer, cuntface. Cuz once school starts again I'm going 2 make ur life a living hell.*

Avery refused to tell Karen about the message, and instead pleaded, for the millionth time, to go back to L.A., while Karen told her, for the millionth time, that Steph traveled too much and Avery would just have to wait one more year. That was when Avery and I knew we had to take matters into our own hands and just GTFO. I picked up extra delivery shifts all summer at Pu Pu Hot Pot and was able to save five hundred dollars, and Avery's rich grandma sent her a birthday card stuffed with hundred-dollar bills, so between the two of us, we had almost a thousand bucks.

IN THE DARK field beside empty Route 83, Avery grabs my arm. "Did you hear that?"

"Hear what?" I peer into the blackness, trying to make out an animal or human shape.

"A whoosh somewhere nearby," she whispers.

I hold my breath, but all I hear are crickets and the faraway revving of a car's motor.

She hugs her arms close to her body. "What if there's an ax murderer waiting for us out here?"

"Yeah, ax murderers tend to wait in desolate fields in the middle of nowhere, Kansas." Just then I hear it, too, or more like feel it: a whoosh of air, a vibration from the ground, a dizziness in my body.

"You just heard it, didn't you?" says Avery.

I nod.

She turns on her phone flashlight and spins in a circle, illuminating a bunch of brittle prairie grass and not much else.

"It's probably just the wind," I say, then google "nocturnal field-dwelling animals" and scroll through images of crazy-eyed possums and flat-faced, sinister-looking owls.

Avery shudders. "I'm starting to have a bad feeling about this."

"About what, running away?"

She nods.

I let out an impatient sigh. "Why?"

"How often do you hear anything good about kids who run

away? Usually something terrible happens, like they end up getting sex-trafficked or killed. By an ax murderer lurking in a field." She wraps her arms around herself.

I smile and shake my head at her joke, then get serious and place my hands on her shoulders, looking into her eyes. "I get why you're scared. Trust me, I do. But if we listened to our fear whenever it started getting loud, we'd never do anything. Do you really want to head back and face whatever Tiffany McGackin has waiting for you when school starts in two weeks? You know how nuts she is. I could definitely see her shanking a bitch."

"No, but—"

"Besides, we've been over this. There are no other options. You already talked to Karen about moving back to L.A., and she said no. And you were right not to tell her about the Facebook message—if you did, she'd probably call the cops, and who knows what Tiffany would do then? It's not like the police would stop her. You saw how much they cared about your house being egged, or the billboard."

Avery's arms loosen and fall to her sides. "I guess."

"Hey, don't worry. I'll protect you," I say, flexing my nonexistent biceps and giving her my most masculine grin.

She laughs. "Okay, okay. Do you want to play twenty questions or something? I need to be distracted."

"Sure," I say, even though I think twenty questions is a pretty asinine game. I volunteer to go first and choose the first thing that flies into my brain.

"Is it a person?" Avery asks.

"Yes."

"Is it someone you know?"

"Yes."

"In real life?"

"No."

"Is it Sam Brinkley?"

"Yes."

She smacks my arm. "You turd! You didn't think picking the guy you've had a crush on for the last year was a little obvious?"

I shrug. Sam is one of my online friends and he lives in Los Angeles, which is a bonus reason for going there. Before AAA, my online friends were what kept me going. When I finally got an iPhone, I created profiles no one at school would be able to trace back to me. I made friends by searching for queer hashtags, then replying to people's posts. Once, when I posted a selfie on Instagram with a caption about being bi, I got 237 likes. Everyone left comments full of prayer-hands and heart-eye emojis, saying to keep being me, that I was cute and gorgeous and anyone would be lucky to date me. Given I always thought I looked like Michael Cera's less-attractive kid brother, this was news to me. Being online was like some incredible alternate universe where I was popular and desirable. Then the task force showed up and I learned it was possible to feel that way in real life, not just in the glow of a screen.

I can feel a blister forming on the outside of my right pinkie toe, where the seam of my sock rubs against the inside of my shoe. "Hang on," I say to Avery as I fish a Band-Aid out of my backpack. I lean down and unlace my shoe, then peel off my sweaty sock. I try to stand on my shoed foot but lose my balance and wobble until the bare one touches the dirt. As I'm fumbling to get the Band-Aid out of its wrapper, something glides across the top of my naked foot, something warm and smooth, like a leather belt left out in the sun. The hairs on my arm stand up and I jerk my foot off the ground, which makes me lose my balance again.

"What?" Avery says, swinging her flashlight toward me, the light catching the very end of a brown, scaly tail with what looks like a piece of corncob attached to the tip.

"Oh, fuck." Rattlesnakes did *not* come up in my search for "nocturnal field-dwelling animals."

"Oh my god oh my god oh my god," Avery says as she follows the snake with her flashlight. "What are we supposed to do?"

I contemplate googling "how to escape a rattlesnake," but before I have a chance the snake lunges and Avery screams, almost dropping her flashlight. In the wobbly light I watch, transfixed, as the snake clamps its mouth around the head of a small cottontail rabbit and struggles to get it down, making me gag a little bit. While the snake is preoccupied, Avery and I take a few careful steps backward, then turn and sprint.

"Fuck your rule," Avery says, "I'm walking next to the road from now on."

"I don't think that's a good idea."

"Dude, we just watched a rattlesnake kill a rabbit. We could literally be next. We'll be able to see a car coming from a long way off, and we can just duck in the prairie grass when it gets close."

"Fine," I say, shuddering at the feeling of the snake slithering over my foot.

After a few minutes of walking in silence, Avery asks, "How mad do you think Karen will be when she figures out we've run away?"

"Honestly, I think she'll be more worried than mad."

"I dunno," Avery says. "Every time she looks at me, I swear I can, like, viscerally feel her disappointment emanating from her eyeballs and seeping into my bones."

I roll my eyes. "I think you're imagining it, the same way you imagine that she wishes you were a lesbian."

She crosses her arms. "You think Karen is so perfect. It's different when she's actually your mom."

"I know she's not perfect, but you've got to admit she's a hell of a lot better than my dad and Nancy." Nancy being my evil Baptist stepmom. I contemplated leaving them a coming-out note before I left, then decided against it, knowing their reaction would probably entail turning a blind eye at best and hateful rejection at worst.

Sometimes I wonder if I'd even have to run away if my mom hadn't died. I like to tell myself she would have loved me no matter what. She took me to the public library all the time and let me read whatever I wanted. Once, when I was about ten, she let me check out *The Catcher in the Rye*. They didn't have it in the school library because it had been deemed "obscene." Jan the librarian gave my mom total side-eye and said, "Is that really what you want your son reading?" My mom just rolled her eyes and said, "Don't be such a prude, Jan." The last book she ever took me to check out was *What's Happening to My Body?* "I won't be around when this starts happening to you, and your father sure as hell won't talk about it, so you better read it now," she'd said.

Two years after she died, when I was thirteen, my dad met Nancy at a potluck. She'd brought a pot of baked beans that weren't even cooked through all the way, but my dad told her they were the most delicious beans he'd ever had. My dad is a Baptist now, too. When I was growing up, we went to church every Sunday because that's what you did, not because my parents had any great belief—my dad would yawn and pick hangnails through half the service. But three months into dating Nancy, he got baptized in Pastor Jim's backyard aboveground pool—a pool they had for that specific purpose. I stood next to my dad and put a supporting hand on his back as he plugged his nose and fell backward into the water. I studied his face as he emerged, trying to see if he really felt born again, but he had the same fixed half smile, the same unoccupied gaze he'd had ever since my mom died.

These days he just goes along with whatever Nancy says. And Nancy says homosexuals are worse than animals, because at least animals know you have to procreate with a member of the opposite sex. I showed her some articles about the gay penguins in Central Park Zoo, but she dismissed that as "liberal nonsense." After AAA came to town, she blamed them for every bad thing that happened: Dylan Ivingston's death, Barb's Boutique struggling to stay open, even coming down with the flu—all the task force's fault.

Nancy and my dad know I don't share their political beliefs, but I don't think they ever suspected anything about my sexuality. They know I dated a few girls, and it would never occur to them that you can date girls and still not be straight. I don't think they have any idea that AAA has become my surrogate family, either—or they don't *want* to have any idea. One time, when I was riding in the passenger seat of Karen's car, my dad pulled up next to us at a red light. He looked right at me, then at Karen, then back at the light. For days after that my stomach would drop whenever I saw him, but he never said a word about it.

"So tell me the plan again," Avery says. "For how we'll get on the bus."

"There's always some weirdos hanging out in Greyhound stations. We'll just find someone who looks like they're hard up and give them fifty bucks to sign our Unaccompanied Child Form."

"What if the Greyhound people ask for ID? Won't they notice that the weirdo's last name doesn't match yours or mine?"

"We'll say they're our legal guardian."

"What if they ask for papers to prove it?"

I google "how to prove legal guardianship" and WikiHow confirms Avery's suspicion. Instead of telling her she's right, I say, "God, Avery, we'll figure it out."

"Don't act like I'm ridiculous for being realistic. There are a million unknowns ahead of us, like how long we'll be able to stay in my friend Scout's pool house without her parents noticing, if Scout will even be able to keep her mouth shut, if someone will recognize me and tell Karen or Steph, if we'll be able to get jobs under the table, if we'll be able to go back to school, if—"

I throw my hands up. "We're taking a risk! There aren't any guarantees. We can question every little thing until we turn around or we can accept the unknowns and plow ahead."

As if to punctuate my words, what can only be described as a spine-chilling scream cuts through the air. Avery and I freeze, exchanging wide-eyed stares as we grab each other's arm. Then another scream echoes toward us. We crouch down and swivel our heads, looking for the source. It's hard to tell if it's coming from close or far away.

"Motherfucking motherfucker goddamn it all to hell," Avery whispers, rocking back and forth on her heels. "I knew it. I knew something terrible was going to happen. I just didn't think it would be us hearing Satan murder a child."

"I'm sure that's not it," I say, even though my heart feels like it's trying to knock its way through my ribs.

Another scream pierces our ears. This time I try to really listen despite my fear. The noise doesn't sound quite human. More like a machine, or an animal. I google "animal scream" and one of the first results is for a barn owl, with a white heart-shaped face and two perfectly round black eyes that look like they were hole-punched into its head. I click a YouTube link and after a few seconds, a scream almost identical to the one Avery and I just heard plays through my speakers.

I hold my phone in front of Avery's face. "It's okay, it's just an owl."

"I don't know," she says. "It sounds different to me."

We wait to see if another scream will come from nearby, but all I hear is a chorus of chirping crickets.

"Even if it is just an owl . . ." Avery stands up and scuffs her

119

sneaker in the dirt. "I'm sorry, but I don't think I can do this, Zach. I'm not brave enough. And I can't disappoint Karen again. One year isn't so long, then I'll be back in L.A."

I cross my arms. "Yeah, *you'll* be back in L.A. And I'll be stuck here."

"What about college? Just two more years and you'll be gone, too."

"You say that like it's a sure thing. No one in my family went to college, my dad can barely make our mortgage payments, and you know my grades last year were complete shit."

"Well, if you work really hard for the next two years, maybe you can get a scholarship."

I blow a forceful gust of air from my nose. "It's not that easy, Avery."

She throws her hands up in the air. "Why the hell not?"

"You grew up in L.A. You have no idea what it's like to grow up in a town like this. To grow up *queer* in a town like this." My voice breaks. "I don't know if I'll make it another two years. I really don't."

"What do you mean, *make it?*"

I take a deep breath and start to explain. About a year ago, right after the task force showed up but before I'd come out to Ramona, the two of us were invited to a party at Billy Cunningham's house. Billy is a wide receiver on the football team—it was unusual, to say the least, for me and Ramona to be invited to one of his parties. But Ramona had recently had a growth spurt in a particular area and we figured one of the guys wanted to see if she would let him get to second base. She hoped it was Seth Braun, whose nickname "Tight End" didn't only refer to his position on the team.

At the party, as I was talking to Avery for the first time, Karen came on the news—though I didn't know who she was then—and Billy did this disgusting pantomimed blow job routine that cut our conversation short. Then Seth took Ramona into the guest room, leaving me with no one to talk to, so I escaped upstairs and wandered around Billy's empty bedroom. Above his bed, there was a poster of Tom Brady mid-throw and the opposite wall was covered in baseball hats for all thirty-two NFL teams. Just as I was about to leave, a football player named Connor appeared in the doorway with two plastic cups. He was the one guy on the team who always smiled when passing me in the hall instead of giving me threatening looks or ignoring me.

"Saw you come up here and thought you could use some company," he said. "Now that your other half is busy." He handed me one of the drinks and sat on the bed.

"Thanks." I sat down next to him and took a swig of what turned out to be straight whiskey.

"What's the deal with you two anyway? You've never . . . ?" He trailed off and smiled, then started bouncing his leg up and down, making the whole bed shake.

"No, we're just friends," I said.

"To be just friends with a girl who looks like Ramona, you must be . . ."

"What?"

His leg bounced faster. "I dunno."

"Okay."

I looked at his leg and he stopped shaking it. "You must be, like . . . not interested."

"Not in her, no."

"But you're interested in other girls."

"Yeah."

"What about—" He coughed, once. "Guys?"

I looked at him sideways. How the fuck?

He pulled his phone out of his pocket. After a few taps and swipes, he tilted the screen toward me. It was my secret Instagram account. Specifically, my post about being bi.

A hot flash snapped through my body. "How did you find this?"

He bolted across the room and closed the door. Then he walked toward me, a determined look in his eyes. Before I could move, he lunged at me, grabbed my face, his hands shaking, and shoved his tongue into the corners of my mouth. I leaned back farther and farther until I was lying down, then rolled out from under him. "Connor . . ." I sighed.

"What?"

"I just . . . I don't think I see you that way."

His face went red. "Don't you want to fuck everyone? Isn't that the point?" He straddled me and unbuckled his belt, pushing his jeans down. His erect penis loomed in front of my face. "It'll be our secret," he said before pushing himself into my mouth. Billy walked in as it was happening and I tried to yell for help, but I couldn't get out the words, since I was choking on Connor's dick. I know Billy saw the look in my eyes, though. I know he understood what was going on, but he just backed away and closed the door.

Over the next few weeks, the scene looped through my mind like it was running on a track. I deleted my apparently-not-so-secret social media accounts, paranoid that Connor would show someone. Whenever I saw him at school, he still smiled at me like nothing had happened, but right underneath the smile was something menacing. "What's going on with you?" Ramona kept asking, but I couldn't bring myself to tell her. I was full of shame—that I didn't know what to call it, that I hadn't done more to stop it, that I was who I was. One night I swallowed a huge handful of Tylenol. I woke up in the hospital, and before I even opened my eyes I overheard Nancy say to my dad, "I told you we should have made him come to church with us. If he believed in God, he wouldn't have done this."

"Jesus, Zach," Avery says, lowering herself to the ground. "I'm really sorry. Did you ever tell anyone?"

I shake my head, sitting down next to her.

"Do you ever think about doing something like that again?"

I nod.

"But you think in L.A. you won't think about it anymore?"

"That's what I'm hoping."

Avery sighs. "Okay. Yeah. You need to get the fuck out of Big Burr, I get it now."

I pull a piece of prairie grass out of the ground and tie it into a knot. "I don't want you to do this just because you feel bad that I tried to kill myself."

"It's not because I feel bad, I promise. I'm in a position to help, and I want to."

I tie another knot in the long piece of grass. "What about Karen?"

"I think she would actually understand, if she knew the whole story. If she were in my position, she might do the same thing."

A tentative smile curls the side of my mouth. "So we're really doing this?"

She nods once, decisively. "We're really doing this."

I grab Avery's hand and we stand up, then I feel it again: that whooshing sensation. My scalp tingles. I turn on my flashlight, but it's too dark to see anything. There's a pulsing noise in the air, like a heart beating through a distant stethoscope. It gets closer. Then a different sound joins in: soft, buzzy chirps. A cloud moves out of the moon's way and the sky brightens. Avery and I exchange a glance: *Is this the beginning, or the end?*

A gust of air washes over us and I tilt my flashlight upward as the sky becomes spotted with the bodies of hundreds of birds in flight. We laugh in relief, spinning in circles as we watch them. They must be migrating south to Mexico or some other warm place. I had no idea birds migrated at night. I start to google it, then make myself wait, awed by the spectacle. They're not flying in a V, but in a dense cluster of dizzying momentum, shape-shifting into different configurations: tadpole, mushroom, speech bubble, hourglass, expanding and contracting in an undulating rhythm. I wonder how they're able to move like that—like a singular organism, their wings beating to the same pulse. How they know exactly where to go. I close my eyes and imagine myself as part of the greater whole, finally, my heart matching the beat of everyone like me as I shape-shift into something new.

I hear a rushing noise like a car approaching, but when I open my eyes I don't see one. I wonder if it's just the birds, but a moment later I feel a slight breeze from movement nearby. The high-pitched whine of screeching tires invades my ears. It goes on for a few full seconds, then it's followed by a heavy thud and a metallic crack. A rolling noise, then another, smaller thud. I look around for Avery, but don't see her. I'd sensed that she'd drifted away from me while we were watching the birds, but I hadn't really been paying attention, caught up in the fantasy of my new life.

"Avery?" I call out, but she doesn't answer. My breath catches in my chest. I look to my left, where the noises came from, and can barely make out the white dashed line in the middle of the road, and a dark, hulking shape with a shiny black surface ever-so-slightly reflecting the wan light of the moon. A car. How the fuck did we miss a car? The lights must have been broken, or a drunk driver forgot to turn them on, or a dumb teenager was looking for a thrill. If the lights had been on we would've had to notice, even if we were looking up at the birds. As I walk closer, trying to see beyond the dark windows to who's in the driver's seat, the tires screech again and the car peels out.

Only then do I see Avery lying on her back in the road, her head turned away from me and one of her legs splayed out to the side like a rag doll's. A scream rises from a subterranean place within me. I run to Avery, but stop short, afraid to touch her. The leg that's splayed out to the side is split open, a jagged tear from the hip to the knee, and I realize I've never seen the inside of someone's body before. The fat and muscle look like large curds of cottage cheese messily stuffed into a red fishnet stocking. My throat spasms and the sky seems to tilt. I lower myself to the ground and look away, willing myself not to puke. But all I see when I look away is Avery's blood, branching into rivulets that follow the grooves in the road.

"Avery?" I force myself to peer at her face and it looks surprisingly placid, her eyes closed and her mouth in the slight smile she always has when she's sleeping. I lower a shaking hand to her head, and stroke her soft auburn hair, then slide my hand down and rub her rough split ends between my fingers. I hesitate before moving to her neck, where I'll need to press my fingers to a vein and wait to feel either the pulsing of her beating heart, or, incomprehensibly, emptiness. Jesus. I convinced her—*guilted* her—into coming with me by telling her that leaving was the only way for me to live, and now she might be the one who dies. Steeling myself, I press my pointer and middle fingers to her neck in the spot below her jaw. It's warm, a good sign, but I don't feel any movement. I wait, applying more pressure. Finally, underneath my middle finger, there it is—a swell, then a thrum. I exhale in a gasp of relief and grief, feeling my Los Angeles dreams vanish one by one, then I dial 911 for the ambulance that will take us back to Big Burr.

Year Two

Gabe

U wanna meet at a motel. On my phone's screen, the blue speech bubble from PB Tall Guy floats over a dark gray background wallpapered with little Grindr logos: a face mask with two round eyeholes. PB Tall Guy didn't put a question mark after *motel*, like he's not asking, but reading my thoughts. I wanna meet at a motel. I do. I wanna meet at a motel real, real bad.

A toilet in the stall next to me flushes. I've been gone five minutes, maybe ten. Jean is out there in Giovanni's dining room, probably watching her chicken piccata get cold, wondering if I'm having diarrhea or if I ran into someone I know. Or she's on Facebook, scrolling past pictures of her cousin's babies and articles about this season of *Looking for Love*. She's definitely on her second glass of wine. I close Grindr and put my phone in my pocket. Sweat slicks my forehead, upper lip, and palms. I wipe it off with a wad of toilet paper, then drop the paper in the toilet and flush.

"You okay?" Jean says when I come back to the table. She says it flatly—annoyed, not concerned.

"My stomach is just a little upset." It's not exactly a lie. QB nausea, I used to call it. The kind that would hit before a big game, when I was excited but knew so much was riding on it.

"Again?" Jean says. "I don't know why you refuse to see Dr. Webber when this is happening every other day."

"It's not that bad, hon."

"It's bad enough to ruin our anniversary. You've spent half the night in the bathroom." She looks down at the table, then back at me with glassy eyes. God, I'm the worst. As of today, Jean and I have been married for fifteen years. Something about that number has sent me into a tailspin. I guess it's because milestones that are multiples of five always feel weightier, more significant. And fifteen years is just a long fucking time. A long fucking time to be pretending. I've been on Grindr for a while now, but mostly just to look. Today, my fifteenth anniversary, is the first time I've considered going through with it.

"I'm sorry," I say, reaching across the table. Jean keeps her hand limp, refusing to close her fingers around mine. "It's not like I can control it."

The sound of something shattering comes from the kitchen, and everyone in the restaurant turns. At a table in the corner, a man sits across from another man. They have coiffed haircuts and visible pectorals underneath their starched oxfords—one of which is covered in a bright floral print. The man in my sight line regards me with a slightly raised eyebrow and I quickly avert my gaze, keeping the pair in my peripheral vision while trying to pay attention to what Jean is saying. Something about probiotics. The other man turns around in his chair and looks in my direction. Jesus Christ.

You're imagining it, I tell myself. *You look like every other straight man in this restaurant sitting across from a woman.*

Before the task force arrived, I never had to worry about being spotted or outed, but now everywhere I go I swear I can feel them looking at me—looking *through* me. Not to mention my online presence. The only Grindr people from Big Burr know about is the kind with pepper in it, but I've seen a few task force members on there. I changed my picture to a generic ab shot and made sure there were no identifying details in my profile, but that makes it harder to catch someone's interest. A lot of guys even say, "No face pic, no chat."

"Dessert?" asks Norm, our usual waiter.

Jean looks at my plate, the square of lasagna almost fully intact. "I don't think so."

We split the tiramisu every time we come for dinner. "Hon, you want some tiramisu," I say.

"You're not feeling well. We should just go home." She folds her cloth napkin into a neat square. Disappointment hangs on her face.

Norm shifts his weight from one foot to the other.

"We'll take the tiramisu to go," I say.

AT HOME, two empty macaroni-and-cheese boxes and an orange-crusted bowl sit on the kitchen counter. The familiar sounds of swords clanging, blood sluicing, and death groans emanate from the living room.

Jean tosses her purse on the table and gives me a do-something-about-this look.

"Billy," I call out.

He doesn't answer. I walk into the living room.

"I'm at the hardest part," he says, his eyes fixed on the TV. A fighter with an octopus head shoots out a tentacle and wraps it around a samurai's neck. The samurai's face turns blue and he collapses to the ground.

I pick up the remote from the coffee table and turn the TV off.

"What the fuck, Dad?" Billy turns to me, his eyes rage-filled like one of the characters from his game, and throws the controller across the room. The terrible twos have nothing on a sixteen-year-old with an addiction to video games and a temper like a buck in the rut.

"You left the kitchen a mess."

"I'll pick it up later."

"Now," I say.

He blows air out from between his lips. "You don't need to take it out on me just because you and Mom had a shitty date."

I blink. Taxidermied heads of deer, elk, and antelope line the living room walls—trophies from hunting trips I've taken over the years. The whitetail buck has a smug expression, his mouth curled up at the edges and his head tilted at a watchful angle. *He knows*, the deer seems to say. Billy huffs by me, his shoulder knocking against mine on his way into the kitchen. Jean sidesteps Billy and hands me a cup of ginger ale—on the surface a sweet gesture, but there's resentment behind it. *Drink this and shut up about your stomach.*

"Coming to bed?" she asks.

"Right after I drink this." As she walks up the stairs, I feel the warm weight of my phone in my pocket. The blue speech bubble drifts somewhere inside of it, lonely, waiting for a response. I lock myself in the downstairs guest bathroom with my cup of ginger ale. *In the bathroom* is starting to feel more fitting than *in the closet*, since it's the only place private enough to check Grindr.

The room is decked out in Jean's late-fall décor: beige hand towels covered in red and orange appliqué leaves, a clear vase full of dried wheat stalks, and a green-and-yellow striped gourd next to the soap dispenser. The one nonseasonal item is a *Far Side* daily calendar that sits on the toilet-tank lid. Every morning Jean rips off the previous day's comic, even though we almost exclusively use the upstairs bathroom. Today's comic shows two wolves standing in the middle of a flock of sheep, holding sheep masks. When you look at the sheep more closely, there are seams connecting their heads to their bodies and fabric patches over their wool coats. The caption says, "Wait a minute! Isn't anyone here a real sheep?"

Writing back doesn't mean I'm committing to anything. *Where and when?* I reply. My yellow speech bubble hangs underneath his, the lonely one now. I take a gulp of ginger ale while I wait for him to respond. The soda is flat, and without the bubbles, it tastes sickeningly sweet. I open up the medicine cabinet and take two extra-strength Tums. The chalkiness never seems to leave my mouth—these days a value-sized container lasts me only a week.

Dry Creek. Motel 6. Tuesday 7 pm, PB Tall Guy writes.

After a few minutes of deep breathing, I head upstairs, hoping Jean is already asleep. But she's propped up on her backrest pillow, reading one of her romance novels. This one is called *The Duke and I*, a pink-tinged pastoral scene on the cover. I'm always surprised she reads them in front of me—they should be a secret, an embarrassing indulgence. Every now and then I peek over and catch a sentence like "He tore off his clothes with the urgency of a man fighting off fire ants" or "She bucked on top of him like he was her prize stallion and they were feet from the finish line." Her face is expressionless, like she could be scanning the paper. But she must get a little turned on reading this stuff. Isn't that the point? And who does she picture when she fantasizes? It can't be me.

I climb under the rose-printed quilt and groan while rubbing my stomach, trying to make it obvious that I'm in no state for sex. I know Jean will be upset, not because she'll miss the physical act, but because of its significance. No lovemaking on our anniversary means we're not keeping up with the Joneses, even though I'm pretty sure the Joneses aren't doing it on their fifteenth anniversary, either.

Jean closes her book but keeps the page marked with her finger. "I'm making you an appointment with Dr. Webber."

"I really don't think that's necessary, hon."

"Gabe," she says sternly. "It's affecting you, and it's affecting us.

It's not up for discussion." She opens her book again and lets out a long, forlorn sigh.

IN THE MORNING, the sun streams through the window for the first time in almost a week, so I decide to go hunting. Deer season is ending in two weeks, and I still haven't gotten one. The last time I didn't bring one home was eight years ago, when I came down with a flu that knocked me out for a month. When Billy sees me in my orange vest, he asks if he can come.

"I don't know if that's a good idea." Hunting has been the perfect way to spend hours on Grindr, Craigslist casual encounters, and Reddit with no fear of Jean or anyone else walking in on me. It also limits my hunting zones to places with cell reception, which is maybe why I haven't shot anything yet.

"You promised you'd take me this weekend," Billy says, looking down at his hands.

"Why do you want to come?"

"I don't know. You got me a permit and all. Shouldn't I use it?" He sees me considering. "Plus, it'll get me away from my video games for a few hours."

WE SIT IN my tree stand staring at the beige expanse of Dave Harnell's field—Dave lets me hunt on his land in exchange for a little meat. It's been two hours, and we've yet to see anything. In the distance, a thin tail of smoke wisps out of the Harnells' chimney. My nose catches a trace of the burning wood. Behind their house, a hill slopes to a small pond surrounded by crispy cattails. To the right, a long tree-lined gully cuts into the field. One oak holds onto a handful of brown leaves, but the rest of the trees are bare. I alternate between keeping my eyes on the pond, where deer sometimes go for a quick drink, and the gully, where they go to eat sumac seed heads, those densely packed clusters of fuzzy scarlet berries.

The tree stand shakes, and I glare at Billy, who's been jiggling his leg off and on all morning. "Cut that out."

His leg stills. "Don't you get bored out here?"

"That's part of it."

He hoists his rifle onto his shoulder and closes one eye, squinting through the sight. He sweeps his gun across the field and curves his pointer finger over the trigger, making firing noises with his mouth as he pretends to shoot trees and birds. Playing a video game even out in the real world. "Why do you like it, then?"

A yellow-rumped warbler trills somewhere nearby. I look for a flash of yellow through the tree branches but don't see any birds. "It's nice to get away from everything."

"What do you want to get away from?"

I shrug. "Nothing specifically."

"Mom?"

"No, not your mom."

He picks up a browning maple leaf mottled with small black spots and rips pieces off. "Are you having an affair or something?"

My stomach surges. "What makes you say that?"

"I'm not blind," he says. "Or stupid. Who is it? I won't tell Mom or anything."

Who is it instead of *Who is she*? Was he making an intentional grammatical choice, or am I just reading into it? I want to press Billy about what evidence he has, but I don't want to seem guilty. Kids can do anything with computers these days. Could he have found my browser history even though I cleared it? Or my Grindr app, even though I hid it in my extras folder? *Dry Creek. Motel 6. Tuesday 7 pm.* I still haven't figured out what I'm going to do. I make endless mental lists with two sides. On the "should go" side, there's (1) I'm dying to; (2) maybe after I do it once, it'll be enough and I'll stop; (3) I should find out if I even like having sex with a guy before I bust up my whole life. On the "shouldn't go" side, there's (1) I've held out this long; (2) maybe I'll like it so much I won't be able to stop; (3) I know I'll like it. I should leave Jean first so I'm not a cheater. No matter how many lists I make, the sides are always even.

"Fine, don't tell me," Billy huffs, and starts swiping at his phone. I peer over his shoulder and see a familiar name on his Facebook: Zach Roland, the kid who was running away with the head of the task force's daughter the night that poor girl was hit by a car. The paper said the car drove right over her legs. The police still haven't figured out who did it. She was in intensive care for weeks, though last I heard she was finally being released from the hospital.

"Hey, is that girl back at school yet? The one who was hit by the car?"

Billy nods. "She's in a wheelchair. The doctors said they're not sure if she'll ever walk again." He scrolls through his Facebook timeline too fast to even see anything.

"That's terrible. Do you know why they were trying to run away?"

Billy shrugs like he's trying to shake something off his shoulder and looks away. "How the fuck would I know? I don't even know them."

"You're Facebook friends with people you don't know?"

"What're you talking about?"

"I saw you're friends with that kid Zach."

He puts his phone in his lap, facedown. "God, Dad, don't look at my shit. Besides, everyone at school is friends on Facebook, even if you're not really friends. Everyone knows that except old people."

I hold my hands up. "Okay, I was just curious."

Billy's eyes widen. "Hey, look." He gestures with his chin in the direction he was staring.

A beautiful buck stands smack in the middle of the field, about thirty yards away. The sun glints off the tips of his expansive rack and I count twelve points. My heart speeds up. The buck on my living room wall is only a ten-pointer. The greatest spread of this one's main beams must be at least twenty-five inches. He turns to the side, giving us a clear shot at his heart.

"Get him, Dad," Billy says.

I raise my rifle, still shaky from Billy's questions about if I'm having an affair. The sight quivers in front of my eye. I center the cross on the buck's heart and take a deep breath. As I breathe out, I squeeze the trigger. The buck's ears perk up and rotate at the sound of the shot. He looks straight at the tree stand and then sprints to the gully, his white tail up.

"Shit." I throw my rifle down and smack my palm against the wood planks of the stand. It vibrates under my knees.

"It happens," Billy says.

"That was an easy fucking shot." I reel my arm back and punch the tree trunk. Rocklike maple bark grinds into my knuckles. I punch again. A piece of bark falls off the tree, revealing smooth brown wood underneath. Notches of blood appear on my knuckles, welling into drops.

"Dad," Billy says, pulling my arm.

I whip him off and keep punching. I punch until I feel the crack of bone.

"How's THE OTHER GUY look?" jokes a customer in Sportsman's Corner the next morning.

I wish I could flip him off, but my hand is covered in a rusty Ace bandage and a white drugstore splint. I give him a courtesy laugh, pretending I haven't heard the same thing all day.

"What happened?" he asks.

I tell him I fell on it, the same thing I told Jean yesterday when I got home. Another lie to add to the bucket. When Jean looked to Billy for confirmation, he backed me up, even saying he accidentally tripped me.

I spend the first part of my shift chewing out the sales team for not reaching their monthly quota, then I go through inventory. A shipment of mallard decoys never arrived, and after an hour on the phone with corporate, I find out the truck crashed. A chunk of the highway had to be closed to pick up all the plastic ducks that spilled out. Around lunchtime, a guy I vaguely recognize walks into the store. I flip through the possibilities: a regular customer, someone who works in town, a husband of one of Jean's friends—no, no, and no. He goes to the footwear section and stands in front of the boots.

I hide behind a clothing rack and watch him pick up and put down various winter boots. His large hands trace the curve of each shoe. He rubs the fleecy linings between his fingers. He has deep brown eyes and a trimmed, gray-flecked mustache. He's wearing a navy-blue sweater and jeans that are just a little tighter than mine. He looks up and starts walking toward me.

"Excuse me," he says.

I pretend not to hear him, shuffling the hangers of plaid flannel shirts.

"Excuse me," he says again, louder.

I turn to look at him. He's holding a Caribou boot. "Do you need a size?" I ask, even though footwear isn't my section.

"I'm not sure," he says, holding up the boot. "I'm debating if these are too hideous." He smiles, and it hits me—I've seen him on Grindr. In his profile picture, he smiles as a man kisses his cheek, and his description says something about looking for a third. I think he messaged me once, last winter, and I turned him down because at that point I was just looking.

My heartbeat pulses in my fingertips. "I don't know if there's such a thing as stylish winter boots for men," I say, searching his face for a sign that he recognizes me, though I'd probably have to lift up my shirt for that to happen.

"I guess you're right," he says. "I'll try them in a ten and a half, please."

I head to the back and wander through the aisles stacked from top to bottom with hunter-green shoeboxes, looking for the boot section. He has to be here with the task force. I wonder how it works, with him and his partner and whoever joins them in bed. I wonder who they've found on Grindr. It's not like there's a huge market in Big Burr—maybe *they've* hooked up with PB Tall Guy. The thought feels distasteful, like we're completely interchange-able and maybe PB Tall Guy didn't message me for a specific reason at all. Though if that's the case, I can't really blame him—it's not like my profile gives anyone much to go on.

PB Tall Guy has a nondescript profile picture, too—just his bulge in a pair of gray Jockey boxer briefs. I imagine a Robert Downey Jr. type with dark features and a five-o'clock shadow. Pull-ing the blinds shut as he bites the back of my neck. Tracing the curve of his ass with my hand. The first flick of his tongue around my tip. Maybe the impersonality of Grindr is what men like about it—because you can imagine whatever you want.

I stand there, staring at a bar code, until my erection goes away. I find the right section and match the boot in my hand to the small black-and-white image on the box. As I walk back out to the floor, sweat from my palm dampens the cardboard.

I hand the box to the man. "Ten and a half," I say.

He sits down on a bench and unlaces his brown leather sneakers. They look expensive. "Those are nice sneakers. Where'd you find them?"

"New York," he says in a nostalgic tone. "Where I lived before I came here."

"New York City?"

He nods and slides a foot into the boot, stamping his heel on the floor to get it all the way on.

"You're here with the task force?"

"Is it that obvious?" He smiles and looks up at me curiously. "And you're . . . from here?" A wisp of flirtation clings to the question.

I nod. "Been here my whole life."

"Wow," he says, shaking his head. "How do you do it?"

"Do what?"

He shrugs. "Exist here." His eyes meet mine, and I understand he's not asking how anyone exists here, but someone like him. Like me. He holds my gaze for a moment, then puts on the other boot and stands up. He walks a few paces and turns around. "What do you think?" he asks, striking a pose.

I blink a few times, coming back down to earth. "Oh, um. Well. They look . . . fine. They look good."

He laughs and looks in the foot mirror at the end of the stool. "Well, they're comfortable. And truly hideous. I'll take them."

I laugh. "Ashlinn can ring you up at the register."

"Thanks for the help." He turns to walk away, then pauses. "I'm David, by the way." He extends his hand.

"Gabe," I say.

He wraps my hand in a tight squeeze. His eyes fix on my silver wedding ring as he lets go. "See you around, Gabe."

I LEAVE WORK early to go to my doctor's appointment. Jean was able to squeeze me in at the last minute because she told Dr. Webber it was serious.

"Gabe! My man!" he booms as he walks in and slaps his wide palm against my back. We went to high school together, so my medical advice always comes with a side of off-putting chumminess. He sets my chart on the counter and turns on the hot water, pressing the heel of his hand against the soap dispenser three times. The antiseptic smell of the foam fills the room. "So how are we doing, buddy?" he asks as he rubs the soap between his fingers.

"Jean made me come. It's really nothing."

He rinses his hands and dries them with a paper towel, then turns around and regards me, looking down at my splint. "Is it about that?"

"No, I'm here for something else."

He picks up my hand at the wrist and holds it in front of his face. "How'd you do this, anyway?"

"I fell on it," I say for the millionth time.

He presses on my middle knuckle with his thumb, and I just about hit the ceiling. "Yeah, and I shit gold. How'd you really do it?"

"I really did fall on it." I shift on the exam table, the crepe paper crinkling under me.

"This here is a boxer's fracture, champ. You don't get it from falling. You get it from punching shit."

I shrug.

"All right, you don't want to talk about it." He holds his hands up in surrender. "I'll get you a better splint and if you ice it once a day, it should be feeling better in about six weeks." He takes a pinwheel peppermint out of his lab coat pocket and tosses it in his mouth. "So what's the thing that you *are* here for?"

I stare at an illustrated poster for prostate cancer. Dr. Webber's brother had it a while back, so he's become a champion for early detection. A bright red lump like a misshapen heart sits at the base of the shaft. "My stomach has been a little off lately."

"Off." He opens my chart and flips through it. "Can you elaborate?"

"Nausea, mostly. Not much of an appetite."

He closes my chart. "Any vomiting or diarrhea?"

I shake my head.

"Hm. Nausea can be psychological. What's going on up here?" He taps his temple with his pen.

The prostate cancer poster warns me that one in six men will be diagnosed with the disease. What if I die having never slept with a man? "Just the usual," I say.

"What are your usual stressors? What makes you punch shit?" He smiles, biting down on the mint. It crunches between his teeth.

"Oh, you know. Money, sales goals at work, the house falling apart, Billy getting F's on his English papers, Jean riding my ass about whatever." *Imagining men riding my ass constantly.*

144

"Tell me about it, man." He makes a note in my chart. "Let's go ahead and schedule you for a barium swallow, just to rule out an ulcer. Depending on those results, we can talk about next steps."

I nod.

He claps me on the back again. "Gotten your buck yet?"

"Not yet," I say. "You?"

"Nope," he says. "But we've got time."

WHEN I OPEN my eyes at 6:10 the next morning, the first thing I think is, *Dry Creek. Motel 6. Tuesday 7 pm.* My stomach churns. There are twenty minutes until my alarm goes off, but I can't fall back asleep. Outside, it's still dark, but my eyes adjust within the room. Jean is on her side, facing me, breathing deeply. Her top lip juts out from the thick night guard that's supposed to help her stop grinding her teeth. She's doing it right now, a tendon on her jawline popping out and her teeth squeaking against the plastic.

I wonder if I'm to blame. Sometimes I tell myself it'd be better for her—kinder—to tell her. She'd ask when I knew and I'd have to say always. Trying to convince my male childhood friends to play doctor. Waiting in the bathroom stall of the locker room for my erection to go away. The night of my twenty-first birthday, when I was falling-over drunk and kissed my best friend Jeremy and the next day both of us pretended we didn't remember. I stuffed it all down. I knew what my life would look like if I followed the path society had laid out for me. I had no idea what it would look like if I didn't. I thought maybe once I was married it would go away. Maybe once we had a kid. Maybe once I got old enough. Wouldn't it be better for Jean to find a man who can love her the way she deserves? She could find someone. But what if I can't? Then I'll be out, but I'll be alone. What's the point of that? Plus, I'd probably have to leave Big Burr, which would mean being away from Billy. Maybe I could wait until he goes to college? But if I don't do it now, soon it'll be too late. I'm already thirty-nine.

I open the app. There's a new message from PB Tall Guy: *U cumming tonight*. Again, no question mark. I wonder if it's confidence or just laziness. The way he spelled *coming* seems juvenile, but I still start to get hard. I wonder who he is, beyond the messages. I've been too scared to ask. Is he part of the task force, like David? Does he want to meet up just so he can out me? Or maybe he's closeted, too, with a wife and kids and an excuse he'll need to make up for tonight.

The alarm blares. I turn it off as Jean slides over and lays her head on my chest.

"I was having a good dream." She slips her hand under my shirt and traces the line of my boxers, brushing against my erection. "You were, too?"

I close my eyes and picture PB Tall Guy's thumb rubbing the underside of my cock. His fingers squeezing my balls. I turn over and pull down Jean's yellow daisy pajama pants. I try to focus on the sensations, but Jean keeps getting in the way. Her breasts rub against my chest. Her neck smells like vanilla perfume. She lets out quiet, high-pitched moans.

"I'm close," she whispers.

I go faster, the way she likes at the end, until she trembles and arches her neck. A streak of pale pink lights up the bottom of the window. One of the neighbor's hens calls out her imitation of a rooster's crow. It sounds like a sick chicken gargling. I kiss Jean's cheek and roll back to my side of the bed. "I might need to work late tonight," I say.

I PULL INTO the Dry Creek Motel 6 parking lot after spending most of the day in the employee bathroom, hunched over the toilet dry-heaving and writing PB Tall Guy, *sorry can't make it*, then deleting it. The only way I got myself here was by telling myself I can sit in the parking lot for a while, then drive away. I don't need to go through with anything. Lights shine from behind the curtains of two rooms on the first floor and three on the second floor. I wonder if he's already inside.

7:12. I wait for a message while chewing on Tums. A streetlight illuminates a blue banner hanging from the second-story railing that says COME AS A GUEST, LEAVE AS A FRIEND. A red Taurus pulls into a space three away from my truck. My mouth fills with spit. The top of my head prickles. Will he look the way I've imagined, like Robert Downey Jr.? Will we talk first? Will he ask me my real name? Will he be gentle or rough? Will he be able to tell I haven't done it before? Will he film it, then use it against me? I watch the car door, holding my breath. A young woman in a plaid coat steps out. She opens the back door and leans over a car seat, unbuckling a wailing baby. I swallow the spit in my mouth and turn up the oldies station. Elton John sings, *It's lonely out in space.* The music swells and rises around the chorus, *I'm a rocket man.* The music sinks back down with a sad mechanical howl.

7:28. 7:29. 7:30. *I'm here,* I write. *Where are you?* I play a game of sudoku on my phone but can't solve it. 7:45. A middle-aged guy with a small paunch pushing out his long-john shirt steps out of a first-floor room and walks toward the parking lot. As he passes my car, his eyes lock on mine through the windshield. He jerks his chin upward in what could be a tic or could mean, *Follow me.* He has a five-o'clock shadow, but not the kind I imagined. I step out and trail him to the back corner of the parking lot, to a black Chevy truck with duct tape covering the cab's back window. I stand near the bumper. He pops open the glove compartment and emerges with a silver condom between his fingers. When he sees me, he freezes.

"What the fuck do you want?" He takes a step forward.

My stomach audibly squelches. I clench my sphincter as I ask, "Are you PB Tall Guy?"

"PB Tall Guy?" he repeats. "What kind of a name is that? That's not *my* fuckin' name."

"I'm sorry." I start to back away. "I was supposed to meet someone here, and I thought you might be him. Sorry to bother you."

"Let me get this straight. You were supposed to meet somebody called PB Tall Guy at this motel?" He sucks air through his teeth and takes a step closer. "That sounds like some fag shit to me."

I hold my hands out in front of me. "No, no," I say. "No fag shit. Just a friend."

He walks up to me, stopping when there's no more than an inch of space between us. He reaches behind him, and his hand emerges with a pistol in it. "Friend?" He lets out a short laugh as he pushes the gun into my heart. His face looms over mine. From his mouth, the smell of old cigarettes and yogurt curdles the air. A small, sallow scar curves across his cheek underneath the dark stubble. "I ain't no friend," he says, pressing the pistol against me more forcefully. The coldness of the metal seeps through my shirt, making my skin ripple. "You hear me?"

I nod.

The man pulls the gun back a few inches. I think he's about to let me go until he says, "Take off your pants."

"What?"

"You heard me, fag." He points the pistol at my crotch and makes a quick down-and-up motion.

Cars race by on the dark road, none slowing down to turn into the parking lot and save me from whatever this is—an assault, a rape, a murder, a joke. With my unsplinted hand, I pull back the strap of my belt until the prong slides out of its hole, then yank the strap out of the buckle. The belt hangs open on my shaking thighs, the metal prong clinking against the frame of the buckle. I unbutton my jeans and look up at the man.

"Hurry the fuck up," he says. "This ain't a striptease."

I push my jeans down my legs until they're bunched at the ankles.

"Those, too," he says, pointing the pistol at my light blue boxer briefs.

I wince, pushing the boxer briefs down to meet my jeans. I straighten up as quickly as I can and hold my hands in front of my penis. The cold night air whooshes between my legs.

"Look who's bashful all of a sudden. Isn't this what you wanted? Some dude to see your dick?" The man taps the barrel of the gun against the inside of my forearms, forcing my hands out of the way, and laughs heartily. "Not much to look at." He lets me stand there for a minute, exposed and humiliated, then says, "All right, give 'em to me," gesturing at my jeans and boxer briefs.

I step out of them, my briefs still slightly warm from my body heat. Out of habit, I fold the jeans with the briefs inside before handing them over.

Before he heads back toward the motel, he says, "See ya later, *friend.*"

WHEN I PULL into my driveway, I turn off the truck and sit looking at the house, trying to see it as a stranger would. In the dark, you can't see the peeling blue paint or the warped shingles on the roof that let water in when it rains. The porch light illuminates the placard on the front door that says THE CUNNINGHAMS and Jean's silver pots full of fake red poinsettias. Billy's video game flashes through the living room windows. A soft light shines from the master bedroom. Jean is probably reading *The Duke and I*, waiting for me.

If I can just make it to the laundry room without her seeing me, I can grab a pair of sweats and not have to explain what happened to my jeans.

The garage's sensor light snaps on, illuminating a buck no more than ten feet away. He nibbles on the evergreen at the side of the house, his antlers scraping against the peeling siding. I count twelve points. Could it be the same one from the other day? I reach behind me, feeling for the smooth wood of my rifle, then I ease the door open just a crack. The deer turns its head at the clicking noise, and I stay still until it goes back to eating. I slowly slide out of the truck, then lift the rifle until the sight is in front of my eye. Bending my pointer finger sends an electric jolt of pain through my body, but I grit my teeth and think, *Twelve-pointer, twelve-pointer*. The buck looks to the right and left as he chews with his mouth open, then his round brown eyes meet mine. He tilts his head to the side, just like the buck mounted on the wall of the living room, seeming to say, *I know*.

I lower the rifle. His white ears swivel, hearing something I can't, and he goes bounding into the woods.

Tegan

S o if someone who's transgender says they're a man trapped in a woman's body, couldn't someone also say they're a white person trapped in a black body?"

I take a long drink of water to stop myself from making my what-the-fuck-did-you-just-say face. Me and some other members of the task force are hosting a Q&A at Town Hall, the most well-attended event we've had yet—probably because we're giving away a bunch of $50 gift cards to locally owned businesses. On the flyer advertising the Q&A, we wrote, *There are no stupid questions! Ask us anything!* "First of all, the rhetoric of trans people being 'trapped' in their bodies is really simplistic and reduces trans people to victims," I say. "If anything, trans people are trapped by society's expectations, not by their bodies."

"That doesn't answer my question," the woman says, crossing her arms.

I sigh. "I guess my question back to you would be, have you ever actually heard of a black person claiming to feel white inside?"

"I'm just playing devil's advocate." The woman shrugs and makes a faux-innocent face. She clearly thinks her question was clever as hell. "Playing devil's advocate" is one of the phrases I've heard the most since being here.

I take another gulp of water and swallow down what I really want to say. "I think most of us can agree that a white person trapped inside a black body doesn't really exist," I respond. "We have no documented instances of that. Trans people definitely do exist. There are approximately seven hundred thousand of them in the United States. That's the easiest answer I can give, without getting into the intricacies of neurobiological theory and identity." The woman doesn't look satisfied at all, but I doubt there's anything else I can say to change her mind.

You came here of your own free will, I remind myself now and a hundred other times throughout the course of a day. When I was still living in Queens and working at an HIV/AIDS nonprofit, I got a call from a recruiter for AAA. She basically performed cunnilingus on my ego, saying my expertise was unmatched for someone my age and what an asset I would be to the task force. A promotion to director of education and training was the dangled carrot meant to distract me from the rest of it. I thought it couldn't be *that* different from running training sessions in New York. Shirin and I had been talking about leaving the city for years—she'd started having anxiety attacks on the subway and I hadn't gotten a decent night of sleep in a decade—but we couldn't decide where to go. Someone

154

else making the choice for us turned out to be the push we needed. Big Burr it was—at least for a couple of years.

After the Q&A, the woman comes over as I'm packing up my bag. Now that she's standing, I notice she has a half-gray, half-brunette braid so long it brushes her thighs. People with hair that long are never normal.

"I get the sense that my questions frustrated you a bit," she says.

"Transgender topics can be very confusing for some people." I wrap my laptop charger cord around itself while picturing strangling her turtleneck-sweatered neck with it. "You'll get there someday."

"You're not transgender, are you?" she asks.

"I don't see why that's relevant."

"Well, you don't look like you are. You look like a nice, normal girl." My blond shoulder-length hair, small frame, and cherubic face have a way of fooling people into thinking my personality must match—tourists in New York would always ask me to take their photo, sure that I'd comply without stealing their phone.

I shove my laptop into my bag, my empty water bottle crunching underneath it. "Yup, a nice, normal girl who eats a ton of pussy." I give the woman a hyperbolic smile before walking away, my heart thumping like I've just run up a hill.

BACK AT THE Acceptance Across America office, David paints over some spray-hate on the exterior of the building.

"What did it say this time?"

"GO HOME HOMOS," says David, pulling the paint roller over the remaining os. "How'd it go at the Q&A?" he asks, blowing air into his cupped, gloveless hands.

"It was great. Everyone asked really respectful questions and told me they learned so much and said they're so glad we're all here."

He laughs. "Yeah, and I had an excellent cup of coffee at the Pancake House this morning." David and I are the resident coffee snobs in the office, although I don't think it's snobby to expect a potable cup of coffee with some real cream, instead of single-serve nondairy creamers.

"I've started dreaming about coffee," I say. "I pour the cream in and watch it turn the perfect dark caramel color, and just as I'm about to take a sip, I wake up. It's worse than waking up mid-sex-dream." A truck drives by blaring Blake Shelton, and I want to kill myself for knowing it's Blake Shelton.

David laughs. "I know it's not the same, but I brought some coffee flan into the office today, and it's pretty delicious. Arturo taught me how to make it over the weekend."

"You and Arturo are always in the kitchen these days. Warming up to each other, huh?" I grin.

"He still drives me completely nuts, but we're finding some common ground, at least through our stomachs. It helps that Miguel and I have started taking those weekend trips to cities where good coffee *and* gay men are easier to find." He winks as he finishes the last coat of paint and sets the roller in the tray.

"Oh, are you guys back on that train?"

He shrugs. "Only when we travel, which helps set boundaries."

"Well, the next time you're chasing tail, can you bring me back some decent coffee beans?"

He laughs and I head inside. Behind the front desk hangs a banner with our sad, too-literal logo on it: an American flag, but instead of red, white, and blue, it's rainbow-colored. To the right of the desk, there's a burgundy fainting couch and, unfittingly, a swoopy modern plastic chair. Beyond the sitting area, the office extends back into eight cubicles arranged two-by-two, like a short ice-cube tray. From Jamal's cube, Salt-N-Pepa plays slightly louder than usual, since Karen is out for the day.

She's been out a lot since Avery's accident, first keeping vigil at the hospital and now driving Avery to countless physical therapy appointments in Dry Creek. The doctors still aren't sure about Avery's long-term prognosis, but Karen keeps mentioning articles she's read about people whose doctors told them they'd never take another step, and lo and behold, they're now dancing and running and climbing mountains. "She'll walk again, I know she will," Karen keeps repeating in this obsessive way, and everyone in the office nods and pats her arm while making doubtful eye contact with each other. I think she has to keep telling herself Avery will return to normal, otherwise she'll feel too guilty about bringing Avery to Big Burr.

Zach has stopped coming around the AAA office, too. I get the sense that he and Avery aren't really hanging out anymore, but neither of them will tell me why. I'm worried about him—one day I spotted him at the diner, curled into a booth by himself. He looked awful, like he hadn't slept in weeks. I started walking over to him, but as soon as he saw me, he threw some cash on the table and ducked out the back. I went to his house the next day, aware that I was veering into what could be considered stalker territory, but I was hoping maybe he'd talk to me in private. He just yelled at me from behind the closed door to go away.

I sit down and open my PowerPoint for the LGBTQ Cultural Competency training I'm leading at Walmart later in the week. *Fifty-three percent of LGBTQ employees nationwide feel they have to hide who they are at work. So whether or not you think so, you probably work with an LGBTQ person. Don't make assumptions about your coworkers' sexuality. Use inclusive words like "partner," "significant other," or "spouse." Instead of making your best guess about someone's gender identity, simply ask them, "What are your pronouns?"* I add an image of gender-neutral name tags that say "Hello, my name is _____. My pronouns are _____." I'll print some and hand them out at the meeting so everyone can practice.

After finishing a few more slides, my hand wanders to my phone almost of its own accord and I start scrolling through Instagram. Jenna and Tiana, both red-lipped, pose with fancy cocktails at a subway-tiled bar. Keir's posted a food selfie of a duck confit sandwich and a beer next to a movie stub for the new Coen brothers flick playing at the Nitehawk. Sawyer makes a faux-horrified face while standing in the never-ending line for First Fridays at MoMA.

I can't believe that a year and a half ago these were the images of my life, too. My body aches with jealousy. My last few Instagrams were of a billboard that said WHISKEY: THE ROAD TO RUIN, a boomerang of an oil pump jack slowly lowering and raising its head like an exhausted bird pecking for seed, and a closed-down pawn-shop on Main Street whose sign read, PAW, the N hanging upside down and askew.

AT HOME, SHIRIN sits at the dining room table, focused on her lap-top. She's in her uniform of plaid pajama pants and a stained gray sweatshirt, her curly hair piled in a chaotic bun on top of her head. Strewn around the table are a family-sized bag of potato chips, an apple core, a half-eaten container of yogurt, a coffee cup with brown, foamy watermarks inside, a granola bar wrapper, a Snickers wrapper, and an aerosol can of whipped cream.

"Thank god!" she says when I walk in the room. "A human!" Shirin is a web designer, and her company in New York agreed to let her work remotely so she could come to Kansas with me. Every day she descends a little deeper into cabin fever, or what I've taken to calling Kansas fever.

I give her a kiss. Her mouth has the tangy funk of unbrushed teeth. "Dare I ask how your day was?"

"Just more of the abyss." She shrugs, pressing her pointer finger onto a chip crumb on the table. It sticks to her skin, and she brings the finger to her mouth.

I tell her for the umpteenth time, "I think you need to make a schedule for yourself, sweets. Like, showered and dressed by ten. A break in the afternoon for a walk, some fresh air. A little cleanup around the house at five."

"I know." She threads her fingers together and turns her palms outward, raising her arms above her head. "But every time I stand up I just sit back down again. It's like the gravitational force of the earth is stronger here."

I open the refrigerator. "You wanna go out to eat tonight?"

"Yes, I want to go to Barosa," she says. Barosa is—was?—our favorite Italian place in Queens. "I want the arugula salad and the homemade taglierini with meat sauce and three glasses of Malbec."

"Don't make me cry," I say. "We could try Giovanni's again. Maybe it got better since the last time." I pull up its Yelp page on my phone. "One person said it'll make you feel like you're in Italy."

Shirin guffaws. "Oh, I'm sure that's just how it'll make me feel."

ON THE WAY to Giovanni's, we pass the remains of the Acceptance Across America billboard. The photo is so faded and frayed you can barely see the two women, much less discern that they were ever holding hands. A flash of white catches my eye near the top right corner—one of the red-tailed hawks who recently built a nest on the beams. The bird perches on the edge of its nest, its frowning beak in profile. A car is pulled over on the side of the road, the driver snapping pictures of the hawk with their phone. I can't help but laugh at the irony: who ever thought the people of Big Burr would want a picture of our billboard? We've asked countless times to put up a new one, but the town claims they can't remove what's left of the billboard because of the hawks, which are a protected species under the Migratory Bird Treaty Act. I had to look that up to make sure it was real. Soon there will be baby hawks, they say. I'm pretty sure they don't give a shit about the birds, but I can only imagine how gleeful they were when they realized they had a legally sanctioned way to stymie us. It's like the billboard has become a permanent taunt—or a warning. *You'll never win, so you might as well stop trying.*

Inside the restaurant, gaudy oil paintings of cookie-cutter Italian scenes cover the walls: a gondolier paddles young lovers down a canal lined with pastel-colored houses; two glasses of red wine sit on a table at a cliffside restaurant overlooking the sea; bright pink bougainvillea spills over Greco-Roman columns. The host, an ancient man with a face like a bloodhound and a name tag that says CLYDE, eyes us suspiciously as we announce that there's two of us for dinner. This happens everywhere we go in town—*the look*. Shirin gets it even when she's alone, due to her tan skin and Iranian features.

"We've got a big party coming in tonight," says the host. "Ray's eightieth." Like we're supposed to know who Ray is. "I don't know if I'll be able to get you girls in."

I peer into the dining room, where there are multiple empty tables.

Seeing my skeptical look, he says, "We're about to set up. All those tables will be pushed together."

Heat suffuses my cheeks. I take a long, deep breath. Shirin gives me a look that says, *It's not worth it.*

"So you don't have a single two-top available, Clyde?"

He shakes his head. "Ray's got a big family."

Just then, Lizzie and her husband Derek walk in. Lizzie is my one Big Burrian friend, whom I met a year and a half ago during an LGBTQ-friendly training at the beef plant where she's the manager. Afterward, she caught me crying in the bathroom. "I was just thinking about that Sarah McLachlan animal cruelty commercial," I told her. She laughed and brought me to her office, where she had a bottle of Jameson stashed, and after two rounds I knew we'd be friends.

We exchange hugs and pleasantries, then I tell them we were just leaving. "The host won't seat us because he's either too homophobic, too racist, or both," I say loudly.

"What the fuck?" Lizzie marches up to the front desk. "Hi, Clyde. Table for four, please."

"I'm sorry, Lizzie. We've got a private party tonight. I already told them." He cuts his eyes at me and Shirin.

Lizzie crosses her arms. "Is that true? You better not lie to me, Clyde."

He leans in and lowers his voice, saying something I can't hear.

Lizzie presses her lips together and shakes her head. "You know where you get your beef from, right? It would be a shame if you had to find another distributor."

Clyde raises his shoulders in an almost-imperceptible shrug.

"Okay, then." Lizzie turns on her heel and storms out, and the rest of us follow.

"What did he say to you?" I ask as we stand in the parking lot.

162

Lizzie rolls her eyes. "You could probably guess."

I shove my hands under my armpits, trying to warm them up. "Would you really stop distributing to them?"

Lizzie looks at the ground. "I doubt the higher-ups would actually approve that. God, I can't wait till I'm CEO and everyone has to do what I say."

Derek shuffles his feet back and forth. "So, should we just go to Applebee's?"

I look at Shirin and she makes a weary, resigned face. "Applebee's it is," I say.

THE NEXT NIGHT we host a listening session at the public library. At the circulation desk, there's a notice about a young adult book the library is refusing to carry due to its "mature themes," "offensive language," and "political viewpoint." A photo of the book's cover shows the close-up face of a teen whose gender and race is hard to pinpoint. Student artwork for a NASA project called "Reach for the Stars" hangs across the library walls. A small placard says that each piece of art is made out of fabric and will be wrapped around a large rocket replica. The fabric squares are supposed to depict the students' hopes and fears about the future. Most of the kids seem to have interpreted the project literally, with stitched rockets shooting into space or aliens shaking hands with humans. Some have focused on platitudey statements like "Positivity is a universal language" or "Believe in peace"—they'll make friends with E.T. but not the queers next door. One that must have been made by an older student shows an austere pink lake below sharp gray mountains. The sky above the mountains swirls with deeper pinks and blues. On the lake's shore, an indeterminate silhouetted figure stands looking out over the water.

I set up donuts and coffee in the main event room, hoping the food will encourage people to open up. The listening session is basically an outlet for residents to vent about our presence; we don't talk other than to say things like, "I hear you," "I can understand why that's frustrating," and "It's so helpful to have your perspective."

I start by asking how everyone is feeling. I've written some words on the chalkboard to help the group express specific emotions: on one side are words like *frustrated*, *afraid*, *angry*, *discouraged*. On the other side, words like *hopeful*, *interested*, *excited*, *peaceful*.

"I feel blamed," Christine Peterson says, her voice shaking. "Blamed for being straight, like it's somehow my fault and I should be ashamed. I can't help that I was born that way."

"I feel unsure of myself," says someone else. "I keep second-guessing everything I say and do. I didn't feel that way before you all showed up."

"I feel interested," says a teenage girl. "Like, the other day I asked my nephew if there were any girls at school he had a crush on, then I remembered that we should say, 'Is there any*one* you have a crush on,' so it's not gendered."

After everyone has aired their feelings, Harley asks what we could be doing differently. The group says things like "It would just be nice if everything didn't have to be so political." "I don't think my children should have to hear about gay issues at school." "Why do gay people always have to be the victim?" "I just don't understand the end goal of the task force, or the gay movement in general. You can get married now. What else do you want?"

At the end of the session, the townspeople seem unburdened. They laugh and take deep, easy breaths, their shoulders no longer scrunched up beneath their ears. I, on the other hand, feel like a soda that's been vigorously shaken and all I want to do is pop the top. I follow Harley to the bathroom. There's no all-gender restroom, so they have to use the women's room—yet another thing we're trying to change. I lean down and check the stalls for feet to make sure we're alone. Then I let out all the urine and the words I've been holding in the whole session. "Did you see how many stale donuts everyone ate? And it was the saddest thing I've ever heard when John Wagner said he loves living here and wouldn't live anywhere else in the world. It's like he has Stockholm syndrome. Not to mention when Christine Peterson said she can't help that she was born straight, it was like, helloooooo, that's what *we*'ve been trying to tell *you* for decades! What a fucking hypocrite." I bust out of the stall, feeling a little better, only to see braid lady from the Town Hall Q&A standing at the sink.

"Speaking of hypocrites," she says, meeting my eyes in the mirror. "You hold a listening session but you don't actually *listen*. You don't care how we feel—it's all for show. You act like you're so much better than us, but you hate us, too, and for the same reasons you think we hate you." She says all of this calmly, like it's a matter of fact, then takes her time washing her hands. Harley is still in a stall, probably hiding until the altercation is over.

A flush of heat avalanches through my body. I try to come up with a retort, something to exonerate me, but my mouth is dry and empty.

Shirin picks me up and drives us home the back way, past pitch-black fields and the beef packing plant.

"You're quiet," she says. "I was ready to get an earful."

"Braid lady said I'm a hypocrite. She said I hate them, too."

"Wow, what an asshole."

"No, she's right. I hate them too much to even try to understand them. And if I'm asking them to do something that I'm not even willing to do, then maybe I'm not the right person for this job." When I started out in nonprofits, I was hopeful about finding common ground with people whose beliefs opposed mine. I thought if I could just present them with all the information, they'd eventually have to see things my way. The right way. It didn't occur to me that hate had absolutely nothing to do with information, or a lack thereof.

A FEW DAYS later, I turn in a resignation letter to Karen. She looks like she's aged ten years in the last few months, a shock of gray hair sprouting next to her left temple and a deepening wrinkle between her eyebrows. She reads my letter as I sit across from her getting lost in the ocean art covering her office walls. An overhead photo of bold, striped umbrellas lining a beach. A vintage ad for the California coast. Now that I've quit, Shirin and I can fly directly to the beach for a vacation. Where's the gayest place we could go? Provincetown? Fire Island? Miami?

"You're just realizing this?" Karen says, folding up my letter. "That you hate them?" She lets out a single laugh, a literal *Ha*. "Of course you do! So does anyone in this field."

"What?" I blink at her.

"If we loved them, we'd sit on our asses. We wouldn't be here, doing this hard work. Hate gets a bad rap, but I think all activists are motivated by it, deep down."

"I can't tell if you're joking."

"I'm absolutely not."

"So you don't think I should quit?"

"You're very good at your job, Tegan. And *liking* these people isn't a necessary part of it. You have to understand them, but that's different." She crumples my letter into a ball and throws it into the trash can. "Now get back to work."

I KEEP THINKING about what Karen said, that you don't have to like someone to understand them, and I come up with a new kind of listening session, one that's ongoing. Instead of asking the residents their feelings about us, I ask about themselves—one-on-one, kind of like therapy, but more guided. *What did your parents teach you?*

What three words would you use to describe your childhood? What is your greatest fear? What is your idea of perfect happiness? What do you think is your best quality? What about your worst? What is your biggest regret? I answer the questions first, so it's not a one-way street, hoping my brutal honesty will beget theirs.

Jean Cunningham is one of the first to show up. She says she came because she desperately needs to get something off her chest, but can't be honest with anyone she knows. Then she tells me she's been having an affair with Jeff Peterson, Christine's husband. I struggle to keep my face composed. She says that finally telling the truth makes her feel like she's on some new, undiscovered drug that's "even better than mushrooms." I never would have guessed that Jean Cunningham had done mushrooms.

One day her husband Gabe comes in. He doesn't seem to have any idea that Jean has been coming, and vice versa. After a few sessions of kicking the can around, he tells me he's pretty sure he's gay and that I'm the first person he's ever told. I practically have to clamp my hand over my mouth to stop myself from blurting out that Jean has already checked out of the marriage. Then we come up with a plan for how he'll tell everyone in his life, and how he'll cope if their reactions aren't ideal.

When Christine Peterson shows up, I look out the window to see if pigs are flying.

"Could you please stop making that face?" she says as she sits down, smoothing her khakis.

"What face?"

"Like you've just *won* something."

"I'm sorry, I'm just surprised," I say, forcing my lips into a straight line. "Why did you come?"

"Oh, I don't know." She scowls.

"Come on, Christine. The whole point of this is to open up. I promise I'm not going to tell anyone what you say." I feel like I'm coaxing a small, scared animal out of a hole.

Using the thumb and pointer finger of her opposite hand, she twirls the diamond on her engagement band around her finger until it makes a full 360-degree turn. "The person who burned down the billboard, why do you think they did it?" she asks.

I shrug. "Probably because they were mad about us being here."

She purses her lips. "That seems a little obvious, don't you think?"

"I don't know why else someone would do it. Do you?"

She keeps twisting the ring around her finger. "Maybe it had nothing to do with the billboard at all."

I cock my head. "Then what did it have to do with?"

"Oh, probably their own life."

"What about it?"

At this, she shuts down, her face hardening. "How should I know? Most people are very unhappy, but they don't have a clue why." She brings a hand to her neck, suddenly covered in red blotches, then stands up and leaves.

I sit there for a few moments, wondering what the hell just happened. Some kind of confession? Nothing at all? For the rest of the sessions, every time I hear a knock on the door, there's a part of me that hopes it's her, returned to finish our conversation. But she never comes back. I tell myself she's like one of those elusive flowers that only blooms once a century in the middle of the night, and even though I still kind of hate her, at least for a glimmer I think I understood her.

Henry

It's in the middle of February, when winter feels like some demented Energizer Bunny that just keeps going and going and going, that my wife of twenty-five years leaves me. I'm walking through the mall in Dry Creek, on my way to inspect Panda Express and make sure there's no longer a pile of dead mice stuck in the grease coagulated behind the deep fryer, when I pass by Victoria's Secret and see my wife in the front window. Lacy bras spill out of her arms. A tall woman with long black hair and huge eyes stands beside her, holding up a pair of black panties. At first I think, dunce that I am, that my wife has asked a friend to help her pick out something special for our anniversary. But then the woman reaches a hand down to squeeze my wife's ass and I realize she's much more than a friend—she's a lesbian. A carnal grin I've never witnessed before spreads across my wife's face before she swats the lesbian's hand away and looks around nervously.

I feel like I'm going to puke, and I can't tell if it's because of what I've just seen or the smell of the fruity tear gas being pumped out from Bath & Body Works next door. I stand there mouth-breathing, trying to decide between marching into Victoria's Secret and confronting my wife or continuing on to Panda Express and never saying anything, when they emerge from the store carrying two pink-striped bags each. They turn toward the food court, and in a split-second decision I pull up the hood of my jacket, shove my sunglasses on, and follow them.

They walk close together, their heads tilted inward and their arms barely touching. They stop at Orange Julius and order drinks. My wife pays for both. The cashier holds out her change but my wife walks off without noticing, laughing at something the lesbian said. The cashier shrugs and drops the bills into the tip jar. I could be standing right next to them, they're so oblivious to everything but each other. Still, I keep a safe distance, trailing about twenty feet behind as they exit the mall. When they turn down a row of parked cars and get into my wife's silver Subaru Outback, I curse that I'm parked in a different lot.

I open and close my mouth for two days, my nerve to confront my wife like a slippery fish in my hands. Then, on the third day, while I'm chopping an onion for dinner, she just walks in and says it. *I'm in love with someone.* I play dumb and ask who. A woman, she says, someone you don't know. I tell her I'm not crying, it's just the damn onion. She does her best to explain, saying it has nothing to do with me, she's just a lesbian. Always has been, she sees now. Nothing to do with me at all.

I HAVE SO MANY QUESTIONS in the days after she leaves. Did she know when she married me? How long had she been cheating? Was this other woman the first? Had she ever actually desired me? I call her with each question, and at first she's good about answering them, but then she starts to get fed up. She says that giving me more information will only feed my "fixation." But there are so many things I still need to know. I call our son Peter instead.

"Yes?" he says, his usual amiable greeting. The clatter of silverware and the din of voices tells me he's in the dining hall. He's in his first year at CU Denver, majoring in psychology and driving me into debt.

"Hey, Petey boy," I say. "How's school? Hitting the books as hard as you're hitting the kegs?" I cringe at my stock-dad attempt at conversation, but it's the first time I've talked to Peter without his mom on the other phone. She usually did most of the conversational heavy lifting.

"I'm about to go to class," he says. "Do you need something?"

"I just wanted to see how things were going, if you need any money for books or anything like that."

"Nope, I got my books at the beginning of the semester. Which was over a month ago." Peter is a passive-aggressive master. When he was a kid and we'd tell him he had to finish the food on his plate, he would pull his face into an exaggerated smile and say, "I'd be happy to."

I drive my knuckles into my forehead. "All right, then. Everything's good, though?"

"Everything is good."

"And your mother . . ." She told me she called Peter to break the news about our separation, but I'm not sure how much detail she supplied.

"What about her?"

"You've talked to her recently?"

"I know she's with that woman now, if that's what you're getting at."

"Oh, she told you about that." I clear my throat. "What do you think about it?"

"I don't know." He finally sounds like he's not about to hang up. "It's kind of weird. Mom, a lesbian?"

"Tell me about it."

"I guess I knew you guys weren't happy, but I didn't know that was why."

"I didn't, either," I say.

"Really? You had no idea? That's so Jungian." Over the past year, this has become Peter's catchphrase. I could sneeze or take out the trash or eat a peanut-butter-and-jelly sandwich, and it would all be so Jungian.

"Right," I say. "So Jungian. So did Mom ever tell you anything about how she met this woman?"

"I didn't really want to know the details."

"Of course," I say, wishing I didn't want to know, either, wishing the urge to know wasn't consuming me. "What about *when* they met?"

"Oh, I get it." Peter lets out a short, bitter laugh.

"Get what?"

"Why you called," he says, the words daggering through the phone. "For a minute there, I thought you actually cared how I was doing."

"Listen, Peter," I begin, but he hangs up. I squeeze the phone in my hand. It hadn't occurred to me that he might be having a hard time, too. I call him back, prepared to ask lots of questions and to listen, but he doesn't pick up.

I sit on the couch, taking stock of the house. Peter's backpack no longer sits on the chair next to the door, the kitchen countertops aren't flecked with flour from my wife's baking, and a sloping pile of unopened mail colonizes one side of the coffee table. I pick up the most recent *Big Burr Herald* from the top of the stack and half-heartedly flip past an article about layoffs at the beef plant and a feature on an exhibit of patriotic quilts at the library before pausing on a half-page ad for a winter social at the convention center tomorrow. Different activities are advertised inside giant illustrated snowflakes: a performance by the high school jazz band, pin the nose on the snowman, a pie-eating contest, an indoor obstacle course, and a raffle. Then I see the Acceptance Across America logo at the bottom of the ad, and it dawns on me. There weren't any gay people in this town before Acceptance Across America showed up, so the lesbian my wife left me for must be with the task force. If I go to this stupid winter social, maybe I can figure out who she is. See what it is about her that made her worth leaving me for.

BUT ONCE I'M THERE I don't see her or my wife anywhere. It's mainly a bunch of young kids running around shrieking like gremlins, clutching half-eaten sugar cookies in their sweaty little hands. The guy who just won the pie-eating contest is hunched over in a chair, taking deep breaths. As I'm putting my name into the raffle box for a chance to win a new iPod preloaded with music by LGBT artists (which I plan on deleting if I win), I see Gabe Cunningham, one of my poker buddies, at the refreshments table. I haven't gone to poker night since my wife's confession. I'm thinking about ducking behind the pin-the-nose-on-the-snowman cutout when Gabe looks over and we make eye contact. Dammit. I reluctantly wave, and he gives me a quick nod—he doesn't seem overeager to say hello, either, but it would be weird not to, so I walk over. "Hey, man," I say. "What the hell are you doing here?"

He shifts his weight from one foot to the other. "I could ask you the same thing."

I rummage around my brain for a plausible excuse, then think, *Screw it, why the hell not be honest? At this point, what do I have to lose?* Besides, it might be nice to talk to someone about it. As you get older and more barricaded by family life, the amount you talk to friends about real things seems to decrease bit by bit until one day it's all work and the weather and vacations. When my wife and I hadn't slept together in weeks, then months, when I thought the problem was sex in general and not sex with me specifically, I wondered if any of my male friends were going through the same thing. But if they weren't, it would be too mortifying to bring up. Sometimes I looked around the table at poker night and wondered what we were all hiding from one another—*why* we were hiding it. "I haven't told anyone this yet," I say. "But my wife recently left me."

"Oh, man," Gabe says. "I'm sorry to hear that." He gives me two rough pats on the shoulder.

"For a woman."

His eyes widen and he coughs up a piece of the cookie he's eating.

"Yeah. This is going to sound pathetic, but I thought maybe the woman she left me for would be here and I could ask her all the questions my wife refuses to answer. But neither of them are here, so now I'm just an idiot at a gay winter social."

He chuckles nervously. "I'm really sorry. You want to, uh, talk about it?"

I shrug. "I wouldn't know where to start."

"Did you have any idea?"

"That's the worst part. Wasn't on my radar at all. I don't even know if it was on *her* radar until recently. Do you think she knew when she married me?"

"Did you ask her that?"

"Yeah, but she couldn't really give me a straight answer. Haha, a straight answer." I make the drum noise that usually follows a bad joke: *bud um bum chhhhhhh.*

"Well, maybe she doesn't know the answer, either. Maybe she

had an inkling but thought if she married you it'd go away and she could be happy. There's a lot of denial with these things." He coughs again. "I mean, that's what I hear."

The jazz band starts to warm up, trombones making long downward-sliding notes like farts and the drummer whacking the snare a mile a minute, so we step outside.

"Are you doing okay?" Gabe asks.

"I don't really know how I'm doing. I was surprised, but now that that's worn off, I can't land on a word that feels right. How do you think you'd feel if Jean told you she was in love with a woman?"

"Relieved," he says, then grimaces. "It would be a relief if she ended it and not me."

"Oh? I didn't know things weren't good between you two."

"They're *fine*," he says, scowling the word. "I just think we could both be a lot happier if we were with other people."

ON THE WAY home from the social, I drive past the Cinephile and I swear my wife and the lesbian are standing outside, but then a big rig goes by and once it passes they've disappeared. Maybe *that* was how they met. It was pretty much the only place my wife used to go without me, other than work. Ironic name for a theater that gets maybe five movies a month. But for some reason, my wife loved it there. She'd see a movie a week, no matter the plot or the ratings. I'd tell her to have fun, and I'd stay home and watch something on the History Channel.

The night I imagine my wife meeting the lesbian, it would have been crowded—a new-release Friday. Some rom-com with that blond woman who's in every rom-com these days, a memory-loss plotline combined with a married-in-Vegas plotline. When the lights dim, a woman with long black hair haphazardly gathered into a clip asks my wife if anyone is sitting next to her. My wife says no, and as the lesbian sits down a subtle gust of lavender flies into my wife's nose. During the previews they guffaw at the same cloying lines. The lesbian tilts her bag of Sour Patch Kids toward my wife. My wife, whose second joy in life after movies is sugar, holds out her hand. She giggles a little as the vaguely human-shaped candies fall into her upturned palm.

"These make me feel like a teenager," she says, her tongue prickling as she places one in her mouth. In the dark, she can't tell what color it is, but it tastes green. A car explodes in the preview, and my wife can't make out the lesbian's response. "Come again?" she says.

"They're my guilty pleasure," she repeats, leaning in close to my wife's ear. "Among other things," she adds, pulling back and smiling. They make offhand comments to each other throughout the movie, even though my wife usually hates it when people talk in theaters. *Is that her mother or her sister? Oh, that's believable. Do you think she's had work done?* At some point the lesbian reaches over and places a hand on my wife's thigh. My wife looks at her, lowering her head in an almost imperceptible nod. The lesbian uses a finger to slowly follow the inseam of my wife's jeans up and down the length of her thigh, and my wife whispers to her, "This makes me feel like a teenager, too." The lesbian stands up to leave even though the movie is only halfway through, and my wife doesn't hesitate to follow her.

Torturous images flash through my mind: my wife leaning down to lick the lesbian's nipple, a strand of her pale red hair unfurling from behind her ear; my wife raising her head from between her legs to say, "You taste so good," her chin glistening with wetness; my wife lying sated and smiling beside her, their bodies striped by sunlight. Sometimes I get hard, thinking these things I don't want to be thinking about. When you find yourself jerking off to your wife and her lesbian lover, there's not much lower you can go.

A FEW WEEKS after the split, we meet up for lunch at the diner on South Street. I inspected it recently, so it's on my safe list. My wife is almost twenty minutes late, and I can guess why. She sits down and unbuttons her coat, releasing a smell of something fruity and sour. Her hair is in a ponytail and she isn't wearing any makeup, the freckles she used to hide glowing like flecks of amber mica. Her hair looks slightly greasy, like she hasn't washed it in a while—certain daily activities become unimportant when you're so in love and in love with fucking.

"I was surprised you wanted to meet up," she says, opening a menu. "You should be mad at me." She says this guiltily yet admonishingly, like my own emotions are yet another thing I can't get right.

"I'm not mad, I'm just . . ." *Curious* is the word that pops into my head. Extremely, extremely curious. "Confused," I say instead, following her lead and opening my menu even though I decided I was getting the grilled chicken sandwich fifteen minutes ago. I *should* be mad. But instead of anger, I feel a kind of sick fascination. How did this person I was with for twenty-five years become someone else?

"I'm getting the tomato soup and grilled cheese," she says, closing her menu and looking toward the kitchen. "This place passed, right?"

"Would we be eating here if it didn't?"

"Right." She smiles and rolls her eyes. "I almost forgot about your golden rule."

"It's a good rule."

"Well, I've been eating at places without your holiness's blessing and I haven't gotten sick yet."

"Yet." It's strange to picture her out to dinner at places I've never been, with a woman I don't know. I want to ask where they've gone just to see if it's a restaurant that's failed inspection, but I stop myself.

"You should branch out, Henry," she says. "I'm worried about you."

"Is that what you're doing? Branching out?"

She sighs and picks at a corner of the menu where the plastic has come unglued.

"Yeah, I should branch out," I repeat. "Because there's so many opportunities for a divorced middle-aged man in Big Burr, Kansas." The restaurant is full of people I've known for almost two decades.

Christine Peterson scolding her two mini-mes. Pastor Jim counseling a distraught-looking young woman over bowls of soup. Lizzie Calhoun, the manager of the beef plant, squinting at some spreadsheet on her laptop.

My wife's phone, facing down in secrecy on the table next to her, makes the double-ding noise that means she has a text message. She picks up the phone and starts typing.

Don't say it, I think, but I can't help myself. "Is that her?"

"Who?" she says, still looking down at her phone, her thumbs tapping away.

I wait, unwilling to repeat it.

She sets the phone down. "Henry, we've been over this. If we're going to have lunch, we're not going to talk about her."

"Friends talk to each other about their . . ." I falter, not knowing which word best suits the situation.

"I don't think we're at that point yet, do you?" I can't stand how she always ends didactic statements this way, with the *do you*? It'd be like if Kim Jong-un went around saying, "I don't think we really need a free press, do you?"

"How's work, then?" I say, not caring how work is.

"This morning I had a phone session with a woman whose parrot stopped talking." My wife is an animal communicator, what most people call a pet psychic—something I sneered at during our first date. I almost didn't go out with her again, thinking she was some kind of crazy hippie, but then she "talked" with my dog Willie and what she told me was so specific, I couldn't discount it. Willie didn't like it when his tail was touched because the previous

182

owner's kid used to pull on it; he hated our neighbor because once, when he got through the fence, the neighbor kicked him. I never told her he didn't like to have his tail touched or that he growled every time he saw our neighbor. My favorite part of the day used to be coming home and hearing all the stories the animals had told her. The lesbian probably gets to hear them now.

"The parrot had gotten out of its cage and saw its owner having sex with her new boyfriend," she says. "The parrot was so jealous it decided to give its owner the silent treatment."

As she goes on, I try to remember the last time we had sex. It must have been at least six months ago. I didn't think it meant anything when she started to keep her T-shirt on, when she would get up to go to the bathroom immediately after and the water in the sink would run and run. A lot of married couples stop doing it after a while, and it doesn't mean one of them is gay.

AFTER LUNCH, I call Peter and leave yet another voice mail. Then I go to the Acceptance Across America website, trying to find a picture of the lesbian. The problem is, I saw mostly her hand grabbing my wife's ass and not much of her face. She had long black hair, that's about all I can remember, and none of the women pictured on the website have that. I stop when I see a picture I recognize— Linda Ivingston, the woman who lost her son last year. Her bio says, "Linda recently left her job at the credit union to become Acceptance Across America's community liaison, serving as a bridge between residents and the task force." Jesus, are they recruiting everyone now? Linda never struck me as the type to want to hang around with a bunch of gays, but maybe if Peter died I'd be doing crazy things, too.

I can't help but read some of the hype on the site. All their pie charts with tiny slivers showing how close-minded we're supposed to be—all because they conducted a few lousy polls and cherry-picked some of our tweets? They make it sound like they're making such great strides, with their listening sessions and trainings, their community events. Don't they know that people only go for the free food and the giveaways? Maybe my wife goes for the actual events, but I bet she's the only one.

She never wanted to move here in the first place. She was pregnant with Peter, and I wanted us to live somewhere more affordable. We settled on Big Burr because it was two towns over from my parents and I wanted to be close to them for the free babysitting. So we packed up our two-bedroom apartment in Kansas City and moved into a three-bedroom house that we bought for $80,000. We were so amazed by the price that we never stopped to wonder if we actually *wanted* to live in Big Burr. Eventually we got used to it, and getting used to something is usually close enough to liking it.

The clock reads 5:06 p.m. I drop two ice cubes in a glass and fill it halfway with vodka, then turn on the TV and fire up Netflix. I'm on episode five of the first season of a soap opera-y lesbian TV show and if anyone knew that, I might have to kill them. My wife and I still share an account—the only thing we still share, because she's either forgotten to remove me or she doesn't care—and this TV

184

show was in the "recently watched" tab. Out of masochism, I tried an episode and quickly became hooked, then got a separate Netflix account so I could keep bingeing without my wife knowing. Yeah, it hits a little close to home with the whole plotline about Jenny leaving her boyfriend for another woman, but at least her boyfriend finds out before they've been married for twenty-five years. How is it possible for something to come out of the blue like that? Don't they say you're born that way? Shouldn't you at least know by puberty? Or, at the very latest, before you vow to spend your entire goddamn life with someone? Or is everyone just walking around with a little bit of gayness incubating inside them, not blossoming until they meet a certain person? I try to picture a penis that's not mine. Reaching over and touching it. Nope. No erection here.

I refill my drink and start the next episode. Fucking Jenny. If she really loves her boyfriend like she says, why can't she just stop? I may not have been perfect, but I never cheated on my wife. Sure, I would flirt with that waitress at Giovanni's when I would go in for inspections, but that was harmless. And yes, maybe I exchanged some Facebook messages with certain high school flames, but again, harmless. That's nothing compared to getting oral sex from your lady lover in the house you share with your boyfriend, like Jenny did. Oh, god, did my wife do it in our house when I wasn't home?

She used to call me in the afternoon, asking what I wanted for dinner and what time I thought I'd be home. I thought it was sweet, her little check-ins, but now that I think about it, she was probably just making sure I wouldn't surprise her in the middle of the day. I can see her texting the lesbian with *The coast is clear. Meet at my house in 20 mins*, followed by the two little ballerina emojis and a pink beating heart. My wife would rush home first, changing into a white mesh see-through bra and matching panties that she'd hidden underneath her winter sweaters in the bottom drawer of her dresser, the kind of lingerie she'd never wear for me. Then she'd sit on the couch with a glass of ice water, flipping through a *Food Network* magazine and folding the corners of pages for recipes like "Ina's Lemon Yogurt Cake" and "Baby Strawberry and Honey Pies." When she saw the lesbian's car pull into the driveway, she'd pinch her nipples, making them push against the white mesh of her bra, and lean back onto the arm of the couch, bending one leg at the knee, tilting it slightly open. Just enough to see the smallest glimpse of red hair between her thighs.

Her skin would tingle as the lesbian appeared behind the glass panel of the front door. She'd barely breathe as the lesbian rushed to her, kicking off her shoes and pulling off her clothes and falling gently on top of her. And then . . . and then what? What is it, exactly, that lesbians do? A lot of dry-humping? Finger-banging? A double-sided dildo? Certainly some cunnilingus, but is that the cardinal act? On that TV show, I can never tell where anyone's hands are or who's doing what to whom. They'll be kissing and then someone does something off-screen that makes the other one moan, and after a few seconds of rolling around, abracadabra, a simultaneous orgasm.

Afterward, my wife would make a Waldorf salad and the lesbian would probably sit at my place at the table. They'd talk about a weekend getaway, maybe to Colorado, where they could anonymously walk down the street holding hands. Where they could eat at a Thai restaurant and stay in a hotel instead of a motel. They'd fantasize about when I'm completely out of the picture. They could leave Kansas for good. They could move to California or Canada or even Europe. Then they'd look at the clock and frown: real life beckoning. My wife would clear their salad plates, and as she washed them in the sink, the lesbian would come up behind her and give her three soft kisses down the nape of her freckled neck.

I splosh another glug of vodka into my glass, then open the refrigerator. A box of week-old pizza, the slices now rigor mortis. A mystery Tupperware full of something orange and pureed. A shriveled cucumber moldering in the bottom of the vegetable drawer, with a few stray onion skins for company. I deduct twelve points for all my infractions. Then I speed-dial the Chinese take-out place that always passes inspection and order my usual: beef and broccoli with brown rice and an egg roll, my wife's order of sweet-and-sour chicken glaringly absent. Twenty minutes later, the doorbell rings.

"Hey, Mr. Plummer," says Zach, the delivery boy for Pu Pu Hot Pot, handing me the stapled brown paper bag.

It's warm on the bottom, soy and MSG wafting out. My vodka-filled stomach percolates. "How're things at school?" I ask, handing him a twenty, a ridiculous tip for an eight-dollar meal, but what can I say, I've got a soft spot for the kid. A few months ago, when I was doing an inspection at Big Burr High, I saw one of the guys from the football team hock a loogie onto Zach's sandwich, and not exactly covertly. Zach just sat there nodding, like this kind of thing happened to him all the time. Then he threw his food away without getting anything else. When I confronted one of the teachers about it, he shrugged and said, "Boys will be boys." I never talked to Zach about it, not wanting to embarrass him, but sometimes I wonder if I should.

"Things are good," Zach says, in a tone that implies *good* is a synonym for *godawful*.

"How's your friend doing?"

"I wouldn't know," he says, pushing dirty-blond hair out of his eyes. "We're not exactly friends anymore."

"Oh, I'm sorry to hear that. Why not?"

"It's a long story, but I convinced her to run away with me, so it's kind of my fault she's in a wheelchair now." His voice catches on the word *wheelchair*.

I reach a hand out to pat his shoulder, then realize that might be a little too intimate and instead swat at an imaginary fly. "No, Zach, it's the person's fault who was driving the car."

He crosses his arms. "Easy for you to say."

"I'm sure she doesn't blame you."

"That's what she says, too. But *I* blame me."

I shift the bag of food to my other hand. "Can I ask you something?"

He shrugs.

"Why did you want to run away? Did something . . . happen? At school, maybe?" The paper said it was unclear why they left, if something specific spurred it, but I can't help but wonder if it was related to what I saw the day I was inspecting the high school cafeteria. Maybe if I had pushed harder, insisted on seeing the principal, the bullying would have eased up and Zach wouldn't have tried to run away.

He stares off into the space beyond my shoulder. "Your wife's having a girls' night, huh?"

"What?" I've been assuming that Peter and I are the only people who know about my wife and the lesbian. I certainly haven't told anyone else, other than Gabe, who knows how to keep his mouth shut. I'm hoping my wife hasn't, either. While she's clearly not ashamed of her new identity, she's never liked gossip and would hate to be at the center of it.

"Oh, I delivered some food to her and her friend about an hour ago."

"Right, yes, a girls' night," I say. "That reminds me, Zach. She left her cell phone here and I need to bring it to her, but obviously she can't text me the address. Do you remember where her friend's place is?"

"Sure," he says. "I think it was the corner of Grubbs and . . ." He presses his lips together as he tries to remember. "Grubbs and Hickory. The blue ranch-style with the red door."

I smile. The naïve, beautiful child! "Thanks, Zach. She'll sure appreciate having her phone. She's like you teenagers, can't be separated from it for a minute."

I close the door and set the Chinese food on the counter, waiting until Zach backs out of the driveway. Then I grab my keys from the hook and run, hunched over like that'll prevent me from being seen, to my car. Grubbs and Hickory. That's right on the edge of town, near the nature preserve. I bet she's the type to take long weekend walks, watching birds and identifying plants using an app on her phone.

I drive down my street, admiring the way the streetlamps illuminate the lines of soft white snow on the dark tree branches. If it weren't for the temperature, it *would* be a nice night to take a leisurely stroll with someone, holding their hand, stopping intermittently for a kiss. I haven't touched another human in over a month. Even when my wife was at her coldest, we still kissed hello after work, or she'd scratch the nape of my neck while we watched TV. Sometimes she'd roll over in the middle of the night and scoot her back right up next to me, her spine pressed to my side, and I could feel her breathing in and out, in and out.

I pull over a few houses early. A woman in a maroon down jacket walks by with a cocker spaniel on a leash. A teenage girl in the house directly in front of me sulkily does dishes behind a large window. I step out of the car, closing the door as quietly as I can. Then I remember that no one would think a man getting out of his car was suspicious unless he was acting suspicious, and I stride purposefully down the street. When I spot the blue house on the corner, I dart into the yard, staggering across the shin-high snow, before I make it to the side of the house. The window next to me is dark, but pots hanging from a rack reflect the silvery glow of a television coming from the other room.

I sidestep around the house, my boot holes in the snow glaringly obvious—winter has to be the worst season for stalking—before reaching the living room window. My wife and the lesbian are sitting on opposite sides of the couch, my wife with her arms crossed around a pillow and the lesbian with a hand to her forehead, her lips pressed together. My wife says something, and the lesbian just keeps looking straight ahead at the TV. My wife gets up and stands right in front of her, angrily gesticulating. When she's finished talking, she places her hands on her hips. The lesbian looks up at her and says something that makes my wife start to cry. She turns to walk up the stairs, and the lesbian doesn't follow her.

THE NEXT MORNING I whistle as I check the internal temperature of refrigerated chicken breasts and hot soups in warming pots. I don't even deduct points for the improper use of a cutting board at the deli on Market Street. By late afternoon, I'm surprised she hasn't called, so I call her while driving to my next inspection.

"What is it, Henry?" she says. "I've got ten minutes before I have to meet with a lame horse."

"I was just calling to see how you're doing."

"How I'm doing?" She's chewing something crunchy, probably her beloved kettle corn. "Why do you say that like I got a cancer diagnosis yesterday?"

"*Did* something happen yesterday?" Fishing for something that you know but you're not supposed to know is harder than it seems.

"What are you talking about? We had lunch yesterday. I'm the same now as when you saw me. Are *you* all right?"

"I'm fine, I just had a feeling something might be up. You know, the old marital intuition."

"Henry, no offense, but you never had intuition even when we were together."

The car behind me beeps. I look up to see a green light, and press the gas. "We never fought, did we?"

"Not really," she says. "What does that have to do with anything?"

"It just seems strange, looking back. Why didn't we?"

"I don't know," she says, sighing. "I think fighting requires a certain amount of . . . passion."

In the distance, the rotating blades of wind turbines make it look like they're blowing thin clouds across the sky until they disappear. I feel like one of those clouds, being blown away from my wife until I fade into nothing. She says it's time for her meeting and hangs up. I pull into the parking lot of Prairie Café, my next inspection, and dial Peter. The rich, charcoal smell of hamburgers wafts in through the car vents.

He picks up on ring five and a half, just as I'm expecting the call to go to voice mail. "Hey, Dad," he says, leery.

"You picked up."

"Your messages were getting pretty pathetic. I didn't think I could listen to another one."

"So you forgive me, then?" The lunch crowd arrives as if on a timer. Men in khakis and oxford shoes get out of their sedans, and farmers in snow overalls and beanies get out of their trucks.

"I guess," he says.

"Oh, good," I say. "Because I have a question about your mother."

He laughs, then I laugh.

"Oh, man, you actually do, don't you?" A long breath of air comes through the phone. "Just ask it."

"Do you remember your mother and me fighting?"

"No," he says. "You mostly avoided each other."

"Do you think if we had fought more we would have stayed together?"

"I think Mom realized she's a . . ." His voice goes down an octave. "A lesbian, and it has nothing to do with you. Do you want her back? Is that what this is all about?"

"No, I don't want her back," I say, realizing it's true. Is it possible that I feel jealousy not about the lesbian, but about Laurel herself? That I don't want her back, but I want to *be* her, the one who has an exciting new life spread out in front of her? You're with someone for twenty-five years, not happy, exactly, but not miserable, either—there's a kind of comfort in bleak predictability, because it requires nothing of you—then everything changes. She's this new person who may have always been there, but you never saw her. You're a tidal pool left by the wave of her sea change. You want to figure out how she did it. You wouldn't know how to become someone else even if you wanted to.

Laurel is probably driving home for lunch—her new home. Maybe once in a while, when she's caught up in her thoughts, she autopilots to our house before remembering and turning around. She's probably listening to the Top 40 station and debating between making apricot-glazed chicken or chicken cacciatore for dinner.

She'll pull into the driveway, admiring how the sun reflects off the ice-covered snow. It reminds her of the ocean. It's been such a long time since she's seen the water. They should plan a vacation, maybe Southern California, where they can walk along the rocky coast, their feet stepping over the shallow pools of trapped water that wait for the tide to come in and draw them back into the endless, shifting depths.

Harley

The smell of sausage and syrup and damp down jackets infuses the air as I walk into the Pancake House to hang more signs. The cashier says I can tape one to the front door. One outside, one inside? I ask. Sure, he says. As I press diagonal pieces of Scotch tape onto the corners of the sign inside the door, I catch bits of conversation from people checking out at the register. Did you hear another storm's coming? The *Farmers' Almanac* says there'll be at least two more before spring. The truck broke down. The roof caved in. The snow blower's busted. My wife here wants to get a new one. Who can afford that? I can't wait until summer. Summer's too hot, winter's too cold. You can't win. It's a cat-and-dog life.

"You lost your cat?"

I turn around and see a young girl in purple mittens that are too big for her. They slide off her hands and fall to the floor. She picks them up and pulls them back on, holding her hands in the air like she's making the signal for a touchdown.

She's standing next to a man who must be her father, who looks at my face and tries to figure out what I am: man, woman, or freak. He pulls on her mittened hand. "Come on, honey. We have to go."

"Does your cat like cheese?" the girl asks, leaning away from her father's tug. "Our cat likes cheese."

Her father jerks her hand so hard that the girl trips over her snow boots and falls onto her knees. Her eyes fill with surprised tears.

"You're fine, you're fine," her father says, sighing loudly and picking her up under her armpits.

She wipes at her eyes with the back of a mitten as he carries her out the door. From over his shoulder she says, "I hope you find your cat."

LORNA HAS BEEN missing for three days. My mother has been dead for exactly one month. Things pile on. That's the rule of the universe. My mother and I were not close. The cat and I are—or were, depending on if she ever comes back. I had taken a leave of absence from the task force to go back to Minneapolis, where I grew up, and take care of my mother. I was an only child and she was a single parent; I didn't have much choice. Her liver was failing. It wasn't a surprise. She had been an alcoholic her whole adult life. A few days before she died, she said I should understand because she was born that way. Just like I was born the way I am. It was never a choice, she said. That may be true. But who I am never hurt anyone. Who I am hasn't killed me. At least, not yet.

When I told my mother I was joining Acceptance Across America, she wasn't thrilled. "It sounds like a scam," she said. "They were stalking you on the internet, for Christ's sake. And it's not like you have any experience."

"They weren't stalking me, Mom. I write essays about my life and they're published online. Remember that one I sent you about airport security?"

"Puh! No one wants to hear about that."

Apparently, Acceptance Across America did. Joining AAA as their social media copywriter was the first time I actually felt legitimized. But with every plus there's usually a minus tagging along somewhere. Since returning to Big Burr from Minneapolis, I have been called "sir," "ma'am," "you," and "ummm." I have driven sixty-seven miles without moving the steering wheel. I have seen a foamy glob of spit floating on top of my corn chowder. I have stared down into the silver orb of an empty grain silo and heard my sigh echo back at me. I have been stared down by countless people in restrooms.

I lurch down the icy sidewalk, putting up signs in Dollar General, Barb's Boutique, Giovanni's, and the entrance of the strip mall. *Lorna is a twelve-year-old orange tabby with a diamond of white fur on her chest. She is skittish, but may come for food. She was last seen near Walnut and 12th St. Call Harley with any information: 218-555-0199.* A few people are sympathetic, but most look at me like I got what was coming. "You let her out in weather like this?" one woman says. "How old did you say she was?" says another, clucking her tongue.

Should I have seen this coming? She was getting old. And I did worry about all the moving around: Chicago (where I lived before joining the task force) to Big Burr, Big Burr to Minneapolis, Minneapolis back to Big Burr. Maybe Lorna was depressed—she had actually liked my mother, who always dropped part of whatever she was eating on the floor for her, claiming that human food didn't give Lorna diarrhea. But my mother wasn't the one who scooped the litter box. As I corralled Lorna into her carrier for the eighteen-hour drive back to Kansas, she gave me a look that seemed to say: *Not fucking again.*

So maybe she did run away. Before I let her out three nights ago, we had gone through our usual routine. Around eleven p.m., when I started getting ready for bed, she'd meow by the back door. If I didn't let her out, she'd knock everything off my bedside table in protest: reading glasses, Casio watch, ChapStick, pens, pocket change, and the framed photo of my father standing on the runway in his olive-green jumpsuit, giving the camera a cocky smile. When I finally capitulated and opened the door, she'd dart outside, where she'd roam around until six a.m., or whatever time I felt like dragging myself out of bed and letting her back in. She was almost always waiting on the front stoop, covered in burrs or with muddy snow caked between her paws, evidence of some kind of nocturnal adventure. Once inside, she'd meow frantically until I gave her a can of shredded beef feast with extra gravy. Every day, the same, until three mornings ago, when I opened the door and she wasn't there, tail twitching impatiently, waiting for me.

What I dread most is ringing doorbells, talking face-to-face with locals who search my body for clues the way I'm searching for Lorna. At every house, I renegotiate whether to act more masculine or feminine so the person behind the door will be more inclined to help me. Should I lower my voice pitch or raise it? Should I introduce myself using my name or not? Should I stand up straight or hunch my back? After stopping at thirty houses within a two-mile radius, I'm exhausted from all the shape-shifting, but I still need to visit my next-door neighbors, who are not exactly neighborly.

When I first moved in, my passing comments of "Nice day, isn't it?" or "Would you like some help carrying that?" were met with frowns or grunts. They have a prefabricated colonial that looks like it belongs in a miniature Christmas village. It has two stories, with two white columns on either side of the red front door, beige plastic siding, and decorative red shutters. To the right of their frozen driveway, a snowman with a black top hat, red scarf, and carrot nose lies on its back in the snow-covered yard. Its twig arms make a Y shape next to its head, two arcs of snow smoothed out on either side of its body, frozen in the act of making a snow angel. On their minivan is a bumper sticker in the shape of a paw print that says OUR CATS ARE REPUBLICANS.

I press the doorbell and my heart speeds up, a combination of nerves and hope. You would think at this point in my life I would have learned to be more skeptical, but I still approach every new interaction with my fingers crossed. I still think, *Maybe this time it'll be different*. Almost every time I'm proven wrong, but the rare instances when I'm not keep the flame burning. A wicker wreath with a wooden placard that says WAGNER in calligraphic script hangs from the middle of the door. I ring the bell again and the wife's face appears. She steps out onto the porch and looks at me suspiciously.

"Hi, Martha," I say, deciding to appeal to her feminine side by raising the pitch of my voice. "I don't know if you remember me, but I'm your next-door neighbor, and—"

"I remember you," she says, crossing her arms. "We thought you had left for good."

"No, I just had some family stuff to deal with."

I wait for her to say something like "I hope everything is okay," or even just "Oh," but after a few seconds of her staring past me, expressionless, I hand her a flyer. "I'm looking for my cat. She's been missing for three days."

Her face softens and she lets out a sympathetic sigh. She presses her hand to her heart as she looks at the picture of Lorna. "Such a cute cat," she says. "I have four, myself." Her head tips down as she reads the flyer. There's a half inch of gray hair in her part, before the blond starts. Her eyes flick right and left. A thick border of eyeliner follows her bottom lash-line, but not the top. I wonder if I've caught her in the middle of putting on her makeup or if this menacing intensity is her preferred style.

A gust of wind pushes against me and a chill undulates through my body. Martha sniffles and takes a folded tissue out of the pocket of her khaki pants. Her nose is short and turned up at the end, a blip in the wide expanse of her square-jawed face. She wears a pink cable-knit sweater over a white turtleneck. There's a small stain on the turtleneck, a faded rust circle directly below her right ear, like a drop of blood fell off the tip of her lobe a few washings ago.

"You poor dear," she says. "I haven't seen Lorna, but I'll be sure to keep an eye out. My kids play in the backyard a lot, so I bet they'll see her." She looks me in the eye, without probing my face or my body. Hope releases a latch in my chest.

AT HOME, I put a frozen burrito in the microwave and pick up the phone to call my mother. Then I remember. I used to dread talking to her, but there's something about going to one's mother in times of crisis. I think of what she would say to me, depending on how many drinks she'd had. If she was at the lower end, it would be something like "She's just a cat. At least it's not your *husband* who went missing." At the higher end: "Oh, how awful!" with empathy, not sarcasm. "Put a can of tuna on the back steps. I'm sure she'll be back in a few days." The more drinks she had, the nicer she became. Sometimes I'd let her get into the double-digits just so she would run her fingers through my hair and tell me how much she loved me, how special I was, how having a "normal" child would have been so boring.

In lieu of my mother I call JJ, my best friend back in Chicago.

"The cat is smarter than you," she says when I tell her Lorna is missing. "She knew to get the fuck out of Kansas."

I crouch down and turn the knob on the radiator, even though I know the heat isn't working. Every day my landlord says he's coming, then he doesn't come. "Maybe, but someone has to help these people."

"You think they see it that way? That you're helping them?"

"Some of them." Maybe not my neighbor, but there are at least modest numbers at all of our events now, and my favorite waitress at the Pancake House even sent me a condolence card after my mom died.

"So what are you going to do about the cat?" JJ asks. "I've read about cats that trekked all the way across the country to get back to their old home. Maybe she's going to Minneapolis to visit the ghost of your mother."

The burrito spins in the white chemical light of the microwave. "I think I might miss her," I say.

"Of course you miss her."

"Of course? How can you say of course?"

"Because she was your mother and you loved her, despite everything."

The microwave beeps. I take the burrito out and cut a piece off, pushing it around the plate. "Honestly, I feel more torn up about Lorna being gone."

"Well, that's a classic case of displacement. You're mourning for Lorna because you won't let yourself mourn for your mother."

"When did you become a therapist?"

"Did you forget I was a psych major before I dropped out?" The toilet flushes on the other end of the phone.

"Are you diagnosing me from the shitter?"

"No, honey, that was the garbage disposal," she says. "So if the cat doesn't come back, does that mean you'll consider leaving Kansas?"

"If the cat doesn't come back? That's a terrible thing to say." I grab a PBR out of the refrigerator and pop the tab before taking two big gulps. "She's only been gone for three days."

"How long *does* one wait for a lost cat to come back?"

I consider this. A few months? A year? Years? I picture myself as an old person, in a wool cardigan sitting in a ratty armchair next to a window, peering out in search of a streak of orange fur. "Indefinitely?"

"That's the saddest thing I've ever heard."

After some more half-hearted consoling, JJ tells me she has to get ready for a date. I take my burrito to the living room and wrap myself in a down comforter. There's a *Law & Order* on about a missing girl, and I can't help thinking of Lorna. I wish she had friends I could interview, phone records I could look up, a diary I could read for clues. Instead I'm left to picture her shivering, trapped under a shed by a wall of snow. Or crossing endless white-blanketed fields, her line of paw prints intersecting with trails of fox, raccoon, and deer. Or jumping fences into backyards, looking for the familiar blue door but never seeing it. Or even worse, knowing exactly where I am but choosing not to come back to me.

As I lie in bed trying to sleep through the cold that wriggles its way through my blanket, I remember a time when the heat went out when I was a little kid. My mother made us hot chocolate, the good kind with milk and Hershey's syrup. I was too young to realize that hers was probably full of whiskey. Then we both got into a bath so hot that it felt cold on my feet. She flipped through a Sears catalog, dog-earing pages of things I said I wanted, like light-up sneakers and a swing set with a slide. Things I knew even then I would never get, but it was fun to pretend.

After she finished her hot chocolate, she stopped paying attention to me. So I slipped my head under the water, waiting to see how long it would take her to notice. I opened my eyes. My mother's dark brown pubic hair waved serenely in the water like seaweed, and the long rust-colored scar on her stomach from her C-section seemed to wink at me. The Sears catalog was splayed open in front of her face. On the cover, a family in pajamas was nestled around a Christmas tree with countless presents underneath. It became harder to hold my breath. Under the water, I grasped my mother's calf, squeezing it hard, until her face appeared from behind the catalog and she scooped me up out of the water. She blinked at me slowly, then burst into tears. She thought I had been drowning. She sobbed while rocking me back and forth, clutching me to her chest. She stopped drinking for a full month after that, or so she claimed.

DURING THE MORNING meeting at work, I surreptitiously google "how to find a lost cat," my phone hidden under the table like I'm in high school. Lostpet.net tells me to "be calm and try to think like your cat." If I thought like Lorna, I would think: food food food food food. So what does that mean? Someone is feeding her? Or she's dead. Or trapped. Or dead. Every now and then I look up and nod at one of the PowerPoint slides outlining our anti-bullying session for the junior high. *Gender nonconforming students feel less safe in school and "play sick" because they're afraid to go. 4 out of 5 kids report they don't know an adult they could turn to for help.* The site says if I've recently moved, I should extend my search to my old neighborhood. It doesn't mention what to do if my old neighborhood is over a thousand miles away.

Back at my desk, I try to write a Facebook post about our new #TrustYourNeighbor campaign, a partnership with HGTV where a townsperson and a task force member pair up and redecorate a room in each other's house. Karen arranged it through her media connections and is really excited about the exposure it'll bring to the task force, but all I can do is laugh, picturing myself partnering with Martha Wagner and her covering my living room with woven baskets, sugar-cookie-scented candles, and reclaimed wood wall art from Hobby Lobby that says something like LOVE LIVES HERE. Instead of finishing my post, I return to my cat search. Catsinthebag .org tells me Lorna may still be inside the house, and I should check behind the books in my bookcase, in the heating ducts, and even inside my box spring and mattress—like I wouldn't know if I had been sleeping on top of my cat.

Jamal sits down at his desk next to mine. "I'm a little nervous to go to this school," he says. "Junior high kids scare the shit out of me."

"I know. I'd rather run into a pack of rabid wolves than a group of teenagers." I sigh and turn back to my computer, trying a different cat-finding site.

"Still no sign of her?" says Jamal.

I shake my head.

"You know what my aunt did when her dog went missing a few years ago? She called a pet psychic and found the dog within, like, two days."

I type "pet psychic Big Burr" into Google, doubting there will be any results, but a woman named Laurel Plummer comes up. She calls herself an animal communicator, which sounds slightly better than pet psychic. On her "About" page, there's a picture of her kissing the bridge of a horse's nose. She has light red hair and wears a white polo shirt and mom jeans. "She doesn't look like a psychic," I say.

"What did you want, bangles and a head scarf?"

I shrug and read her testimonials. *Laurel really knows her stuff! My parrot Ruby stopped talking, and Laurel helped me figure out that it was because Ruby was jealous of my new boyfriend. Now I have my boyfriend give Ruby a treat every time he comes over, and she's back to talking a mile a minute!* Another says, *My terrier Jack had a bad habit of eating only when I'd hand-feed him. Laurel showed me that Jack thought he was the pack leader, and once I changed my behaviors to assert that I was the leader, Jack only ate out of my hand metaphorically!* I click on the rates page. The cheapest option is seventy-five dollars for thirty minutes on the phone. "For that price, she better know the exact latitude and longitude of Lorna's location," I say.

FIVE DAYS LATER—Laurel's first available appointment—we talk.

"So how does this work over the phone?" I ask.

"I understand how it might be confusing, Harley," she says in an overly empathetic voice. "Animal communication is done through mental telepathy, so neither of us need to be physically present. I may see images or feel emotions that I then translate into words."

"So you think you can find Lorna?"

"Let's start with the basics. Can you tell me about Lorna, Harley?"

I tell her that Lorna lives for food, that her favorite is beef feast with extra gravy, that she likes listening to Nick Drake, and sleeps with one paw on my arm. That when she sees a bird outside the window she makes a plaintive mewling sound, that she hides under the bed when the doorbell rings, that her favorite toy is a ball of tinfoil on the end of a string and she won't play with any store-bought toys. That she doesn't like to be petted on her back, only her head, and that she gave me that look when I moved her back to Big Burr, the look that said, *I don't want to do this again.*

"Okay, I'll be quiet for a few minutes while I connect with Lorna," she says.

I watch the snow fall out the window, piling up on a branch before it gets so tall that it topples over.

"I'm getting an image," she says after a while. "Newspaper. Wet newspaper."

I wait for her to go on, but she doesn't say anything else. "Is that it?"

"I understand it's a little frustrating, Harley, but the images I get are usually singular."

"Well, can you at least tell if she's inside or outside?"

"All I see is the newspaper, very close up, from her perspective, like she's sitting on top of it."

"I don't know what I'm supposed to do with that."

"In shelters, the cages are normally lined with newspaper. Have you called all the shelters in your town?"

"Of course I have."

"Wait—now Lorna is talking to me. She's telling me she didn't run away. She wants you to know that."

"So if she didn't run away, then what happened?"

"That's all she's saying."

"Great. So she didn't run away, she saw some newspaper at some point, and I still have no idea where she is."

"I know losing a pet is so hard, Harley. Sometimes the information I give needs a chance to marinate, so to speak, and then in a day or two, you'll say, 'Newspaper!' And it will all click."

I SPEND THE WEEKEND standing for abnormally long amounts of time in front of the newspaper rack at the grocery store. When I see a piece of stray newspaper blowing around an abandoned lot next to Barb's Boutique, I climb over the chain-link fence and dig through the snow with my bare hands, looking for Lorna's frozen body. The hawks that have taken over the old billboard screech at me indignantly. I'm convinced one is giving me side-eye, like I've lost my mind. Could a hawk have gotten Lorna? One time she came home with an odd circular puncture wound at the base of her tail. Could it have been a talon? Could they be digesting her right now?

I call in sick to work and spend days watching *Law & Order* marathons. On day three, I get a call from an unknown number. At first I'd get excited every time my phone showed a number I didn't recognize, thinking someone must have seen the flyers and knew something about Lorna. I answered calls promising a free vacation to the Caribbean, lower interest on my credit card, and a "do-not-miss investment opportunity." This time, I don't pick up. After a minute, my phone chimes, letting me know I have a voice mail. It's a guy named Ed who sounds like he has a head cold. In Big Burr for the day. Saw my flyer. Works at a shelter in Dry Creek. (*Newspaper!*) Thinks he might know what happened to Lorna. Can I meet him at the Dunkin' Donuts on Wilson in an hour?

Ed might not know anything about Lorna. He might say, *Why don't you get in the car and I'll take you to her?* When we're far enough out of town, he'll lock the doors and undo his belt, saying something like *Let's find out what you really are.* After, he'll push me onto the frozen ground and kick me until the snow is red, the attraction and the revulsion feeding off of each other. I hold my trembling pointer finger over the number, going back and forth, until I decide my need to know trumps my fear.

A generic recording about the person I'm trying to reach

being unavailable kicks in after the fourth ring. I throw on my coat and get in the car. Dry Creek is almost an hour away. How would Lorna have ended up there? He thinks he *might know* what happened to Lorna. Meaning she is not currently in his possession. What happened. Past tense. Not where she *is*. And he wants to see me in person. People deliver good news on the phone and bad news in person. The possibilities race through my mind: (1) someone else adopted her; (2) she's injured or sick; (3) he saw her but then she ran away again; or (4) she's dead.

I pull into the Dunkin' Donuts parking lot without remembering the drive there. When I walk in, a man sits in the corner with my flyer on the table in front of him. He has thick ears that stick out from the side of his head and a large, rounded nose. He reminds me of a Smurf, which makes me feel better. Then he looks up and our eyes meet, and it is not the look of someone who has something good to say.

I sit down at the table and decide to just be myself. The man seems kind, and I'm too upset to devote my energy to something other than Lorna. "Please. Just tell me what you know. No preamble."

He pulls back the tab on the white plastic lid of his coffee cup and presses the pill-shaped knob into the drinking spout, then pulls it out and presses it in again. "I'm so sorry," he says, my heart constricting. "I think we euthanized your cat a couple of days ago."

"You think?"

"Well, she looked just like the photo on your flyer. She had the diamond on her chest and everything."

"A lot of tabbies look alike," I say. "How did she act?"

"Well, her favorite thing seemed to be food, but I think that's true for a lot of cats," he says. "She didn't seem to like being petted on her back. Her skin would ripple and she'd give you this testy look. But otherwise she was really sweet."

Outside, a Dunkin' Donuts employee stabs at the ice-coated sidewalk with a flat shovel. The metal crunches against the ice and clangs against the cement in a steady rhythm. *Crunch crunch clang. Crunch crunch clang.* I nod. "That's Lorna."

"I'm so sorry," he says again.

"How did she get all the way to Dry Creek?" I ask, more to myself than to him.

"Some lady brought her in," he says. "Said her kids found the cat under their shed in the backyard."

"Did she say anything else?"

"She said she wished she could keep the cat, but they already had four at home."

The hair on my neck stands up. "What did she look like?"

"Oh, medium build. Blond hair. I'm not very good with faces."

I STARE DOWN the wicker wreath that says WAGNER and repeatedly press their bell. I can hear it ding-donging inside the house.

When Martha opens the door and sees the expression on my face, she gives me a long, satisfied look. "You're that poor dear with the lost cat, aren't you?" She brushes her bangs out of her face. "Did you ever find her?"

"I'd really appreciate it if you stopped playing dumb and just tell me why you did it," I say.

She crosses her arms over her purple cardigan. "I'm sure I don't have the slightest idea what you're talking about."

"You knew I was looking for her. Why would you take her to a shelter over an hour away? So I wouldn't find her? So she would be euthanized? For what?"

"I think you're very upset and very confused," she says, starting to shut the door.

I slide my hand between the door and the frame. "Please." I can feel my face contorting, my eyes starting to burn.

She blinks at me and her face hardens. She swings the door shut and I pull my hand out at the last second, before my fingers get crushed. The dead bolt clicks. I stand there, wiping hot tears from my cold face, before I turn around and see that it's started to snow. The flakes fall steadily to the ground, settling on top of that stupid snowman. I yank out its carrot nose and chuck it into the street. I break its twig arms into little pieces. I stamp on its face, pressing its button eyes and button smile deep into the snow. I keep stamping until all three circles are flat, the snow compact under my boots. Then I lie down on top of its flattened body and close my eyes. Flakes fall onto my face, first melting but then accumulating as my skin gets colder, eventually numbing. I imagine how my face must look, blanketed into featurelessness. I imagine how nice it would be to not have to be any sort of person at all.

Lizzie

"We do artificial insemination here," says Neal, the rancher whose cow-calf operation I'm visiting for the day. Cow-calf operations are just what they sound like: a rancher keeps a herd of mostly heifers whose only job is to crank out calves. My company, King Beef, buys these calves when they're ready for slaughter. I'm here to make sure everything is up to code and to see if we can *create any efficiencies*, my boss's favorite phrase since profits started falling.

"We call artificial insemination AI for short," Neal goes on. "Not to be confused with artificial intelligence." He chuckles. Neal has a face like a potato: wide, chinless, unremarkable.

We're standing at the end of a long pole barn, where Rosie, the heifer about to be inseminated, waits between a red metal head gate. Her irises, so dark they appear to be all pupil, stare straight ahead. They look vacant, hopeless. Or maybe I'm only assigning such human emotions to the cow because the other night my husband, Derek, asked me if I thought it was time we start trying. The question echoed in my ears like it had fallen into a dry well. *Trying.* You know what I'd like to try? All sixteen flavors at the frozen yogurt place. I don't want to try to have a baby, then try to lose the baby weight, then try to make VP after I just took two months off, then try to have pleasurable sex with Derek when my vagina is still stretched out like the waist of decade-old gray sweatpants.

The rest of the cows are grazing in the field. Their colors remind me of a spice rack: turmeric, cinnamon, clove, black sesame. A group of exclusively cinnamon-colored cows cluster underneath a small tree, and I wonder if they know they're all the same color. If they're the cinnamon clique. It's a sunny, warm day, and I'd like to ask Neal for a refill of my lemonade, but I haven't been able to find a break in his steady stream of cowversation. I don't think he gets many visitors, much less visitors who are interested in all the details of a cow-calf operation.

"A lot of places still use bulls, but I've found a better success rate with AI. We get our semen from this distributor called Select Sires. It's virile stuff," he says, winking.

The most ironic thing about artificial insemination is that it all starts with a male-on-male sexual encounter. Semen distributors use a steer "teaser" to arouse the bull—they don't use female teasers because they don't want to risk actual intercourse and the spread of venereal disease. The bull will mount the steer but before it can get too far, an actual person has to insert the bull's penis into an artificial vagina to collect the semen that eventually impregnates heifers like Rosie.

Neal pulls on a breeder's sleeve, a plastic glove that extends to the armpit, and rubs mineral oil over it. "We're about to get to the unladylike part," he says. "There's a bucket of pears up there next to Rosie. You can go feed her one so you don't have to watch."

"It's my job to learn about this operation, and that includes watching you stick your arm up that cow's ass," I say. I'm the only woman in a leadership position at King Beef, a fact the men make hard to forget. My dad is the owner, and since I'm an only child, I'll be taking over when he retires. When I was in college I resisted the idea, but after I graduated with a business degree and saw the non-nepotistic prospects out there, working at the beef plant didn't seem so bad. It was a business just like any other, and at least I wouldn't have to start at the very bottom of the ladder.

"Whatever you say, ma'am." Neal raises Rosie's tail with one hand, and with the other he begins to reach inside. Rosie steps from side to side in the small amount of space within her head gate, then stills as Neal's hand disappears from view. A moment later, shit starts shooting out with surprising force. Neal steps back so it doesn't hit him.

"Got to clean out the feces so I can feel what I'm doing in there," he says, grinning, and I wonder if he chose this job or if it was circumstance or desperation. I try to breathe out of my mouth. He continues pulling out more feces than I would have thought could be contained in one animal, even one that size. A friend has a one-year-old son, and the other day she posted on Facebook about how diapers couldn't contain his BMs, how poop would spill out and pour down his legs. Other mothers commented about how this had happened to their kids, too. *The joys of motherhood!* they wrote, followed by the laughing and crying emoji.

I notice something else coming out of the cow, a strand of clear, shiny liquid streaming out of her vagina. Like water, but thicker.

"That's the slick," says Neal. "That's a good sign."

I turn away, trying to focus on how idyllic the cows look scattered throughout the field, eating grass and flicking their tails. But now I can only picture this being done to all of them, over and over again, for their whole sad, predictable lives. Neal is still rooting around inside Rosie, his hand making suction sounds, the shit splatting onto the ground below.

"You want to go feed her that pear now?" he says with an I-told-you-so overtone.

"I'm fine." I swallow hard and force myself to look back.

He takes a wad of paper towels out of his pocket and wipes at the cow's crap-covered vagina. Then he pulls the AI gun out of his overalls, where he had been keeping the "business end" body temperature. He inserts it, making a face of intense concentration.

"Now I'm feeling through the wall of the rectum to make sure the tip of the gun has reached the cervix," he says. "Bingo." He depresses the plunger.

Only then do I walk around to the front of the head gate and pick up a pear from the bucket. I hold it out to Rosie. She sniffs it, then turns away. She blinks slowly, her long, pale lashes swooping over her dark irises. I reach out my other hand and let her sniff it before scratching the brown tuft of hair on top of her head. I hold the pear out to her again, and this time she swings her head to the side and knocks it out of my hand. I kneel down and peer into her eyes, searching for something behind the black inertia, but all I can see are my own eyes reflected back.

"BABIES ARE LITTLE DICTATORS," says Tegan, whom I've met for lunch to discuss the Baby Freak Out. She's the only one I can talk to about it, since all my other friends either have kids or are chomping at the bit to have them.

"I'm picturing a baby wearing Kim Jong-il glasses," I say.

"Oh my god, yes, and that khaki safari suit he always wore." Tegan cracks up, spitting iced tea back into her glass. "I'd have a baby if I could just perpetually dress it up like a dog on Halloween."

"And that's exactly the kind of thing a person who doesn't want a baby would say." Who am I now? A person who wants a baby or who doesn't? I always figured I'd have kids. It's not really something you question when everyone around you is doing it and has been doing it for like five million years. What was it we sang on the playground? *First comes love, then comes marriage, then comes baby in a baby carriage.*

On cue, a mom walks in with a screaming baby Björned to her, and a preschooler on a scooter. The kid on the scooter bumps into a woman in line, and when his mom tells him to apologize, he says, "Why don't *you* apologize!"

I throw my head in my hands.

"Aw, Lizzie, you need to relax," says Tegan. "You're thirty-one. You have plenty of time to figure it out."

"But when I made my five-year plan five years ago, I said I'd have my first kid by thirty."

Tegan reaches across the table and steals some of my chips. She crunches them openmouthed. "This is part of your problem, the lists and the expectations and the constant 'shoulds.'"

"It's not just my expectations this time," I say. "I think Derek really wants this. The other day we were unloading groceries from the car, and the neighbor's kid wandered into the road with his ball. Derek made this judgy face and said, 'Our kids will never play in the road.' Our kids. Like it was this foregone conclusion. What do I tell him?"

"Tell him the truth. You need time to think about it."

Scooter kid and his mom sit down at a table near us. The kid takes a bite of his sandwich and does a happy wiggle. He holds the sandwich in front of his mom's face. She leans down and takes a bite, then she does a happy wiggle, too. They laugh together, a happy family once more.

BACK AT WORK, I meet with an employee who lost her index finger while putting a beef shoulder through the saw blade. Something we don't tell new hires is that if you make it five years at a meatpacking plant, you've got a nearly fifty percent chance of suffering a serious injury, and Carla has been here for four and a half. I know it's the company's fault, with their impossible quotas for production lines—we're up to four hundred cows an hour now—but the chain cannot, and will not, stop. Not if our workers can't keep up, not if we see cow shit smeared all over the place, not if they lose a finger or even an arm.

"I'm sorry this happened to you, Carla." We're instructed to apologize in the vaguest way possible, so it doesn't seem like we're admitting fault. If we can, we should try to turn the situation back around on the employee. It wasn't *our* quota, but *their* negligence.

She nods. "Thank you, ma'am."

"You know how important it is to stay alert while on the line," I say, hating myself.

She nods. "I know, ma'am."

I wait for her to say something about the increased quotas, the impossible speed with which workers have to move, but her mouth stays closed. She must need this job. She must need it desperately.

"On a separate note, I thought you could use some good news. Your five-year anniversary is coming up, and the company is prepared to offer you a five percent raise." This is far less than we owe her, even if she hadn't lost a finger.

Carla's eyes widen; the corners of her mouth rise. "Really?"

"Yes." *Ask for more! Ask for more, you dummy!* I scream at her telepathically.

She lets out a sigh, not of resignation but of relief. "That's great news, ma'am. I really appreciate it." She looks down at her watch. "Is that all? My break is almost over. I should get back to it."

The diligent employee, even as she's getting screwed. "That's all," I say. "But go ahead and take an extra fifteen minutes today. Maybe you could step outside and enjoy the sunshine. If anyone asks, tell them I said it's okay." A scrap I can toss her.

She presses her lips together. "Maybe I will," she says, and I know she won't.

After she walks out of my office, I feel so guilty that I watch cat videos for half an hour. In a compilation called *Kitties vs. Kiddies*, a toddler tries to throw a cat in a pool, but the cat whips around and the kid ends up falling in the pool instead. I laugh out loud and am about to send the link to Derek when I realize its anti-kid implications. So I send it to Tegan instead. *Cats > kids always & forever*, she writes back.

"WHAT DO YOU want to do tonight?" Derek asks when I get home. A few weeks ago, he was laid off from his job as assistant manager at Applebee's, and he hasn't had much luck finding something new, though to find something you generally need to expend some amount of energy looking. After glancing at the classifieds for a few minutes, he spends the rest of the day playing video games. By the evening, he's usually dying to get out of the house.

I'm tired and could easily spend the night zoning out in front of the TV, but instead I say, "We could see a movie."

"We've seen all the movies that got decent ratings."

"We could see a bad movie. What about that one with Jennifer Lopez—"

"I'm going to stop you right there."

"Okay, we could . . ." I open the dishwasher and start loading in dirty dishes. "Babe, remember what I said about the coffee cups? You have to soak them, otherwise the brown ring won't come out."

"We could go to Pizza Hut again," he says, even though we've already been this week.

"Do *you* want to go to Pizza Hut?"

Derek throws himself onto the couch and pulls down the skin below his eyes, making a zombie face. "See, this is why we should have a kid, so we won't care that there's nothing to do."

"*That's* why we should have a kid?"

He shrugs. "Or, you know, to *give our lives meaning*," he says, too sarcastically for it to actually be sarcastic. "You haven't said a word about it since I brought it up last week."

I hold a knife encased in peanut butter under the hot stream of water and wait for it to melt off. "That's because I don't really know how I feel about it."

"I don't understand where this uncertainty is coming from. We've always said we want kids. I meant it. Did you?"

"It's easy to say it when it's hypothetical, Derek. When it's far away." I think about the part in our vows that said, "I take you as you are now, and who you are yet to become." We got married nine years ago, right after college. We were both twenty-two. We've been together since our junior year of high school, when—true to teen movie tropes—Derek was a quarterback and I was a cheerleader. We lost our virginity to each other. Got our acceptance to KU on the same day. After we graduated, we agreed we'd move back to Big Burr so I could eventually take the reins at King Beef. We've always moved in tandem. Some part of me assumed that if I was unsure if I wanted kids, Derek must have been feeling the same way.

Derek sits on the couch, pulling on his earlobe. The skin turns bright red between his thumb and forefinger. "So you don't want to, then?" His voice is sharp, accusatory.

The knife is still slick with peanut butter. I drop it back into the sink and it clangs loudly. "I literally just said I'm not sure. That doesn't mean no."

"Okay," he says. "Just let me know whenever you make up your mind, I guess."

"I know you're upset because I *might* be changing my mind about a baby," I say. "But what if you never change? Isn't that just as bad?" I try to picture Derek as an old man, but it's impossible. In my mind he looks exactly the same, just in a sweater vest and orthopedic shoes. He's barely changed since I met him: his hair still parted on the left, his lower lip sticking out due to his overcrowded teeth and his refusal to ever get braces, the gray polos he buys in bulk at Old Navy.

"Why do I need to change?" he asks, incredulous. He reaches for his earlobe, then stops himself, clasping his hands in his lap and pressing his fingertips into the spaces between his knuckles. "If we didn't have a baby, what would you want to do that's so different?"

I open my mouth, then close it.

"Right," he says. "That's what I thought."

WE GO TO a party at Tegan's boss Karen's house the next night. Mid-century modern furniture is artfully placed around the living room and synthy electronic music pulses from bamboo speakers. Somehow, it smells like the beach: salt water, coconut sunscreen. A photo of a vintage orange Beetle parked next to a squat palm tree hangs over a polished chrome dining table. Avery, Karen's daughter, sits at the table reading a book despite the party going on around her. Derek wanders off to find the bathroom, so I sit down next to her.

"What're you reading?" I ask.

She turns the cover to face me: *The Sun Also Rises* by Hemingway. "It's funny," she says. "I've read it before but now it's hitting me in a whole other way."

"How so?"

"Well, you know how the main character lost his dick in the war?"

I nod, laughing a little bit at her bluntness.

"The first time I read it I barely registered that part. But now it's, like, all I can see. He'll never be able to have a romantic relationship. Not really. And it's the same for me."

"What do you mean?" I had thought just her legs were paralyzed but now I wonder if the injuries were more widespread.

Avery gives me a dead stare. "Come on. Who's going to want to fuck a girl in a wheelchair?"

I fumble for the right thing to say. "There might be some people who wouldn't, but who would want anything to do with them? Besides, things might change. You're still doing physical therapy, right?"

She gives me another, deeper, stare. "I go to physical therapy to humor my mom, because she can't accept the truth. I'm never going to walk again."

"You don't know that for sure."

"I do," she says. "My life will never be the same, all because we came to this stupid town. It's not fair, but it's what happened." She presses her lips together and shrugs, then wheels herself down the hallway.

I hold my hand to my chest, my heart thumping hard. What do you do, as a mother, when something like that happens to your kid? It's one thing to know you can't protect them from everything. It's another to feel partially responsible for something catastrophic. Derek comes back from the bathroom and joins me at the table. "It's a little . . . chichi in here," he says, squinting at the photo of the Beetle.

"Oh," I say, still distracted by the conversation with Avery. "I think it's nice."

Derek surveys the snacks on the table and scoops a mountain of hummus onto a pita chip. "This is really good," he says. "Tastes homemade."

I nod and dip in a cucumber slice. "We could make our own, too. It wouldn't be that hard, if we used canned chickpeas." When we woke up, we agreed to let the fight go, but all day we've been making small talk like we're coworkers in a break room waiting to use the microwave.

We sit there, dipping and chewing, dipping and chewing. "Okay, we've gotta stop," says Derek. "It's really rude to show up to a party and eat all their homemade hummus."

We move to the couch and eavesdrop on a conversation-in-progress between Tegan's coworker Jamal and Karen.

"So my brother and his husband told the adoption agent they wanted a black baby," says Jamal. "And she says, 'Well, at least it'll be cheaper.'"

Karen grimaces. "I take it they're looking for another agency, then?"

"They're thinking of using a surrogate now, despite the cost, because they're so tired of dealing with this bullshit. It's been years of nothing going their way."

I take a drink of my gin and tonic so I won't have to make eye contact with Derek. If we had to go through all that to have a baby, would we? I feel like I'm wasting some gift I've been given but didn't ask for.

"And I thought choosing a sperm donor was hard," says Karen.

"What's this, more baby talk?" says David, another one of Tegan's coworkers. He wanders into the living room and drapes himself across an armchair, clearly a little drunk. "Babies babies babies. You can't meet a man these days who doesn't have one or want one. I need a time machine back to the days when guys were sucking each other off in back rooms, not painting their picket fence white like straight people." He looks at me and Derek. "No offense."

"What makes you think I want a picket fence?" I say.

"You don't?" David says. "Tell me more."

Derek shifts uncomfortably in his chair and stares into his drink.

"I don't know. Never mind," I say.

"All of a sudden she's not sure if she wants kids," Derek says, chuckling meanly.

David puts a hand on my shoulder. "I feel for you. Straight women have it better than me in some respects, but not this one. No one *expects* gay men to have babies."

"That's the problem," Jamal says. "Anyone who doesn't fall in line feels that pushback. You're straight? Why haven't you had a baby? You're queer? Who said you could have a baby? You can't win."

I RUN INTO Carla in the break room the next day. She stands in front of the microwave, watching a plastic-covered tray rotate in the bright light.

"How are you, Carla?" I ask.

"Fine," she says. "Another day, ya know. How are you?"

"Fine, I guess." I pour a cup of coffee.

"I heard you visited my uncle's cow-calf operation the other day."

"Neal is your uncle?" I search her face for potato-y resemblance. She nods. "What did you think?"

"It was something," I say, and almost leave it at that, but for some reason I go on. "Honestly, it was a little depressing. All those heifers cranking out babies that are just going to come here to be slaughtered."

She shrugs. "The circle of life. We're not so different."

"I know," I say. "That's why it's so depressing."

"What can ya do?" She takes her tray out of the microwave and pulls off the plastic film, steam billowing out. Her meal looks like some kind of Alfredo pasta with cubes of chicken. She lowers her hand over it like she's going to poke her index finger in the middle, then stops. A thick square of gauze covers the stub where her finger used to be. "It's the darnedest thing. I keep forgetting it's gone," she says.

"Carla." I lower my voice. "If you had pushed, I could have gotten you more than five percent."

"Oh." She dips her pinkie in the food, then licks her finger. "Well, it'll still really help out."

"I could get you more. I could tell them you reconsidered."

"It's all right, ma'am," she says. "I'm glad for the five percent." She sits down at the plastic folding table and takes a bite of her Alfredo while flipping through an *Us Weekly*, her mouth moving in small, efficient circles.

"I DON'T KNOW how you do your job," Tegan says. We're at Applebee's for happy hour, and I'm drinking my third blue agave 'rita. A midsummer thunderstorm pounds the roof.

"Being a vegetarian helps."

"Yeah, I'm thinking about it, after hearing all your stories," says Tegan.

I let out a long sigh and signal the waitress for another round of drinks. "Tell me something terrible from your day."

"You know how I told you that someone from town came out to me a while ago? And I was so excited for them to tell their family and finally start living their truth?"

I cross my arms. "I still can't believe you won't tell me who it is."

"Well, I'm realizing I'm probably the only person they're ever going to tell. They said talking to me about it is 'almost as good' as being fully out. I was, like, you know what'll be really good? Having a dick in your ass!"

I laugh, then gasp. "So it's a man!"

Tegan clamps a hand over her mouth, then slowly lowers it. "I've thought about just coming out for him. Getting on a loud-speaker and letting the whole town know."

"You wouldn't." I cock an eyebrow at her. "Would you?"

"No," Tegan says. "Most days I'm pretty sure I wouldn't."

I look out the window. A shelf cloud that looks like a round cake with piped white frosting hangs in the dark sky. On the TV above the bar, a weather alert for a tornado watch cuts into the Jayhawks game.

"Should we leave?" Tegan asks, her face turning slightly pale.

"We're fine," I say. "A tornado watch just means it's possible. They'll issue an actual warning if we need to leave."

Tegan peers out the window nervously as the waitress delivers our next round. "I've never lived somewhere with tornadoes. It feels so apocalyptic."

"Relax." I push her drink toward her. "Have another 'rita."

She takes a deep breath in and out. "What were we talking about?"

"Our jobs."

"Oh, yeah," she says. "Would you say you *like* your job?"

"You say that like you're asking if I like diarrhea."

She laughs. "Sorry. Do you like your job?" she asks again, brightly.

"I'm really good at it."

"That's not what I asked."

I take a drink and try to think about if I like my job. "Climbing the corporate ladder is kind of fun." I mime climbing a ladder.

"You're so Type A," says Tegan. "And so drunk."

"What about you?" I point my finger in Tegan's face. "Do you like *your* job?"

"Uh-oh, the finger's coming out," says Tegan. "I'm cutting you off."

"Answer the question." I guzzle my 'rita until the straw sucks at the bottom, just to spite her.

"I don't like it, but I think it's important," she says. "Is that the same thing?"

I shrug. "Maybe liking things is overrated. Maybe I don't have to like being a mother. I know I'd be really good at it."

"You would be," says Tegan. "Your kid would, like, grow up to be the president. Or at least secretary of state."

"That's probably nice," I say, "watching your kid grow up and achieve things, and knowing you had a part in it." My head spins, a carousel of images flitting by: reading *The Giving Tree* before bed, sitting in the stands at the debate championships, ripping open the acceptance letter from their first-choice college. My heart swells, then I burp, sour 'rita rising in my throat.

"WHERE HAVE YOU BEEN?" Derek asks after Tegan drops me off and I stumble in, soaked from the rain. He's sitting on the couch with his arms crossed, a repeat of *Seinfeld* on mute. Another weather alert flashes across the bottom of the screen.

"I was out with Tegan." I stand in the hallway between the living room and the bathroom, trying not to hiccup. I hiccup.

"You're drunk."

"Yup."

"You've been spending a lot of time with her lately."

"Yup." I hiccup, then take a big breath and hold it in. Thunder cracks so close that I imagine the sky splitting in two. By the time I've breathed out, Derek hasn't said anything else, so I go into the bathroom to brush my teeth.

He follows me and stands in the doorway, watching me squeeze an inordinate amount of Colgate onto my toothbrush.

"What?" I say.

"I just wonder if Tegan's been putting this no-kids idea into your head."

"Why?" I say through a mouthful of foam. "Because I couldn't possibly have put it into my own head?"

"No, because she talks about it all the time. How kids are life-ruiners and shit machines and all that." He makes air quotes around "life ruiners" and "shit machines."

I spit. "So she has strong opinions about it. But it doesn't mean she's influenced me. If anyone's trying to influence me, it's you."

"Jesus Christ, I'm not trying to influence you. I'm just trying to follow through on what we've talked about for years. I want a kid, and if you actually don't—"

I grab his mouth and press his lips closed with my fingernails. "Do you want to do it right now?" I pull him into the bedroom, my fingers still locked around his lips. I let go to whip off my wet clothes, then jump on the bed and lie on my back, legs splayed. "Come on, honey, let's see how fast your little guys can swim!"

"Stop it."

"I'm serious. All my doubts are gone now. I'm so ready. I'm wet just thinking about making a baby with you."

His face flashes from annoyed to angry to scary as he unbuckles his belt and looms above me. He grabs my hands and holds them above my head, the bones of his wrists pressing into the soft skin of my inner forearm. His mouth is a flat line. In the half-light of the room, his pupils have subsumed his brown irises, turning them black. All at once, I understand this is it. Unless I agree to this baby, he *will* leave. His desire for a certain kind of life will outweigh his love for me, and he'll change. Just not in the way I expected or hoped. The flash from a bolt of lightning pulses through the room, catching us in a freeze-frame. Derek blinks and lets go of my wrists. He sits back on his haunches and covers his face with his hands.

"I'm sorry," he says. "I never would have—"

"It's okay," I say. "We were upset. We didn't mean it."

I spend all night in the bathroom puking, and when I wake up in the morning, my face indented with lines from the tile floor, the sky is blue and calm. Derek makes eggs and we never talk about that night again.

TEGAN AND I meet up for lunch like the old days. She claims I've been avoiding her, but I knew I wouldn't go through with it if I talked to her about it, and if I saw her, I wouldn't be able to *not* talk about it.

"Holy shit," she says as I approach the table. "You're pregnant."

I nod and sit down, pulling my cardigan across my stomach, finally rounded at fourteen weeks.

"I knew it," she says, shaking her head. "I knew that's why you disappeared."

"Don't say congratulations or anything." Everyone else I've told has gotten so excited, like a few weeks of lying with my legs in the air after sex is some huge accomplishment.

Tegan smacks my arm lightly. "You know I'm happy for you." She picks up a piece of straw wrapper and rolls it between her thumb and pointer finger until it forms a pea-sized ball. At my first ultrasound, my doctor told me the baby was the size of a pea. "A little sweet pea!" she said, giving me a saccharine smile. She stood there, holding the lubed-up wand, waiting for me to coo at her adorable analogy. Instead, I said, "Don't you think it's weird we compare the baby's size to fruits and vegetables? It makes me feel like I should chop it up and put it in a salad."

"Are *you* happy?" Tegan asks.

"I am," I say. "I really am."

"Good," she says. "Because I've already planned its first Halloween costume."

"Kim Jong-il?"

"I'm leaning more toward Steve Buscemi, with the bug eyes and jowls and receding hairline."

"So my future kid is fugly."

She shrugs. "Some would say Steve Buscemi is the male ideal."

I laugh. "I've missed you. I'm sorry I was MIA. I just needed some time to figure things out."

"I get it."

"I really am happy," I say.

"I can tell," says Tegan. "Scientists say your pupils dilate when you're happy, and yours are taking up almost your whole iris."

"Really?" I squeeze my eyelids shut. In the pulsing darkness, I wait for something to take shape.

Elsie

Outside the large window in the common room, cars full of families pull into the parking lot of Manor Pines, the scorching summer sun reflecting off their windshields. As they walk toward the door, some holding flowers or baked goods, resignation hangs on their faces. *But I don't want to visit Nana*, the small children might have protested. Their parents probably promised them ice cream or extra television time to get them in the car. My own children, Jillian and Kyle, live far away and are too busy with their own families to visit—though not too busy to take vacations to Fort Lauderdale or Vancouver or the Bahamas. But I can't say I blame them. Who would choose to spend their time visiting a dying, crabby old woman in a urine-scented long-term care community?

Harley, I suppose, who's been visiting me every Sunday for almost two years. Harley came to Big Burr with the task force, so at first I assumed volunteering at Manor Pines was part of AAA's outreach. Then I learned that Harley came on their own time, for their own reasons. Originally I had no idea what those reasons were, but now I think they come because they see me as a friend. In the beginning, I had a hard time with everything about Harley. I had heard of transgender people, so I wondered if Harley really wanted to be a man but was too afraid to go all the way with it. Everyone has to be something—you can't just float in the middle. After I said something to that effect, Harley stopped visiting, saying they wouldn't come back unless I got better about everything. They left me a book called *Beyond the Binary: A Handbook for Families and Professionals*, and even though I don't know if it was Harley's intention, I took the gift to mean they considered me family, so I read the whole thing. Then I read it again. I called Harley and told them I'd do my best. A lot of people at Manor Pines do brain teasers or crossword puzzles to keep their mind sharp—try calling a single person "they" for a few days and you can practically feel your brain doing backflips. I messed it up almost every time for the first few weeks, then every other time, until eventually I got down to just a few random slips here and there. I still can't say it feels entirely natural, but maybe someday it will.

Here Harley comes now, walking with their back slightly hunched as usual. They sit down next to me and set a box of muffins from Dillons on the table. "They finally had peach," they say, taking a muffin out of the box and pulling the wrapper away from its sides. A middle-aged woman I've never seen before gapes at Harley, no doubt trying to figure them out. I used to get embarrassed when this happened and wish Harley would try to blend in, but now it just annoys me. I stare at the woman until she looks away.

These days it seems funny to me that Harley could have ever been considered one gender or the other: they seem so perfectly placed between the two, like the fulcrum of a seesaw. They have short, half-kinky hair that frizzes out from their head in unpredictable peaks and swirls, and their cheekbones cut a diagonal line from the middle of their ear down to the corner of their long, wide lips. A few weeks ago a movie about Bob Dylan was screened in the common room. Different actors played him at different times in his life, and when Cate Blanchett appeared with that equilibrium of slack-jawed masculinity and discreet femininity, I thought: *Harley*.

When the muffin is free from its wrapper, they hand it to me. I take a bite. It's too sweet, like grocery store muffins always are, and the peaches are canned, but I tell Harley it's good because it's the thought that counts.

"Can you believe last night's episode of *Looking for Love*?" Harley says. I was surprised when Harley first mentioned they watch the show, too—a dating show didn't seem like something they would be interested in. "I watch it *ironically*," Harley said, which I think is just something young people say when they like something but are too embarrassed to admit it. I only started watching the show because my daughter Jillian lives for it and I figured it would give us something to talk about on the phone.

I click my tongue. "I knew Ashley L was only in it for the fame."

Harley shakes their head and smiles. "You're so cynical, Elsie."

Rose's daughter paints Rose's fingernails a bright pink, the chemical smell of the polish rudely filling the room. Thea's granddaughter Lizzie rubs her pregnant stomach and shows Thea pictures of the soon-to-be nursery. "We decided Derek is going to stay home with the baby," Lizzie says. "He's more maternal, anyway. If only *he* could carry the next one!"

"Do you think there'll ever be a gay contestant?" I ask Harley.

Harley shakes their head decisively. "No way."

"Really? Why not?"

"Try to picture someone from Big Burr watching that. Men making out with men? Women making out with women?"

"Well, maybe they just wouldn't show all that."

"Then what's the point?"

I chuckle. "I guess you're right."

Sid's son sits with him at the computer, flipping through photos on Facebook. A fat-cheeked baby covered in birthday cake. Relatives all wearing the same green T-shirt, posing next to a tractor. Sid's son holding up a very big fish. Sid nods politely at each picture—he has dementia, so he has no idea who the people in the photos are.

Harley looks at their watch and groans. "I have to leave for work in a few."

"How has it been lately?"

Harley looks down at the table, sweeping muffin crumbs into their palm. "It feels so strange knowing our time will be up in a month. I don't know whether I'm happy or sad."

I blink. Harley told me, when they first started visiting, that they would only be in Big Burr for two years. Has it really been that long?

I wonder if the task force actually made things any better here. I think of the stories Harley told me over the past two years, like when stores around town put up signs barring task force members from shopping there, or when someone tried to light the Acceptance Across America billboard on fire. The worst was when Harley's neighbor took Harley's cat to a faraway kill shelter. Can you even imagine? But there were bright spots, too. Linda Ivingston, a woman from town, started working for the task force. Harley said Linda is going to move to D.C. to work at Acceptance Across America's main office. My roommate Shirley told me her great-grandson came out and that he never would have done it without the task force. Shirley didn't mean that as a positive, but I decided to take it that way. Big Burr High got one of those gender-neutral bathrooms a few months ago. And the town finally let AAA put up a new billboard on Main Street that says HATE IS NOT A FAMILY VALUE over a photo of two smiling children.

I force myself to smile at Harley. "You should be happy. Where will you go?"

"I'm thinking about San Francisco," they say. "My friend is the editor of a magazine there and said she might be able to hire me as a writer."

"The world is your oyster," I say.

IT NEVER FELT like there was an oyster for me. I was nineteen when I had Kyle. His birth moved me to a different plane of existence: a deep sea, without light or oxygen, and it took all I had to struggle back to the surface. In those years no one talked about stuff like that. You were supposed to cry in the bathroom, powder your eyes, and come out smiling.

Kyle was only four months old when I got pregnant again. My whole body vibrated with *no no no no no*. I'd always assumed I'd eventually have another child, but at that time it felt inconceivable. Phillip said the baby was a gift from God and we should be grateful. I called my best friend Faye, who once whispered to me that her cousin had "a procedure" after a married man got her pregnant. Faye wasn't any help—she said her cousin was forbidden from ever contacting that doctor again, and in any case, she had been blindfolded during the procedure and was never told his real name. "You're married," said Faye. "Why wouldn't you want the baby?"

I had no one else I could ask—no friends I trusted enough; no coworkers, because I didn't work. It had never occurred to me how cut off from the world I was, how powerless. I drove for hours until I reached Wichita. I turned down streets aimlessly, until I spotted a few women wearing heavy makeup and dresses with higher-than-usual hemlines sauntering up and down a particularly dicey-looking block. I asked if they knew someone who could help me end a pregnancy. One of them told me to follow her down an alley, where she whipped out a Swiss Army knife from her bra and stole my purse. Back home, I drank paregoric and ran into the corner of the dining room table until finally I accepted I was having the baby. After I had Jillian, I learned to track my cycle and make up excuses during certain times of the month. I stared down the long path of my life and understood there would be no off-roads—at least none of my choosing.

"DID YOU HEAR Henry Plummer moved to Denver?" says my room-mate Shirley, sitting on her bed and flipping between a daytime talk show and a soap opera. "That's why that new guy has been inspecting the food here." Shirley is the queen bee of Manor Pines. Her social status is mostly due to the fact that she can still walk, and has a long mane of soft white hair that she sweeps into an opal barrette. "I suppose Henry was so disgraced by his lesbian wife that he had to leave town," Shirley goes on.

I roll my eyes. "Maybe he just wanted a fresh start."

"That's not what *I* heard," she says, puckering her mouth in a self-satisfied way.

"If I believed everything you heard, I'd probably be one of those crazy conspiracy theorists by now," I say. I used to confide in Shirley until I realized her interest in my life was really just an interest in gossip. Now I strategically control the information she spreads about me. Sometimes, when I hear her coming back to the room—because you can always hear Shirley coming—I pick up the phone and pretend to be talking to Kyle or Jillian. *Oh, a promotion?* I'll say. *That's wonderful.* Or, *Thank you for the gift, it was so thoughtful,* or *I miss you, too. I'm sorry you can't get any time off from work.*

"I have to do something to keep myself entertained in this place," Shirley says, hoisting herself off the bed. She stands in front of her closet, thumbing through a rainbow of cardigans. She must have a different color for every day of the month. She lays a beige cardigan with pink buttons on the bed, then places a pair of pink capri pants next to it. Shirley is obsessed with matching. Sometimes she even coordinates the beading on a blouse to the flowers on her brocade socks. "They canceled current events class today, so I have nothing to do until arts and crafts at four."

"You could read a newspaper."

"I don't go for the news, Elsie," she says, like this would be a ridiculous reason to go to a current events class.

I don't go to many of the activities, myself. I used to garden, but I don't have the mobility now. I asked for wheelchair-height planting beds, but that kind of thing costs a lot of money, so I don't blame them for not following through. Jillian sent me some potted herbs for my birthday, but they're already drooping and paling. Plants aren't meant to live inside, just like humans aren't meant to live in places like Manor Pines.

Jillian loves to tell a story about how I once made her weed the whole front yard on a scorching summer day. I had asked her to weed a portion of the garden, and she didn't pull any of the weeds up by the roots—just picked off the leaves. After I must have explained to her half a dozen times that if she was sloppy about it, the weeds would grow back. "But new weeds will just take their place," she said. "What's the point?" Ten years old and already such a nihilist. She claims her punishment for not properly weeding the garden was to weed the entire front lawn. She says it took her all day, and she had to miss Peggy Larson's birthday party, and she had such a bad sunburn on the back of her neck that her skin peeled off in a bubbly sheet. Her most ridiculous claim is that she passed out from dehydration because I wouldn't let her come inside for a drink. I don't remember any of that. Probably we'd fought about the weeds in the garden and then she stayed outside all day, sulking and giving herself a sunburn to make me feel guilty.

"WAS YOUR MOTHER mean to you?" I ask Harley as they wheel me around the short path that makes a figure eight behind Manor Pines. Harley and I always roll our eyes at the name—the only pines to be found in the whole place are a sad single line that barely hide the truck route on the other side. You can hear the big rigs revving and popping at all hours, billows of dark gray smoke rising over the tops of the trees.

"Oh, sure," says Harley. "Especially when she was trying not to drink."

"What would she do?"

"She'd yell at me for the smallest things, like forgetting to clean my hair out of the shower drain or leaving a dirty napkin on the table. Once, I accidentally left a big Tupperware of chicken soup sitting on the counter and it went bad. She made me eat a bowl of it and I was up with diarrhea half the night."

"That's terrible!"

"Yeah, but you know, I never forgot to put food away after that."

"And you still went to take care of her in her last days."

"Death is the great equalizer," says Harley.

Maybe that's what I need to do, I think. *Die, so my kids will forgive me for God knows what sins I committed against them.* It might happen soon. Two months ago, my legs started to swell. Now they've ballooned to double their normal size. I couldn't fit into my pants, so Harley had to bring me long skirts from Walmart. I've tried four different kinds of diuretics, compression stockings that made me feel like an overstuffed sausage, and even switched my heart medication, all to no avail. The nurses talk around it, but I know the swelling is because my heart is failing, and I know my heart is failing because it's been broken by my children.

"ANNABELLE IS WALKING NOW," Kyle says on the phone from Detroit. He calls every other Monday evening at seven o'clock, like I'm a chore to be checked off a to-do list. Annabelle is Kyle's granddaughter, which makes her my great-granddaughter, although it feels strange to call her this when I've never met her, and probably never will.

"When did that happen?" I ask.

"Last weekend," he says. "Would you believe she did it while Patti and I were visiting? Like she'd saved it for us." Kyle has gotten sentimental now that he's a grandfather—everything is kismet, a blessing, a celebration.

"Or maybe she just felt like walking that day," I say.

"Everything okay, Mom? Did that new diuretic help?"

"What new diuretic? The one they put me on two weeks ago? It did nothing, just like all the others." I reach a finger into my pot of herbs and poke at the soil. It feels moist but not too moist, the way soil should feel. But the plants still look sad, their stems spindly and their leaves wilted. Harley even brought me some organic fertilizer, but it didn't seem to do a thing.

"Can they try another?"

"There are no more to try," I say. "We've tried them all."

The clacking of a keyboard comes through the phone. Kyle spends half our conversations googling things, like the internet knows better than my doctors. "You tried Diuril?"

"I can't remember all the names, Kyle."

He sighs. "Did Harley talk to the doctors? I know it's hard for you to take in all the information."

"Harley's leaving soon. So I can't depend on them anymore."

"Leaving?" His voice goes up an octave. "Where is she going?" I used to correct Kyle about Harley's pronouns, but after a while it became clear it wasn't an accident. I let it slide so he wouldn't have an excuse not to call.

"The task force was only supposed to be here for two years, and their time is almost up. They're all leaving. Harley's moving to San Francisco or something like that."

"Well," he says. "That's too bad."

"Yes. But I can't blame them. Who wouldn't want to go to California?"

I THOUGHT ABOUT leaving once. I was home with the kids on one of those endless afternoons when they were small and Phillip was gone all the time, traveling around the state selling encyclopedias. I heard something on the front porch and peeked out the window to see a man in a suit taping a piece of paper to the front door. When he looked up and saw me, he scurried back to his car. I waited until he drove away, then opened the door to read "FORECLOSURE" printed across the top of the paper in bold capital letters. I ripped it off and crumpled it into a ball, hoping none of the neighbors had seen.

When Phillip came home two days later, I set the crinkled paper down next to his plate of spaghetti. He glanced at it and nodded matter-of-factly. Lit a cigarette and took a few slow drags. "We'll probably need to move," he said. I took the cigarette out of his mouth and stubbed it out in a meatball. It took days to find out what had really happened.

He told me the encyclopedias weren't selling, which didn't make any sense, because a few months back he had gotten a best salesman award. After he left for another trip, I searched his office and discovered a false bottom in one of his desk drawers. Inside, there was a manila folder full of bank statements from an account I didn't recognize. My hands shook as I scanned a statement: monthly payments to a mortgage company, a gas and electric company, and a Chevrolet dealership, all based in Wichita, where he frequently went for work. A large charge at a store called Toy Emporium. Heat flushed through my body. I grabbed the trash can under Phillip's desk and vomited. With Phillip gone at least half of every month, of course I wondered if he strayed. But in my head, it was always one-night stands with call girls or women he met in bars. I had decided I could live with that and kept it closed off in the back of my mind. I never imagined there could be someone serious. Someone like me, with a house and Phillip's children to take care of. Someone who probably had no idea about me, either.

I would leave him. Take the kids and go to California, where it's always warm. Find a job as a secretary and rent a small apartment. The kids could take the bedroom, and I'd sleep on the couch. Maybe we'd be able to see some palm trees from the window. My mind went down this road for a day or so, until Faye said to me, "Oh, honey, they like their secretaries young and single over there. Future wives, not former." Then the doubt started creeping in. I had never had a job. Never had any money of my own. What if no one would hire me or rent me an apartment? What if I left only to find myself worse off? So I never said a word to Phillip, afraid he would leave me for his other family. After the foreclosure notice, we moved to a smaller, shabbier house. When he'd come home from one of his trips, I'd kiss him on the cheek and set a plate down in front of him. When he wanted to have sex, I stared at the ceiling and projected Jillian and Kyle's future onto it. They would go to college, get jobs that made them happy, start their own families that would be better than ours. I never said a word to the kids about what I'd discovered, either. I didn't want to ruin their idea of our family, since it was already so fraught—better for them to think I was angry and distant for no reason. I stayed with Phillip until he died of a heart attack six years ago. Then, when Jillian and Kyle became convinced I couldn't take care of myself after a few minor falls in the house, they wrote a check and I came here.

OUTSIDE MY ROOM, the bottom of the sun touches the tips of the dark pine trees. A light orange creeps onto the edge of a white cloud, then the color spreads outward until the whole cloud is blazing orange. The sun set an hour ago in Detroit, and has yet to set in Seattle, where Jillian lives. Kyle and Patti are probably watching TV; Kyle loves those reality shows like *American Pickers* and *American Restoration*, anything with *American* in the name. Jillian is probably packing up from a catering event, putting leftover mini-quiches on a tray to bring to the homeless shelter. She thinks of the homeless, but not me, stuck in this place watching the sun set because there's nothing better to do while I wait for someone to help me to the bathroom. Then, like she heard my reprimand, Jillian calls. I never call Jillian because I like to see how long it takes her to remember—this time it's been a month since we last spoke.

"Sorry it's been a while," she says. "We just got back from . . ." Her voice is garbled, cutting in and out. Jillian always calls me on speakerphone from the car, an excuse to keep our conversations short when she reaches her destination.

"Got back from where?" I say. "You know I can't hear you when you call from the car."

"I'll call you some other time, then," she says.

Some other time meaning another month from now. "Never mind," I say. "Where were you?"

"Alaska," she says. "On that cruise."

"Another cruise? You never told me."

"I'm sure I did, Mom."

Through the phone, a motorcycle revs, then fades away. "I don't know how you stand being cooped up on those little ships."

"It helps that it's free." Jillian's husband works for Royal Caribbean, and she claims every vacation they take is on the company's dime. They'd come visit me, she says, if only they had the money. Manor Pines isn't cheap, she says. Managing to guilt me about how they pay for a place I don't want to be while also getting out of the one thing she knows would make me happy. "We saw a glacier so blue it looked like it had been dyed with food coloring," she says.

"I thought glaciers were white." Traveling, seeing things you didn't know existed—it must be nice.

"Some are white, some are blue," she says. "The funny thing is, glaciers that look blue to us have actually absorbed red and yellow light, and the blue is just what's reflected back to the human eye. I learned that from a tour guide."

"So the color it is isn't the color we see?" I say, more impatiently than I meant to. "That doesn't make any sense."

"Never mind, Mom." She audibly sighs. "How are you? Kyle told me Harley is leaving soon. That's such a shame."

"Yes," I say. "I doubt I'll have any visitors now." I rub a basil leaf between my fingers and, to my surprise, it easily detaches from its stem. Barely visible white lines squiggle across its surface: leaf miners. I'll have to ask Harley to bring some insecticide.

"I'm sure they'll assign you a new volunteer," Jillian says.

"I don't want a new volunteer."

"Maybe I can get out there sometime in the fall," Jillian says. "If I can get the time off. It'll be so much easier when I'm retired." *Maybe, sometime, if.* Such tenuous words. She won't be retired for another three years, at least. I shiver, wondering if I'll even be alive then. "I'm at the grocery store now, so I've got to hop off. I'll talk to you soon, Mom."

WHEN KYLE WAS FIVE, we got separated in the grocery store. I had warned him to stay close to me countless times, then he wandered off to the snack aisle to salivate over the cookies. Always such a sweet tooth, that one. Most of his teeth are fillings now. I stood at the top of the aisle, watching him pick up packages of marshmallow sandwiches and Oreos and hug them to his body, then I continued on to the produce section. He would be scared when he looked up and didn't see me, and that would teach him not to run off again.

When my cart was filled with everything to make celery trunks and melon ball cocktail for the party later, Kyle still hadn't found me. I went back to the snack aisle. He wasn't there. Panic pinged softly in my chest. I walked-ran to the meat department at the other end of the store, looking down each aisle, then back to the produce department. He knew better than to go off with a stranger, didn't he? An image flashed by—Kyle in the passenger seat of a run-down car, a box of cookies on his lap, munching away happily. What had I been thinking? How would I explain to the police how we got separated? Then an announcement rang through the store: Kyle's mother to the front desk, Kyle's mother to the front desk. I rushed over to find Kyle sitting on a pregnant woman's lap. When he saw me, he blinked in recognition but didn't move.

"I saw him wandering around all by himself," the woman said sharply.

"Thank you for your help," I said. "You know little boys, always running off." I held my hand out to him. He reluctantly got up and waved goodbye.

"You should really keep a better eye on him," she said, rubbing her hand over her rounded stomach.

"Is that your first?" I asked.

"Yes." She smiled serenely.

"You'll see," I said, walking away, Kyle following closely behind.

HARLEY COMES FOR their last visit. They bring a chocolate cake with pink flowers made out of frosting, like it's a celebration—or a funeral. Today Rose's daughter is giving her a pedicure, using an emery board to buff away a callus on Rose's big toe. The fine white dust of dead skin drifts to the floor.

"Do you think there's such a thing as a truly selfless act?" Harley asks after we've discussed this week's episode of *Looking for Love*.

"Sure," I say. "And my shit doesn't stink."

Harley laughs. "People tell me I'm selfless, because I went to take care of my mother, and because I came here with the task force, and because I hang out with you."

"People say the same about motherhood. But if you resent having to be selfless, is it still selfless?"

Arturo Garcia deals cards for another round of rummy as his son Miguel lectures one of the employees about Arturo's clothes going missing in the laundry. Shirley heard that Miguel hadn't wanted to put his father in a home, but Miguel's partner had insisted after Arturo had a second stroke.

"If children only call or visit or take care of their parents because they feel guilty, is it still love?" Harley asks.

"Impossible riddles. Sometimes I think the only true relationship a person can have is with someone they're not bound to in any way."

"So friendship," says Harley, smiling.

HARLEY HAS BEEN gone for twelve days. I go to a current events class, but I leave halfway through, after someone asks if ISIS can read her emails to her grandson. I try a "garden meditation social," which might as well be called "garden wheelchair napping." Shirley takes pity on me and joins me in watching *Looking for Love*, but she chatters the whole way through, so I can't follow anything. I ask the staff if there are any new volunteers. They shake their heads and suggest I try to make some friends.

My potted herbs are steadily declining. The basil is going brown at the stalk, and the squiggly white lines have become more numerous and pronounced. The sage leaves, once soft and fuzzy as rabbit ears, are now dry to the touch and look singed around the edges. The parsley has faded to a sickly yellow. I water the plants excessively, hoping all they need is moisture, and slide them across the windowsill in tandem with the sun. Then one day I discover a young grass-like weed next to the basil's browning stalk. The herbs have never been outside—how the hell a weed found its way into the soil is beyond me. As I pinch the weed's root between my fingernails, an image shoves into my mind: me, standing behind the locked front door, watching Jillian's pale neck turn pink as she bent over the lawn. Did I really force her to stay out there all day? Did I refuse to give her even a glass of water? I release the weed from between my fingers, deciding to let it grow.

A few days later, in an unprecedented act, I call Jillian instead of waiting for her to call me. I tell her to get Kyle on a conference line while wheeling myself up and down the short length of my room until the phone cord becomes taut.

"Mom? Is everything okay?" Jillian asks.

"I think I understand about the glaciers now."

"Are you having a stroke?" Kyle says.

I wheel myself to the pot of herbs, which are now a desiccated purplish brown, and examine the weed. It's gotten slightly taller and is still green, but droops from the top as if hanging its head. "I'm trying to say I'm sorry, if I wasn't the mother I hoped I was. If I really did make you weed the whole lawn that day, or other things I've forgotten. And I know you two are probably sorry. I forgive you. Do you forgive me?"

"*You* forgive *us*?" says Jillian. "For what?"

"For putting me in this home. For abandoning me."

"This is just classic," says Kyle.

There's a few long seconds of silence before Jillian softly says, "Are you dying?"

"Not presently," I say. I fill the watering can and shower the dead herbs with water, hoping the weed's stubborn tenacity will ensure its survival. I'm probably the only gardener to hope for such a thing. "So? Do you accept my apology?"

"I don't really know what to say, Mom," Jillian says.

"Maybe it would help if we got together. You two could come visit. I know I don't normally ask, but I'd really like to see you."

"So that's why you apologized," says Kyle. "Because you're all alone and finally want us around."

A click on the other end.

"Kyle?" I say.

"I think he hung up, Mom," says Jillian. "I'm really sorry, but I have to go, too. I'll get back to you about the visit."

"You're sorry?" I say into the emptiness of the dial tone. "You're really sorry?"

Ten Years Later

Gabe

Even in my most private fantasies, I never pictured myself marrying a man. The farthest I'd let myself imagine was a relationship, probably covert, but hopefully there'd be love. And yet somehow, at fifty years old, I've found myself looking out our bedroom window at a large white tent sitting in the field behind our house, while trying to force a pair of stupid silver cuff links through the holes of my brand-new button-down. The cuff links and tailored suit were a compromise; Brad had wanted a wedding with violins, ornate flower arrangements, a three-course meal, and white *doves*, for crying out loud, whereas I would have been happy to go to the Town Hall in my flannel. So we met somewhere in the middle: a bluegrass band, a barbecue buffet, Tegan officiating, and jars of wildflowers arranged by Jean.

The funny thing is, Jean ended up leaving *me*. About ten years ago now. Told me she hadn't been happy for a long time, that it always felt like something was missing. A few months later I ran into her and Jeff Peterson at Giovanni's and she blushed and wouldn't meet my eyes. Then I started seeing them everywhere—in line at Dillons, on walks in the nature preserve, once even with Jeff's kids in tow. Later, she'd admitted that they had been having an affair for months before she'd left me. She told me they met at Dunkin' Donuts, where they both went for their morning coffee, and one day they just "got to talking."

I never cheated on her. After I came out to Tegan and we started talking through the logistics of how I'd tell Jean and Billy and what my life might look like afterward, I got scared shitless. Who would I possibly meet in Big Burr? I could leave, but to go where? I had no desire to live in a city, with everything crammed so tight and no open space, but what would be the point of going to another small town? If I was going to do that, I might as well stay in Big Burr, where at least I could be close to Billy. Even if it meant living alone in some crappy apartment with dingy wall-to-wall carpeting and a single window, my nights a long pathetic blur of frozen dinners eaten on the couch while watching *Naked and Afraid* marathons and compulsively checking Grindr, only to see that there was no one new within a hundred miles.

And that's exactly what my life did look like for a long time after Jean left me. I took to sitting in my tree stand for hours, well past hunting season, seeing how long I could go without moving. Fooling nature into thinking I didn't exist. Fooling myself, too. It was the one way I could get myself to stop thinking about what my life had become. One day I watched a robin build a nest step by step in the tree next to me, gathering beakfuls of dead grass and twigs and depositing them in a protected nook until she had a big enough pile that she could stamp her feet in the center, spin around in a circle to make a cup shape, then fill the cup with mud.

Another day I watched a red fox trot across the field and stop partway, tilting its head back and forth in intense concentration, then launch itself off its back legs and dive headfirst into the snow up to its shoulders. It did this countless times until it emerged with a mouse clamped between its teeth. Perched high up in my tree stand, watching the animals while pretending I didn't exist—that was the closest I ever got to a sense of peace.

Eventually I found a guy on a new app called Myxr. He lived in Kansas City but was taking a leave of absence to come back to Dry Creek and care for his mom, who had early-stage dementia. For our first few "dates" we met at a bar, then hooked up in my truck. Once I was sure he wasn't going to pull something, I let him come over when Billy wasn't at home—Jean and I shared custody, so Billy was with me every other week. When Billy was at home, we'd meet at a Holiday Inn Express in Dry Creek. At that point, I still wasn't out to anyone other than Tegan. This went on for about six months, and just as I was starting to picture a possible life in Kansas City, one day he just didn't show up at the hotel, where I'd been waiting in a room for him for hours, and instead texted me that he thought we should stop seeing each other.

On my way out of the hotel, picturing my miserable return to a life of frozen dinners and mind-numbing TV, I ran into the manager, Brad, who always seemed to be working when I checked in. He was very obviously gay, with a high singsongy voice, overblown hand gestures, and a bubble butt in tight khakis that he sashayed from side to side when he walked. Dry Creek was slightly more metropolitan than Big Burr, but not metropolitan enough for drawing that kind of attention to yourself. On my third or fourth time checking in, he'd remarked on how often I was staying at the hotel and asked if I was in town for business or pleasure, a knowing glint in his eye that made my stomach drop.

"Neither, I guess," I said, hoping that would be evasive enough to conclude the small talk.

"Hmmmm." He drummed his fingers against the desk and I noticed that his right pinkie was painted with a sparkly silver polish. "If it's not business and it's not pleasure, that must mean you have family in the area?" He smiled in an exaggerated way, his teeth apart and his tongue just slightly poking through, like a golden retriever freeze-framed mid-pant.

I got the sense that the questions wouldn't stop until I said yes to something, so I said yes, my tone just short of rudeness, and looked pointedly at my watch.

Seemingly oblivious, he glanced down at my driver's license, a strand of chunky-highlighted hair releasing itself from the gelled coif on his head. He reminded me of a Ken doll, with the immovable hair and the plastered-on smile and the generically proportioned features. "I don't think I know any Cunninghams, and I'm the town's official busybody. Where do they live?"

"In Big Burr, actually," I said. "I just like staying in Dry Creek. Better hotels and restaurants and everything."

"Ah, yes," he said, putting on a stuffy British accent. "You're craving the refinement and endless options that Dry Creek has to offer."

I let out a short laugh while snapping my wallet shut, hoping that would bring an end to the conversation, but Brad plowed on. "So where are you visiting from?" he asked.

I pressed my lips together, forcing myself to take a long breath, then said the first place that occurred to me, New York City.

"I've been there once," he said, his blue eyes widening. "Magical place. I saw a woman on the subway rubbing herself down with Orange Glo, that wood cleaner, while the woman sitting next to her puked into a handbag."

Tegan once complained to me that people who didn't live in New York only wanted to tell you about the grossest things that had happened to them there. "Yup, it's a crazy place," I said, shaking my head like I was all too familiar with these scenarios.

Finally he let me leave, though I swore I could feel his eyes on me until I hit the parking lot. Every time I saw him after that he'd say, "Hey, New York City!" and we'd talk for a while, my nervousness that it was only a matter of time until he discovered I'd made up everything lending an extra dose of awkwardness to our conversations. When it became clear we were becoming friends, or something like it, I thought about telling him the truth, but there was never the right opening and it had already gone on for so long. How could I explain why I lied without sounding nuts?

But the night my boyfriend, or whatever he had been, decided to break it off, I was so irate that when Brad said, "Hey, New York City!" I completely lost it and started yelling at him about how I

261

didn't live in New York and had made it all up because I actually lived in Big Burr and was still closeted to almost everyone who lived there and I had been coming to the Holiday Inn Express for the last six months to meet up with a guy who had just ended it via text message.

Brad listened with a bemused, sympathetic expression, then when I was done yelling he insisted on taking me out for a drink at the sports bar down the street—where he ordered a Budweiser, to my surprise—and we got to know each other. He was from Salt Lake City but lived in Dry Creek because it's where his husband was from, his husband who had died a few years earlier from a rare form of cancer. He was extraordinarily close to his husband's family, who loved him better than his own, so he had decided to stay in Dry Creek and see if he could build a new life for himself. Being a hotel manager wasn't his dream job, but it paid the bills. He was taking business classes at the community college because he wanted to open his own coffee shop that served "actual coffee," which, according to him, was impossible to find in small Kansas towns. It reminded me of Tegan and David, which made me smile.

"And what exactly is *actual* coffee?" I asked.

"It should be as velvety as a velour tracksuit, pleasantly bitter like Dr. House, and have body like Beyoncé," he said.

I laughed. "I have no idea what that means."

He started singing a song I didn't know in a too-loud voice while bouncing his shoulders up and down. "I ain't worried, doin' me tonight, a little sweat ain't never hurt nobody," he sang in a slightly off-key falsetto.

I glanced around us at the men with beards wearing flannel shirts; men who looked like me. "People are looking at you," I said, even though they might have just been looking in our general direction.

He kept shaking his shoulders. "So? I don't care."

I humphed. "No one who says that really means it."

"So says you." He arched a brow.

We left shortly after that. In the parking lot, he put his number in my phone, saying I should call him if I ever needed to talk again. Then he got in a pastel-green Fiat and drove away. I assumed that was the last time I'd ever see him.

But a few days later, as I was sitting in my tree stand practicing invisibility, watching a shiny black beetle that had fallen onto its back frantically kick its legs in the air, I kept thinking about when the men in the bar were looking at Brad and he said he didn't care. He really did seem completely unbothered. I picked up a twig and used it to flip the beetle over, then I called Tegan and told her that the guy I was seeing had ended it.

"Oh, Gabe, I'm sorry," she said. "How do you feel?" At the time Tegan was in grad school for clinical social work, with a focus on mental health counseling. Her goal was to become a therapist for LGBTQ youth, which nicely summed up our current dynamic—me a gay baby in my forties and Tegan my confidant, still relentlessly trying to persuade me to come out to the rest of the world. I never thought Tegan would end up as one of my best friends, but over the years she'd become the person I turned to first.

"Originally I thought I was sad," I said. "But if I'm honest with myself, I don't think it was ever going anywhere. We were just two warm bodies."

"Well, maybe now you're ready for something a little more serious," she said. "Now that you know your way around a penis."

I laughed. "Something serious. How does one go about finding that?"

"Maybe instead of starting with sex, try starting with, like, talking. To someone whose *personality* you like."

I thought about Brad, how nice it was to just talk to him—until he burst into song. "There is this guy," I said. "But I don't think he's my type."

"Why not? What's your type?"

"I don't know. I don't know that I've ever pictured anything."

"Well, maybe that's the problem."

A FEW WEEKS passed. A cold front came through and I couldn't sit in the tree stand for more than fifteen minutes without my feet going numb, but staying in my apartment felt even more numbing. When Jean and I listed the house, I felt so weirdly outside myself that I tossed all my hunting trophies except the deer, which I mounted above my bed in the new apartment. I never bothered to put up any other decorations, so even after two years, the rest of the walls were still bare. Folding chairs surrounded the wobbly kitchen table abandoned by the previous tenant. I kept my toiletries on top of the toilet tank, since there were no cabinets in the bathroom, and I probably knocked my deodorant into the toilet bowl at least once a week. I decided it was time I went to Target for some apartment upgrades. Target was in Dry Creek. When I drove past the Holiday Inn Express I jerked the wheel to the right and pulled in.

"Oh, hi, New York City!" Brad said when he saw me hanging around in the lobby. "Are things back on with your guy?"

"No, I just figured I'd stop in and say hi on my way to Target. My apartment needs . . . something."

He laughed. "Something?"

"Well, it could feel a little more lived in."

"Ah. I imagine that'll be really easy for you, picking out decorations and such." He pointed all his fingers at me and rotated his wrist in circles around my midsection, indicating my ten-year-old Carhartt jacket and paint-stained jeans. "My lunch break is in ten minutes. Do you want some help?"

"You wouldn't mind?"

"I *live* for a trip to Target," he said, dead serious.

WE WANDERED UP and down aisles filled with screaming babies and arguing couples as Brad determinedly placed various items in my cart, saying things like, "A nice big mirror on the wall in your bedroom will really open up the space," "Overhead lighting is worse than a Kay Jewelers commercial," and "Storage doesn't have to be ugly." In his own cart, he added a grapefruit-scented spray cleaner, a gigantic tub of trail mix, two cases of sparkling water with some very eighties branding, and the new Halo game.

I scrunched up my face. "Wait, you play Halo?"

He shrugged. "Who doesn't?"

I asked him a question to gauge his seriousness as a player. "Okay, you know the beach level? Have you beaten it?"

"Maybe," he said coyly.

I widened my eyes. "How the fuck?"

He leaned in and lowered his voice. "You have to jump off the cliff."

"I tried that."

He smiled his golden retriever smile. "There's a cave halfway down. You have to press the over arrow at just the right time, then you can go through." A vibrating noise emanated from his pants. He took his phone out of his pocket and glanced at the screen. "Do you mind if I take this? It's my mom-in-law, and I've been a little concerned about her."

I told him to go ahead.

"Hi, Debbie, is everything okay? Oh, really? That's crazy!" he said in the overly interested tone someone uses when they're not very interested. He put his hand over the microphone and whispered to me, "She wanted to let me know there's a picture of a dog in the paper who looks just like my dog." A series of mm-hmms, yeses, and okays. "Oh, I'm just out with my new friend Gabe. I don't know, let me ask him." He turned to me and said, "Debbie would like to know if this is a date."

I coughed, then choked on my spit and coughed some more.

"I'll have to get back to you about that," Brad said into the phone. "I think Gabe is trying to decide if I'm too gay for him." He laughed at something she said. "Okay, I'll talk to you soon. Love-youbye!"

I stared intently at the end cap we were walking by that had all the ingredients for nachos: corn chips, queso, refried beans, salsa, and pickled jalapenos. My stomach gurgled.

"So, am I?" Brad asked.

"What?" I said, pretending not to know what he was talking about.

"Too gay for you," he challenged, crossing his arms, though his blue eyes looked especially vulnerable. "Don't pretend like you haven't been thinking it."

"I don't know, Brad," I said. "I don't really know anything."

"Well, there's only one way to find out," he said, leaning in and kissing me right there in front of the nacho display. It was a soft kiss that only lasted for about two seconds, but I felt something in my stomach rev, like an old car trying to start. I wanted to see what it would feel like for the engine to turn over.

We went on five dates before it finally happened, and when it did I said, "Oh my god" so many times it was like I was praying. Being with Brad felt easy and natural in a way nothing ever had before. A deep calm spread throughout my body; even the nervous stomach

I'd had since puberty disappeared. When I took him to my tree stand and he sat with me silently for a full hour and only afterward told me all the things he'd noticed—how the thick sheet of clouds had parted like someone pulled a zipper through them, how he'd heard the vibrating drum of a pileated woodpecker but hadn't seen it, how the veins and ridges on the back of a leaf looked like a mountain range seen from a plane—I knew I was in love. Forty-three and in love for the first time in my life.

The thing about falling in love is that it forces the issue of coming out; makes it urgent in a way it wasn't before. I kept promising Brad I'd tell Jean and Billy, then kept not doing it. I started to wonder if maybe it wasn't the fear of hurting Jean that kept me in the closet all those years, maybe it was just the fear. I wasn't sure if Jean and Billy would accept me—I guessed Jean would likely be more sad than angry, and Billy would be aloof and unreadable—but their potential reactions weren't what scared me the most. It was the simple fact that they'd *know*, that everyone would know. People would see me at Sportsman's Corner or Dillons or Walmart and think, *There's Gabe and he's* gay. It wouldn't be so bad if I could go somewhere different where no one knew me, but I didn't *want* to go somewhere different. The ideal scenario would be if everyone in town had their memories of me replaced, so in their minds I was always gay and no one would look at me any differently.

Brad, who had been out since he was a teenager and had a "Fuck 'em if they care who I fuck" motto—thus why he didn't talk to his own family—didn't understand. "But Jean left you almost three years ago," he said. "Why wouldn't you just tell her?"

"Because it'll set the wheels in motion. Then everyone in town will know."

"And?" He widened his eyes and clenched his hands in the air. "Wouldn't that be a good thing?"

I cut my eyes at him. "You know it was only a few years ago that we were labeled the most homophobic town in the nation."

"Yeah, but why do you care what homophobes think? Plus, the task force must have made things even a tiny bit better, right?"

"It's not that simple," I said. After the task force left, things got worse for a while, like the recoil of a rubber band after it's stretched. What was it Newton said? Every action has an equal and opposite reaction. Some kids—or maybe adults, who knows—took a sledgehammer and a can of spray paint to the all-gender restroom at the high school. The governor proposed that state funding be taken away from HIV/AIDS research and instead used for conversion therapy. A young woman came home from college for Thanksgiving and, maybe emboldened by the task force's recent presence, brought her girlfriend with her. One night as they waited at a stop sign, someone hurled a brick through the driver's-side window and sent the young woman to the hospital for twenty stitches. But she healed, at least physically, the governor's proposal went nowhere, and the bathroom was eventually repaired. After a few months, things died back down.

They even got a little better, bit by bit. The high school hired a new principal, who implemented a zero-tolerance bullying policy and actually enforced it. I'm sure not all the teachers were happy about it, but they didn't want to lose their jobs, so they went along.

The businesses on Main Street signed a "Pledge to Serve Everyone." The most surprising change was that Pastor Jim's Baptist church tacked a rainbow flag up on the reader board above the message ALL ARE WELCOME UNDER GOD. I'd be shocked if any gay people saw that and suddenly decided to join the congregation, but it was a gesture, no matter if it was made in earnest or just for the sake of appearances.

But even with these nods toward acceptance, I still couldn't shake my fear. After Brad and I had been together for a year, he told me that if I didn't tell Jean and Billy about us, he would leave. Tegan yelled at me at the top of her lungs over the phone; she even threatened to fly to Big Burr and drive me to Jean's place herself, but it didn't matter—I couldn't do it. Brad gave me a month, and during that time we didn't see each other. "So you have the space to think," he said, but I knew he was just trying to give me a glimpse of how miserable my life would be without him. And it was miserable. My stomach went back to being a bubbling, queasy mess. I retreated to my tree stand, but no amount of nature could distract me from the decisions circling in my head. I thought maybe I should just let him leave; he'd surely be better off with someone more emotionally mature, someone who wasn't a gay baby. I could go back to the hookup apps, keep it simple. Eventually—maybe in a few long years—there would be someone else. Maybe I might even love him, despite him not being Brad. But soon enough I'd be confronted with the same situation all over again. Love is a persistent force, like a stray cat you feed once—it'll keep coming back around forever, mewling outside the door.

Right before the month was up, I drove to Jean's new house, which she and Jeff had bought not long after she left me, stopping once to throw up on the side of the road and almost getting into two accidents, before marching up the front steps and pounding on the door like a crazed bill collector.

"Jesus, Gabe, what's wrong?" asked Jean when she opened the door. "You look like death."

"I have to tell you something," I said, swallowing down the bile rising in my throat.

"Oh, god, do you have cancer?"

I hunched over, then sank onto the doorstep, folding myself into a ball.

Jean squatted next to me and put a hand on my back, trying to look at my face. "Gabe, you're scaring me. What is it? Is it Billy?"

"I'm . . ." I blinked, seeing the quivering sliver of life between present and future. "I'm gay," I croaked.

Jean's hand fell from my back as she slid down next to me. She nodded slowly. "I always had my suspicions," she said. Jeff was in the backyard blowing leaves, the constant mechanical bleating making the situation even more stressful and surreal. "Have you always known?" she asked, looking at her moccasin-slippered feet.

"I guess. But I thought I could suppress it enough that it wouldn't be an issue."

Jean pushed air out from between her lips in a look-how-that-turned-out gesture. Her eyes flicked from left to right like she was reading a book, and I wondered what she was seeing: our first date at the movies when I spilled soda all over her lap, our wedding

271

when the officiant kept accidentally calling her "Joan," the days we spent in the hospital eating strawberry Jell-O cups after Billy was born five weeks early. Her face went somber. "Were you ever in love with me?"

The leaf blower roared closer, followed by the sound of brittle leaves hitting the side of the house. I waited until the racket receded, then said, "I loved you, but now that I know what it really feels like, I don't think I was ever *in love* with you."

She looked down again, picking a piece of leaf out of the welcome mat, then swiped a finger underneath her eye.

"I'm sorry, was that too honest?"

"No, it's okay. It's just . . ." She *tsk*ed her tongue. "So many years wasted."

When I told Billy later that week, all he said was, "Okay," in a completely indiscernible tone, then told me he was running late to PT and hung up. Billy had signed up for the Army right after high school, a decision I wasn't crazy about, but he seemed to like it, and was good at it. He was stationed at Fort Benning in Georgia, training to be a sniper—his childhood video-game dream come true. When he finally visited for the weekend, months after our very abbreviated conversation, I tried bringing it up again.

"Are you upset?" I asked.

"Not about you being gay," he said.

"But about something else?"

He sighed and cracked the knuckle on his thumb. "My whole childhood, I thought it had to do with *me*. You seemed distracted all the time, like there was nothing I could do to get you to notice me.

Sometimes I just wanted to run around banging pots and pans or blowing an air horn in your ear. I thought I just wasn't interesting enough, or important enough. I thought there must have been something wrong with me."

Tears burned behind my eyes. "Oh, Billy. There's nothing wrong with you. I'm sorry I made you think there was."

He shrugged. "It's okay."

"No, it's not, but hopefully now that you know the truth, we can move on. Really get to know each other."

He smiled weakly. "Sure." It looked like there was something else he wanted to say, but instead he got up and went to the bathroom.

I TOLD SOME friends and some people at work, and after that Brad and I started getting *the look* whenever we were out together. I'd been so terrified of how people would react, I was surprised to discover I didn't really care at all. Sometimes I even looked them right in the eye and smiled. One day Christine Peterson came up to us in Walmart, hands on her hips, and said, "Now I understand why Jean had to steal my husband."

Before I realized that my mouth was moving, I said, "Jeff left you because you're a miserable person, Christine." Her eyes widened as red splotches crawled up her neck, then she turned on her heel and stormed away. Brad looked at me, his mouth hanging open. I shrugged and took his hand.

In general, though, life went back to normal, or I guess what you'd call the new normal. My and Jean's old house never sold, so Brad and I decided to move in and remodel it ourselves. It took almost two years, but when we were done, it looked like an after-shot of a house on HGTV: a subway-tiled backsplash in the kitchen, exposed reclaimed-wood ceiling beams in the living room, an "accent wall" with black-and-white herringbone wallpaper. Brad let me keep the deer mounted above the fireplace, and we tied a little bow tie around his neck. The first time we had Jean and Jeff over, Jean kept smacking my arm, saying she couldn't believe it was really our old house. The *Herald* even sent a photographer and gave us a spread in the Home and Family section. In the lead photo, Brad and I are sitting next to each other on the couch, Brad leaning back, his feet resting on the ottoman, me leaning forward, my leg crossed toward Brad with my ankle over my knee. Brad's hand is casually placed on my shoulder. Neither of us is smiling, exactly, but we look content, our faces open and relaxed.

When Brad's mother-in-law gave him a big chunk of money after her father passed away, Brad bought the empty storefront that used to be Barb's Boutique and turned it into a coffee shop, Big Burr's first LGBTQ-owned business. On Friday nights, he hosts an open mic for the high school students; a few have even felt brave enough to read poems with some pretty gay undertones. The coffee shop is now the number-one-rated place in town on TripAdvisor, and even people who don't approve of us come for the coffee— including Christine Peterson, who always orders a Brazilian pour-over and then proceeds to complain about how long it takes and how much it costs. Ever since I confronted her in Walmart, we've come to a kind of truce. I like to think that she grudgingly respects me for calling her out.

From the window, I can see our guests starting to file into the rows of white chairs facing the cottonwood tree that Karen draped in rainbow-colored ribbons. I never expected Karen to come back, but she said she *had* to see the first gay wedding in Big Burr. Avery, who writes for that TV show *Feminazi* that keeps racking up Emmys, is sitting next to Karen in her wheelchair and her boyfriend, a muscular movie producer, sits next to her. Karen told me that Zach lives in Los Angeles now, too. Avery persuaded him to move out there after college, and they're back to being close friends. Sitting next to Avery and her boyfriend and Karen are David and Miguel, still happily swinging after all these years. David is the research director at an AIDS nonprofit, and Miguel is the principal of a high school in Brooklyn. And standing under the cottonwood, shuffling through her notes for the ceremony and rubbing her palms on her dress, is Tegan. She's a licensed clinical social worker now, helping gay babies other than me. She and Shirin broke up a few years after moving back to New York, because Shirin wanted kids and Tegan didn't. She's been single since then, dating on and off but never settling down again.

"Hey, New York City," says Brad, walking into the bedroom in his black-and-white herringbone-printed suit, an homage to the accent wall in our house. He smiles his golden retriever smile at me. "Are you ready to do this?"

"I can't get my cuff links on," I say, holding my wrists out to him.

He gives me a you're-so-helpless eye roll and crosses the room. When his warm, dry fingers gently touch my wrist, I blink back tears. He twists the T-bar on the back of the cuff link, securing it into place with a quiet click that echoes through my body. Sunlight slants through the curtains, falling on the bedside table where there's a half-full cup of coffee in Brad's YOU HAVE THE SAME AMOUNT OF HOURS IN A DAY AS BEYONCÉ mug, the most recent issue of *Outdoor Life*, and the antique jadeite honey pot where we keep our spare change. Outside, the ribbons on the cottonwood tree flutter in the breeze. All the people who love us wait in their chairs. Brad takes my hand, and we walk toward them.

Acknowledgments

Thank you, firstly, to Ashley—for sniffing me out and thus starting my life, for giving me access to the emotions necessary to write, for being my most trusted reader, and for moving to New Mexico with me so I could write this book. None of it would have been possible without you. Thank you to Alexa Stark, my agent, for taking a chance on an unknown writer and supporting me along the way with your calm confidence. Thank you to Michelle Koufopoulos, my editor, for your fierce belief in this book and pushing me to make it better. Thank you to the whole team at Riverhead, my dream publisher, for making the dream a reality. Thank you to Marisa Clark, for being the first official reader of the book and for being a queer mentor when I so badly needed one. I'll always remember the speech you gave about me at graduation, which allowed me to see myself in a whole new way. Thank you to Lori Ostlund, also for being a mentor, and for sharing your incredible knowledge of craft. Thank you to Dan Mueller for teaching me how to write better sentences. Thank you to early readers Emily Rapp Black, Tim Johnston, Abigail Lloyd, Bell Kauffmann, Charles Theonia, and Erika Turner. Thank you to the literary magazines that published some of the stories from this book. Thank you to my parents for never discouraging me from being a writer, and for being open to all the ideas I rant about on the phone. Thank you to my chosen family—you know who you are—for inspiring a lot of this book, giving me such a sense of belonging, and bringing me frequent joy. Lastly, thank you to all the queer people who have come before, who have been visible and thus allowed us to see possibilities for the future, and who fought to get us to the point where a book like this could be published.

Don't miss Celia Laskey's new novel

SO HAPPY FOR YOU

She'd kill for the perfect day...

When Robin agrees to be the maid of honour for her childhood
best friend, she knew she'd have to make a few sacrifices.

She just didn't know one of them would be her life.

Coming July 2022
Hardback, ebook and audio

ONE PLACE. MANY STORIES

Bold, innovative and
empowering publishing.

FOLLOW US ON:

@HQStories